Praise for Sarah J Naughton

'Dazzlingly inventive'   *Sunday Times*

'A meticulously plotted exploration of friendship, foe-ship and the lies that bind, which builds to a gripping and powerful conclusion'   Cara Hunter, author of *All the Rage*

'The perfect dose of thrills and suspense, this will keep you engrossed to the very end'   *Heat*

'Original and stylish . . . will keep you guessing to the last page'
Sharon Bolton, author of *The Split*

'We couldn't put this thriller down . . . brilliant'   *Closer*

'Tautly thrilling . . . This has hit thriller written all over it'
Evening Telegraph

'A perfect example of how a psychological thriller should be written – intricately plotted and full of shocking surprises'
Lisa Hall, author of *Between You and Me*

'A clever, twisting story of obsession'   *Woman & Home*

'Delivers suspense, twists and sharp writing'
Lisa Jewell, author of *Then She Was Gone*

'Deliciously clever. The   ctive'
                                                        Hours

Sarah J Naughton was born and brought up in the West Country. She is a Costa-shortlisted author of psychological thrillers and books for young adults. Her last thriller, *The Mothers*, was a *Sunday Times* Crime Book of the Month. She is married with two sons and divides her time between London and Dorset.

Also by Sarah J Naughton
The Other Couple
Tattletale
The Mothers

THE FESTIVAL

Sarah J Naughton

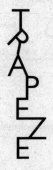

First published in Great Britain in 2021 by Trapeze
an imprint of The Orion Publishing Group Ltd
Carmelite House, 50 Victoria Embankment
London EC4Y 0DZ

An Hachette UK Company

1 3 5 7 9 10 8 6 4 2

A CIP catalogue record for this book is
available from the British Library.

ISBN (Mass Market Paperback) 978 1 4091 8469 0
ISBN (eBook) 978 1 4091 8470 6

Typeset by Born Group
Printed and bound in Great Britain by Clays Ltd, Elcograf S.p.A.

MIX
Paper from
responsible sources
FSC® C104740

www.orionbooks.co.uk

For my wickedly clever friend,
Rhian John, with gratitude.

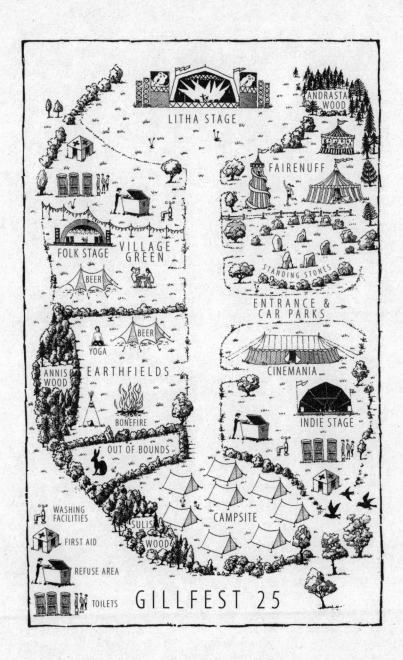

LITHA STAGE

ANDRASTA WOOD

FAIRENUFF

FOLK STAGE

VILLAGE GREEN

BEER

STANDING STONES

ENTRANCE & CAR PARKS

YOGA

BEER

ANNIS WOOD

EARTHFIELDS

CINEMANIA

INDIE STAGE

BONEFIRE

OUT OF BOUNDS

WASHING FACILITIES

FIRST AID

REFUSE AREA

TOILETS

SULIS WOOD

CAMPSITE

GILLFEST 25

@GillingwaterFestival
We'd like to thank everyone for the amazing support you've given us over the past 25 years, but after the tragic events at this year's #GillFest25, the festival will not be returning. If you have any information about the incidents, please contact @ASPolice.

1

For the first time that day, Orly finds herself alone, on the periphery of the milling groups. By now the sombre facades are slipping and occasionally a low laugh will escape, to be swallowed guiltily or met with disapproving looks. Orly understands how they feel. You can only be miserable for so long.

An old man she doesn't recognise comes up to her, clasps both her hands in his and says, in a trembling voice, 'Congratulations.'

His blue irises look like they've been dissolved in milk and his moist lips continue to move after he's uttered the word, as if he's still talking but at a frequency she cannot hear. He's so old that perhaps he has already begun to speak the language of the dead. Perhaps Harry can hear him and is laughing.

'Thank you,' she says, squeezing the papery hands.

He moves away, satisfied, smiling, nodding. He's done something right. A middle-aged woman bustles over. She explains to Orly that he has Alzheimer's and apologises if he has said anything to upset her. Orly says no, not at all. And it's true. She would burst into laughter, but once she started, she might not be able to stop.

The sense of release is terrible and wonderful. The moment the nurses confirmed that Harry was gone, that her duty of care to him was fulfilled, she felt as if she might float out of the hospice window with the sheer relief of being free. Free of fear and pain and indignity and the ridiculous suffering a human body can tolerate before it finally succumbs.

Free of Harry.

An image of him swims up in her mind. Not one of the ones liberally scattered across the tables and fastened to the flower displays – proudly brandishing a football trophy, picking up his degree, laughing with his best man at their wedding – but just a normal memory. Him reading the *Guardian* at the kitchen table with the sun spilling over the back of his hand, turning the hairs to strands of gold. Why does her brain retain this pointless image of him? He's not even looking at her. And then, out of the blue, the sense of loss punches her so hard in the chest that she almost doubles over.

She makes it to the patio doors, slightly ajar on this bright winter day to air the overcrowded room – dying young guarantees you a full church – and breathes deeply to try and prevent the incipient panic attack.

Out on the lawn, her friends' children are playing. Among the dull greens and browns, they are flags of colour, twittering to one another like birds, before scampering away out of sight.

The sun goes behind a cloud and for a moment she can see her ghostly reflection in the glass, her face a landscape of sharp white peaks and deep black troughs. A shadowy figure stands beside her.

Harry?

She turns, but the shadow is only the lumpen bulk of the curtain. For a moment her vision blurs with disappointment. She blinks the tears away. There will be time for that later when she is on her own. Endless time.

In the corner of the room, Thea and Lenny are talking. It's a relief not to feel the familiar prick of jealousy. To think she used to worry about that sort of trivial shit. When she moaned to Harry that she felt left out, he would roll his eyes and tell her she was being stupid, and now of course it's perfectly clear he was right. Thea and Lenny both live in London; it's natural for them to get together more often than the whole group can manage.

4

Bruno comes over and murmurs something into Thea's ear, and she turns and walks over to Orly.

Approaching forty, Thea is still as beautiful as ever. In fact, more beautiful now that she's toned down the brassy gangster's moll look for something more in keeping with her banker's wife role. Well, not quite wife, not just yet. She's wearing a beautiful black wrap dress with bell sleeves, which clings to her tiny waist before flaring out to show off her shapely legs. Orly wanted them to put 'no black' on the invitations, but Heather and Graham vetoed this idea. *It's not a celebration of his life, Orly. It's a tragic loss.*

'I'm so sorry, but we have to go,' Thea says, wincing.

'That's okay. Thanks for coming.' Orly attempts a smile, but it quivers at the edges and Thea reaches for her hand. Orly clutches it as if to save herself from falling. She and Thea have been friends since school. There was a Before Harry and there will be an After.

'It was good of Bruno to come,' she says. 'Please thank him for me.'

'He wanted to,' Thea says. 'He really liked Harry.'

'Didn't everyone?' Orly says. 'Mr Bloody Perfect, eh? But they didn't have to live with him, ha ha!' The fake jollity jars, but Thea smiles nevertheless.

'I tell you, that man was a shit patient,' Orly babbles on. 'If there was something to complain about, he'd complain. The sheet was rumpled, the pillow was too hard, the lines were itching.'

'It must have been so hard for you,' Thea says, squeezing her hand. 'At least now you'll . . .' She tails off, clearly afraid of saying the wrong thing. Orly wishes people wouldn't do that. It doesn't matter what they say, as long as they keep talking and don't abandon her to the terrible silence.

She nods. 'It was . . . it was so . . .' The nod becomes a shake and then her hand goes to her face.

'Oh darling.' Thea pulls her into her arms and strokes her hair. It's nice to be held, and Thea is so fragrant and warm that Orly

5

doesn't want to let go. Then she sees Bruno over Thea's shoulder, far enough away not to have to engage in conversation, but close enough to make it obvious he's waiting. She extricates herself.

'You have to go,' she says, wiping her eyes.

'I'm sorry,' Thea repeats. 'It'll get better, I promise. And we're all here for you. Me and Lenny were just saying we haven't seen enough of each other these past few years. We need to change that. Not just because of this, because of . . . Harry . . .' she takes a breath after saying his name, 'but because we're friends. Best friends for ever, right?' She gives a weak smile and Orly returns it. Then, clearly sensing Bruno's impatience, she becomes brisk again. 'Now, where did I put those pesky children?'

'I saw them in the garden. Hope they're not too muddy for the Porsche.'

'Call me any time. Any time at all. Just pick up the phone.'

As long as it's before Bruno gets home, Orly adds silently, then feels guilty.

'I will, thank you.'

Bruno comes over. 'It was a lovely service. Really lovely.' He kisses her on both cheeks. 'Sorry we have to go so soon. Work thing. A real pain.'

'No problem,' Orly says, her gaze flicking to his cool eyes and quickly away. Bruno's sheer size and the aura of money that surrounds him like a fur coat has always intimidated her a little, and Harry too, who seemed to feel the need to stand up straighter and talk louder and plummier whenever Thea's partner was in the vicinity.

'We really must have you over for supper soon,' Bruno says.

'Sure, yes,' Orly says vaguely. Bruno clearly has no idea that she lives in Bath: rather too far to come for a supper date.

He takes Thea's hand and leads her away, and Orly feels another stab of loss. If only they were fifteen again, her friends would never let her go through this alone, even if she wanted to. They would smother her with their attention, sleep on her bedroom floor, adopt her grief as their own. She and Thea and Mel and Lenny, the four of them as inseparable as sisters.

But she's not alone for long. Mel comes over, her hair bursting from the constraints of its clips to coil around her face like friendly snakes.

'Oh my God,' she mutters. 'I got stuck with this old duffer for twenty minutes, listening to him explaining the mechanics of oil-well shaft-boring devices. I tried to throw in the odd joke about deep penetration, but he didn't miss a beat! On the plus side, I didn't have to say anything, so at least I managed to stuff my face in peace for a while.'

Mel's nerves are making her gabble, but Orly is glad of the change of energy. She's had about all she can take of murmured commiserations.

'You okay?' Mel is looking at her, really looking into her eyes, where Thea's gaze slid across her face.

'Getting there,' she says.

'Oh God, I wish I didn't have to go. I'm so sorry.'

'That's okay.'

'Billy's been on his own all day, which is fine – he's seventeen, not five – but if I'm not there he'll just game all night, and he's got school tomorrow.'

'Of course. Don't worry, honestly.'

'Hun,' Mel lowers her tone. 'You've lost so much weight. Are you sleeping properly?'

'I've got some pills . . . Don't worry, they're not the addictive ones. I'm getting a couple of hours a night.'

'I can't believe it's been so long since we saw each other.'

Eighteen months, but Orly forgives her. Though he might not think so, Billy is still a child, and Mel works her arse off in the café six days a week. She shouldn't have to traipse forty miles to see her friend's dying husband.

'This has been wonderful. Really. Harry would have been proud of you.'

'Heather and Graham arranged it all.'

'Did I say wonderful? I mean average, ha ha.' Mel grins. She knows how Orly gets on with Heather and Graham. 'You were brilliant. So strong. The slide show pictures were gorgeous. Was the one of him diving off that rock from your honeymoon?'

'He lost his trunks when he hit the water and everyone was standing watching. I had to wade in with a towel for him.'

Mel chuckles.

'I wanted to try for a baby that holiday, but Harry said we should wait until we'd been working longer and would get all the maternity benefits. I should have followed my heart, eh? Then maybe . . . then . . .' *Sorry*, Orly mouths, and her face crumples.

Mel holds her for long minutes, rubbing her back, kissing her hair, shushing her as she sobs and trembles, and eventually the fit passes.

She can't meet Orly's eye as she takes her hands to say goodbye. Orly has always tried to keep it to herself, her envy of the other three for their beautiful children, and now she's made Mel feel guilty. Pregnant at twenty, it wasn't easy for Mel. People shook their heads and muttered about the waste, but even way back then, Orly felt a pang of envy. And now, nearly two decades on, the pang has hardened to a shard of glass twisting in her heart. They started too late; the cancer was already gnawing at Harry's bowel and the chemo ended all that for good.

'Oh babe, I wish . . . I wish . . .'

Now Mel is crying, and in the end, it is Orly who dries her friend's tears, gently smoothing them away with her sleeve, as she does with the kids at school when they fall and graze their knees.

'We're going to see more of each other, okay?' Mel says, sniffing. 'I'm not just saying that. We are. These things are gonna happen to us in our lives, and we need to be there for each other. We always have been and we always will be, yeah?'

'Yes.'

'I love you.'

'Love you too.'

She watches Mel pass through the dwindling crowd, nodding at those with whom she has chatted. The smile she receives from Harry's mother is brittle as she clocks Mel's jumpsuit and heels, perhaps catching the whiff of Primark. Mel's phone is already pressed to her cheek as she passes out of the door, to tell her son that she is coming home.

Home.

Without Harry, the flat will never be home again.

Orly goes to the bar and orders another drink. While she's waiting for it to be poured, she feels eyes on her back and turns to find Heather, Graham and Lucy looking over. Heather crooks a finger at her, and with a sinking heart, Orly picks up her glass and goes over.

The twins have been great. Lenny is proud of them. They sat quietly in the church with their colouring books, answered politely when people spoke to them, didn't fight when they were left to their own devices back at the hotel, and now they come when she calls them, emerging from the dusk of the garden, only a little bit muddy. She was slightly concerned to see them playing with Lewis and Jade earlier on, but there don't seem to be any obvious injuries as they run into her arms.

They're still just about light enough to be carried, one in each arm, up the mercifully shallow treads of the hotel's sweeping staircase. She pauses halfway to catch her breath, gazing out of the tall window at an overcast sky washed pink with dusk. Their suite is on the first floor, looking out across the bleak garden to the Mendips beyond. The main bedroom has a king-size, but Lenny walks past it to the interconnecting room beyond, where two little beds are lit by the honeyed glow of a bedside lamp.

As she's helping them clean their teeth, she puts a call through to the main desk to summon the hotel babysitter, and a minute or so later, a teenager appears. Her pale face is marred with acne and her limbs are as rickety as a young lamb's, but she smiles when she sees the children and sits down on Greta's bed and asks the name of her cuddly monkey.

Lenny kisses them, tells the girl to help herself to soft drinks and snacks from the minibar, and heads back downstairs.

The staircase is lined with photographs: stiffly posed Victorians, smug Edwardians surrounded by the trappings of empire, tragic soldiers and old men with Labradors, and finally, gaggles of privileged children riding ponies and skippering yachts. Families are supposed to endure through the ages, but Orly's has been cut off before it began. Though perhaps it was for the best that she and Harry never conceived. He lingered for so long in that hushed room of pain that smelled so strongly of air freshener whenever Lenny visited. It would not have been fair to inflict that on a child; better no parent at all than one so diminished, so unavailable. That's what she told herself more than once throughout Harry's illness. Her own children will never know their father, so they'll never feel his loss.

Carrying the twins up the stairs has really taken it out of her, and she pauses to puff her inhaler; then a thought occurs to her that makes her lean heavily on the banister.

This could easily have been her own funeral. How many asthma attacks has she had in the past year? Four? Five? She's come to terms with the fact that it will be this that kills her, but what if she doesn't make it to the twins' adulthood?

The banister creaks as she pushes herself upright. She needs to take better care of herself. When she gets back home, she'll order several more inhalers to make sure she has one in every room of the house; she'll cut down on the booze, do more exercise, try to reduce her stress levels. She owes it to the twins. One parent *is* enough – her wonderful happy children have proved that point – but that parent has double the responsibility to stay alive.

Downstairs, the room is emptying out. Only close family remain. Lenny recognises Orly's parents talking to the vicar. They look so much older than when she last saw them, the summer that school ended. More aged than the twenty

10

intervening years could account for – and somehow lost. They must have thought their daughter was safe, that their lives would be a smooth transition to overindulgent grandparenthood. Now they will be contemplating the worst kind of parenting duty: attempting to nurse their broken child back to life.

Orly is in the clutches of her in-laws. Lenny orders a gin and tonic, and as she waits at the bar, she watches them talking quietly. Now that the tragi-gracious masks have been removed, their expressions display the bitterness of a family convinced that their son would still be alive if he'd had a better wife. Orly looks terrible. As emaciated and ill as Harry did on Lenny's final visit to Bath six months ago.

Six months.

How could she have left it so long?

She's a bad friend, she thinks, as she sips the drink (cheap gin and flat tonic). There were plenty of excuses – the twins, the merger, the distance – but she knows in her heart that she was just weak. Too weak to face Harry in the extremity of his anguish. Too weak to stomach the horror. Well, she will do better.

Downing the drink, she orders two more to be delivered to the library, and goes over to the group surrounding Orly like papal inquisitors. As she draws nearer, she hears the conversation. It's about money. About items loaned and required to be returned. Life insurance payouts and next of kin. Grief translated to hard numbers, to avenge emotional wounds with material ones.

'Hello,' she says loudly. 'We met at the wedding. I'm Leonora.' She shakes hands with enough firmness to make the father wince. 'It was a lovely service. Particularly the eulogy.' Harry's sister smiles and can't restrain herself from casting a glance up and down Lenny's trouser suit.

'Do you mind if I borrow Orly?'

Not at all, the family murmur. It's time they thanked the vicar.

'Perfect.' Lenny beams, then, taking Orly by the shoulders, she propels her out of the room and into the library next door. Earlier on, a few stragglers were hanging out here, but now the place is empty, the cushioned hush broken only by the crackle of a log fire in the grate.

'Sit,' Lenny says, pushing Orly into a leather club chair. 'Drink.' She picks up the gin (a better brand, fresh tonic) and puts it into her hand. 'Tonight, my love, we are getting wasted.'

Orly leans back against the creaking leather, closes her eyes and drinks.

How many times have they been drunk together? Lenny wonders as she sits down opposite, watching the flames dance in Orly's glass. The first was at the Oak when they were in the fourth year at Summer Hall. Two pints of cider added to the bottle of cheap wine they'd sunk in Lenny's bedroom to start the evening off. They'd met Thea and Mel in the pub for a prearranged rendezvous with the local boys' school. Rich might have been there, she can't remember now. Certainly by nine they were outside, vomiting in the quaint little gutter that ran down the street, wondering how they were going to get through the next hour before Lenny's parents came to collect them.

Could it be possible that one sip has brought a little colour back to Orly's cheeks? Or is it just the glow from the fire? A log shifts, collapsing in on itself in a shower of sparks, and she thinks of another fire: a bonfire surging up into a night sky fluttering with bunting.

The last time they were properly off their faces was at GillFest, the summer they left school. They'd learned to take their drink better by then, and the festival was a last hurrah before they went their separate ways, vowing to be best friends for ever. And they have been, Lenny supposes. At least, that's how she refers to the three of them: her best friends. Or, more recently, her *oldest* friends. The ones who know you best in the world. Except this isn't true. Lenny has no concept of what life is like for Mel: a single mum working in a café in a small market town a stone's throw from where she grew up. Or for Thea, who, with her cashmere, her perfect highlights and her size 8 frame, is the clone of every other kept woman of a certain age in London, desperate to hang on to her rich man. And then there's Orly. How can she possibly imagine what Orly's going through?

'Good girl. Drink up. Plenty more where that came from.'

Orly opens her eyes, looks at her watch and winces. 'I can't get smashed. I'm at Mum and Dad's tonight.'

'Listen,' Lenny says. 'I booked a suite. You don't have to stay, but I just thought a little company and a lot of alcohol wouldn't go amiss. I totally understand if you'd rather be with your folks, though.'

'Yeah, right,' Orly snorts. 'No, I think I'd rather get royally trashed.'

So they do, carrying on long after the last straggler has enjoyed his final free drink, after the staff have cleared the room and ushered them to the conservatory, until the poor boy standing sentry at the bar is wilting against the optics and the sun is pinking the sky behind the bare winter trees. Then finally, too drunk to hold a train of thought for more than a few seconds, they wend their way upstairs.

At some ghastly hour in the morning, the twins climb into bed with them. Jackson has brought his book about trains and Greta snuggles between them and starts plaiting Lenny and Orly's hair together.

When the sun is fully risen, Lenny untangles herself and gets up to order breakfast. While she's on the phone, she watches her children playing with her old best friend. They like Orly, probably because she's always taken the time to talk to them, instead of over their heads to the adults. She even found time for them during the funeral, telling Jackson that he was taller than any of the boys in her class at school and sitting with Greta to draw crayon rainbows on the order of service.

It brings to the fore a thought that has been playing on Lenny's mind ever since Harry's illness brought home to her how terrifyingly fragile life is. That she might have made a mistake when she chose a guardian for the children. When they were tiny, she

13

just assumed they would be best off with someone whose lifestyle reflected her own: a life of private schools and exotic holidays. But – and her EQ has always lagged far behind her IQ – she's come to realise there might be more to a child's happiness than money.

And now, watching Orly reading, for the fourth time, a book about trains to a five-year-old boy, the morning after she has buried her husband, Lenny makes a decision.

After breakfast, Orly takes the children into the garden while Lenny pays the bill and checks out. Joining them afterwards, she finds them in the middle of a leaf-throwing battle, just as Orly is splatted right in the face by a particularly accurate shot from Jackson that makes her slip over. Lenny hurries to check she's okay, but Orly, lying on her back on the muddy lawn, is laughing. The twins rush over to pelt her with leaves, romping over her like puppies, while she laughs and laughs, her cheeks pink, her eyes as bright as they were when they were children themselves, with the whole sparkling world laid out for them.

Lenny waits, smiling, until the game is over and the participants, muddy and wet and panting, are staggering to their feet. Then, giving the children a twenty-pound note, she tells them to go and buy Orly a present from the glass cabinet of hotel-themed goods in the foyer. They skip off, delighted by this responsibility, and Lenny hopes they return with the teddy bear and not the dreadful paisley scarf.

Orly, coming to stand beside her, smiles wistfully after them.

Lenny turns to her. 'Can I ask you something?'

Orly's smile fades. She's got too used to bad news.

'If anything was to happen to me, would you be Greta and Jackson's guardian?'

Orly blinks in surprise, then beams. 'Of course, I'd love to! The kids are gorgeous. But . . .' The smile fades. 'I'm on my own now and my salary isn't exactly . . . I'd hate them to miss out on the stuff they love.' She lowers her eyes and rubs a smear of mud from her pale hand.

14

Lenny grasps the hand. 'I don't give a shit about any of that. All that matters to me is that you love them. I know that's a hard ask, to love someone else's children . . .'

'It's not,' Orly says simply.

'In that case, say yes.'

Orly laughs. 'Yes. And thank you. It's a privilege to be asked.'

They embrace, then Orly pulls away and looks intensely into Lenny's eyes. 'But I don't want you going anywhere any time soon, so please look after yourself.'

Coming from Orly, this is not just a platitude.

'I promise,' Lenny says, pleased. Not only was this the right decision for the twins, but it has made her friend happy. It might even be a relief to the original guardian: after all, there aren't many people who'd be happy to be saddled with someone else's children. 'In that case, I'll contact my lawyer and get my will changed.'

The children come running out, the paisley scarf flying above their heads like a banner of war.

After the gift is handed over, the two women hug quickly, saying little, to try and preserve the magic of the moment, and then Lenny leads the children back to the car.

'You've been so good today,' she says as they set off. 'As a treat, when we get home, you can order anything you like from Just Eat.'

'Dough balls?' Jackson says.

'Including dough balls.'

'Cheesecake?' Greta shouts.

'And cheesecake.'

The cheering lasts all the way to the M4.

Gillingwater

From Wikipedia, the free encyclopedia

Gillingwater is a small village in west *Somerset* with a population of 2100. It has been in constant habitation since the *Bronze Age*, and whilst it boasts one of the oldest *Saxon* churches in the country, *pagan* offerings have been discovered in local wells and springs and streams dating from prehistory all the way to modern times. There is evidence that the ancient woodlands around the village were used by *Druids*, and *neo-pagans* claim that the village lies in the meeting of *ley lines* that connect directly to *Glastonbury, Stonehenge* and *Badbury Rings*.

Since 1994, a music festival has taken place on farmland near the village over the closest weekend to the *Summer Solstice*. From new-age themed folk beginnings it is now a lucrative annual event that attracts visitors from all over the world and showcases some of the biggest international bands.

Local residents make regular attempts to get the festival banned, citing issues around pollution, antisocial behaviour, safety and crime. Defenders of the event argue that they are reviving earlier traditions of a midsummer festival that took place at this site in prehistory, involving worship, ritual and, some claim, *human sacrifice*.

2

Orly

She watches Jago from the staffroom window. He's standing alone at the furthest edge of the playground. He can't breathe properly because his sinuses are permanently blocked by the array of allergies that mean he has to be watched almost constantly, and his mouth hangs open to gape at the oxygen. It makes him look stupid, as do the centimetre-thick glasses – he's not. The other children move around him as if he exists in an entirely different dimension to their own. Which in a way he does.

His is the kind of SEN they don't normally see at Stonebridge Primary. Usually it's dyslexia, ADHD, Asperger's. Problems so familiar they aren't even problems, just 'types of learning'. But Jago is different. If she supports him as she intends to, he might get a bursary to King Edward's and then the sky's the limit. Oxbridge. Harvard. Somewhere the glare from his intelligence will mask the oddities of his appearance – the greying shirts, the unwashed hair, the holed shoes.

He raises a hand and she raises hers to mirror it, a V gap between the two sets of fingers: the Vulcan salute. He loves *Star Trek* and anything else to do with space. He has promised that when he grows up he will build her a wormhole that will let her time-travel. Just a couple of years back would do it. To a time when food had a taste and she slept more than four hours a night.

The door behind her opens and there is a waft of perfume. She turns and smiles, but the head's PA doesn't return it.

'Orly, Miles wants to see you in his office if you've got a moment.'

'Sure,' Orly says. 'Any idea what it's about?'

'I don't know, sorry.' The young woman turns to the counter and starts bustling about with the kettle.

With a final glance at Jago, who's watching the other children play 'it' in the way a zoo animal watches humans stroll past its cage, she goes out of the staffroom.

Miles has been head for seven months, and it's clear he's struggling. He stammers when addressing the staff, is unpredictable with the children – a prank he laughed at one day receives heavy-handed punishment the next – and has started palming the worst parents off on the deputy head.

The first thing she thinks when she walks in is: he's got cancer. His face is a queasy yellow and the fluorescent light above his desk gives it a clammy sheen. Then she notices the shaking of his hands and the sweat patches on his shirt. Perhaps it's just flu.

She sits down, smiling warmly. 'Hi.'

'Um,' he says. 'Orly. I just want to say, on the outset, I mean *from* the outset. At the outset. That you've done wonders with some of the children, you really have. Jake is on year eight stuff already, I hear.'

'Jago. He's doing year nine work. I think he could get into King Edward's given a bit of preparation, past papers, that sort of thing. I don't mind giving him some extra tutoring.'

'Um . . .' Miles swallows and looks up at the ceiling with such intensity that she follows his gaze to see if any magic words are written there.

'The thing is . . . Cuts. Have to be. Made.'

She retracts her jaw, blinks as the sudden new reality sinks in.

'One-to-one SEN provision . . . is a . . . luxury we just can't afford . . . any more.'

It's like he's reading from a script in a different language, one he has to translate each line of before uttering the words.

'But . . .' she says, wondering how many *buts* she will utter before she leaves the room.

18

'It comes down to a choice between you and Judy . . . She's been here fifteen years and . . . you've had . . . so much time off. If she took us to tribunal she would win.'

'But—'

'I know it was because of what happened to Harry. I know, Orly.' His voice is becoming shrill and she feels a rush of pity for him. 'This is not what I want to be doing. And you don't have to tell me how it's going to affect the children. I know how much they all—'

'Miles.'

He looks at her. The pupils of his eyes are pinpricks and the whites go all the way around his irises. He's terrified that she will make a fuss: cry or rage or argue.

'It's okay,' she says.

He blinks.

'I understand. If I was in your shoes I'd do the same. The school has no money and Judy's far more expensive than me to get rid of.'

He exhales like a steam train coming to rest at its final destination. 'Thank you. Thank you, Orly.'

And then it's over. He reaches across the table and shakes her hand with his own sweaty one, tells her she doesn't have to work the notice period and she's free to leave whenever she likes. He looks as if he might burst into tears. Imagine going through your life and the worst thing you've ever had to do is make someone redundant. She wants to say that it doesn't matter, that when you've lost your husband, losing a job just doesn't seem that big a deal, but it will only make him feel worse.

She goes to find Judy and tells her about how wonderful Jago is, about how he needs books for teenagers but to watch the sexual content. About how he is allergic to the ink in the ballpoints and has to use a pencil, about how he must, he really must, get that bursary for King Edward's.

Judy nods earnestly, pity pouring off her in waves.

And then Orly goes home.

The first call she makes is to the landlord to give notice on the flat. The second is to her parents to ask if she can please move back in with them. Of course she can. They will come and collect her whenever she likes. Orly can hear the relief in her mother's voice when she realises it's just a redundancy, not another breakdown. It was her mother who eased the hand holding the fruit knife away from her daughter's throat when Orly had a psychotic episode just before Harry went into the hospice. Her mother who stayed with her for the first month after he died, changing her sheets, cooking her meals, picking up her medication, making her take it. She left the flat, crying, when Orly said it was time she learned to manage on her own again.

And she was managing. She was getting by. Moving on.

Though she hasn't quite got around to taking Harry's stuff to the charity shop. She'll have to now, though. Her parents' house is hardly big enough for an extra living adult and her belongings, let alone the possessions of a ghost.

She goes into the bedroom and opens the wardrobe.

Hanging on the left side is an array of shirts and trousers that have long since lost their Harry scent and reverted to the limp hanks of fabric they always were. She doesn't cry as she folds them all into bin bags, or when she hands them over to the girl with Down's syndrome at the charity shop.

Is there something liberating about it? she wonders as she walks home, through the pretty streets of Georgian townhouses they always imagined they might be able to afford one day, that they might fill with children and dogs and mess and happiness. About divesting yourself of unnecessary possessions, freeing yourself from the tethers of the past? Certainly she feels a lightness that seems to lift her from the solidity of the paving slabs into thin air. As if the top of her head has opened and everything – thoughts, feelings, memories – is pouring out of it like the ash cloud of a volcano.

Then her legs go out from under her and she falls to her knees on the pavement.

*

All her possessions – two decades of adulthood, three of those years as a wife – fit into the back of her parents' Volvo. She doesn't turn round as her father pulls out of the little street. It was *their* little street, not hers. Harry and his wife. A woman who no longer exists.

As they pass slowly through the centre of Bath, she sees familiar faces. Mums of the children at school, wandering in pairs with their toddlers and babies. They look tired, but not with that bone-weary exhaustion that strips every pigment but yellow from your skin. Later they will curl in front of the TV and complain to their partners that *they* have it easy, that the kids fought all day and drove them crazy. Later still they will fall into bed and sleep: a deep, delicious sleep from which they will be woken too early and a new day, full of promise and wonder, will begin.

Of all the things she has lost, she misses sleep the most.

'Are you sure you're all right to drive,' her mum says as her dad uncharacteristically grinds the gears.

'Yes, yes, I'm fine,' her dad snaps.

Orly's heart jumps into her mouth. 'Why shouldn't he be? What's wrong?' She can hear the rising pitch of her voice.

'Carol, for goodness' sake . . . It's nothing to worry about, Orly,' her dad says. 'My left leg has started to swell up a bit. It can happen sometimes with diabetes.'

'But that's all it could be?' Orly says, leaning forward. 'Just diabetes?'

'Not *just*, darling,' her mum says. 'Diabetes can be very ser—'

'Carol!'

It's only a short drive to Newton Collard. She didn't stray far: didn't need to. She was happy in this modest part of south-west England, with none of the moneyed swagger of Devon or the flashy gorgeousness of Cornwall. Harry was too. They didn't want much more than a continuation of that happiness. It was good, he always said, that both sets of parents were close, for babysitting.

21

Heather and Graham live in the opposite direction. She hasn't even told them she's leaving Bath. They haven't been in touch with her since her birthday in March. They sent a card. No message, just their names. The next won't reach her.

As she gazes from the window of the back seat, the years fall away. She's a teenager being driven to university, a twelve-year-old travelling to a ballet exam, a little girl returning from a visit to her grandparents, looking out for the turning into the close that leads to their little family home. The thought of coming home used to fill her with such fuzzy warmth that muscle memory still makes her heart lift as the Volvo clunks up the ridge of the drive, where the builders didn't level it out properly. Then the reality of what her life has become hits her. She will live in this house as her parents grow old and die, and then she will live here alone until she herself dies, lying undiscovered for months because there's no one left to care. The thought of herself as a lonely old woman, shuffling around the kitchen as she microwaves a meal for one, leaves her so weak she can barely get out of the car.

'We can unpack later,' her dad says. 'Let's just have a cup of tea.'

'Oh no,' her mum says. 'You can't leave things in full view like that. It's an invitation to burglars. Last week Helen's son had all his gardening equipment nicked from the back of his van, and it was only parked outside hers for ten minutes . . .'

As her mother warbles away, Orly helps her dad unload, carrying the big wheelie cases – unused since the honeymoon – straight up to her bedroom.

They never expected her to need it again, so the room has been painted beige and decorated with the bland soft furnishings that will appeal to visitors. Despite the paint job and the new bed linen and curtains, it smells the same as it always did. It's a comfort, triggering memories of cramped sleepovers filled with giggling conversations and scandalous revelations. Mel was always proud of her sexual adventures, not hamstrung by shame as Orly was, or strait-laced like Thea, whose prudishness seemed to belong to a different era. Lenny seemed to consider her sex life just another uninteresting part of her weekly routine: like eating and sleeping and homework.

Orly sits down on the squashy mattress she used to sleep so well on, where she dreamt of beautiful boys from films, because real ones were so rare in her all-girl life. The wall opposite used to be covered in Blu Tack bullet holes in the plaster, from a constant cycle of posters being hung up and taken down. But these little markers of her journey to adulthood have been filled and painted over. A slate wiped clean. A fresh start.

A flood of desolation washes over her.

Her mother calls up to her to wash her hands because it's time for dinner.

3

Thea

Thea stands at the back of the room with the other mums while the children watch chocolate coins being produced from Lewis's ear. There are gasps and claps and shouts of 'Look!' and the mums lean forward and raise their eyebrows at Thea in a *How on earth did you find him?* kind of way.

Thea smiles. The guy came recommended by the Russian mum in Lewis's class, and she was right. He is amazing. There are no silly jokes, or cheap bunches of paper flowers pulled from sleeves, just incredible feats of sleight of hand that even this group, with their villas in the South of France and basement cinemas, cannot fail to be impressed by. Best of all, he's managed to hold Lewis's attention. Lewis hasn't hit anyone, broken anything or thrown a tantrum for coming on an hour.

The magician has built a house of cards, four storeys high, and now he asks each child in turn to try and blow it down. None of the children manage it, even after the hugest intakes of breath. Finally it's Lewis's turn, and this time the magician asks him to click his fingers. On the third attempt her son's soft little fingers make the quietest of snaps. The card house collapses and the children howl and point.

Thea can hear the caterers laying out the plates in the kitchen, and the clink of champagne flutes. She hopes they haven't damaged the cake, with its fragile sugar filigree goal net. She's learned not to baulk at figures on invoices, but the price was astonishing.

But it was the guy Bruno's ex-wife always used for Anais and Socrates, so why shouldn't her own kids have the best too?

The magician is now helping Lewis levitate his sister. He is young, barely thirty, and as darkly handsome as a sorcerer ought to be. He reminds her, for a moment, of Tony, and her heart beats faster. She takes some long breaths. Those days are long gone, never to return.

The adults applaud and the magician bows and begins putting away his equipment. But then Lewis jumps up and snatches the string of scarves, and this is the cue for anarchy. The children scream and throw the fragile items at one another. Silk scarves are torn. Plastic cups crack. Brightly coloured balls roll under the furniture. The mothers smile and shake their heads. The magician shouts angrily and snatches his wand from the girl jabbing her friend with it. There is a shocked hush, then the girl bursts into tears.

An American mother rushes forward. 'Oh honey, did he hurt your hand? Let me see.'

The girl holds out a trembling palm and there is a full minute's silence while her mother examines the pink skin. Finally she looks up at the magician and gives him a look of pure loathing. 'Where do you get off assaulting a child?'

Thea claps her hands and says, 'Right, everyone! Pizza in the kitchen!'

The incident forgotten at once, the children rush in a screaming mass for the door. The mums follow and Thea touches the arm of the American, making her brows tilt with concern.

'Is she okay?'

'Oh, it was nothing,' the woman says, all brisk practicality. 'And *so* not your fault. You need to contact the company, though, in case he does that to another child.'

'I will,' Thea says. 'Now go and have a glass of champagne while I speak to him.'

They air-kiss and the woman goes out.

The room is a bombsite.

In the corner, Lewis's presents are forgotten in a tangle of ribbon and torn paper. A drone, a huge Lego set, various remote-control vehicles, PlayStation games. The present-opening soon became a dull-eyed chore for Lewis. It's five years since they moved in with Bruno, and the kids take for granted the lifestyle they now lead, but Thea never will.

She goes up to the magician, who has gathered up all the items and is slipping on his denim jacket.

'Sorry,' she says.

He doesn't even look at her. 'I'm used to it. Why do you think I charge so much?'

'I can reimburse you for any damage.'

Looking up at her, he takes in her cashmere cardigan and kid leather trousers. 'I'm sure you can.' He pushes past her and goes out. A moment later, she hears the door slam.

She sits down on the sofa and drops her head into her hands. A minute is all she needs and then she can be all tits-and-teeth again with these women. She can't leave Lewis in there unsupervised for long. Private school mothers aren't as understanding as state school ones, even at the sort of private school Lewis attends.

She notices that the sleeve of her cardigan has started to bobble. None of the other women wears bobbly cashmere. She should get a new one. Except that when she asked for Bruno's credit card to buy herself some boots from the White Company summer collection, he asked what was wrong with the spring collection ones. He's never done this before. The creeping fear that maybe he has some financial issues sends a chill through her marrow.

'Fuck, what a fucking mess.'

She looks up. Bruno's son stands in the doorway with his sister. 'What have you done to this place?'

'Birthday party,' Thea says, putting on a smile.

'Well clear it up,' Anais says. 'I need to work in here.'

'I will.'

'Like, now. I've got an assignment that needs to be in tomorrow.'

Thea gets up and begins gathering up the wrapping paper. In the kitchen she can hear the hubbub of adult conversation and the wonderful peace of children eating quietly.

'You know, it would take a lot less time if you gave me a hand,' she says as she pushes the enormous sofa back into place.

'Right,' Anais says, and Socrates sniggers.

She is about to tell them *So, do it!* but stops herself in time.

Picking up the armful of paper, she totters out and down the hall in the direction of the utility room, her boot heels clattering in a way that sounds ridiculous. Sure enough, their sniggers follow her.

Five months and they'll be gone, she thinks, off to universities that cater for the thick progeny of the wealthy. And then it will be just the four of them. Perhaps without the distractions of his own children, Bruno will start to bond more with hers. Whatever happens, Thea knows she is doing her best for them. And once a half-brother or sister comes along, they will all be safe for ever.

When she returns, Anais is standing in the doorway. She inhales ostentatiously as Thea passes. Thea stops. *Give me strength.*

'What?'

'Oh, nothing. You're wearing the same perfume as usual.' Anais smiles. 'I liked the one you had on yesterday, that's all.'

'Yesterday?'

'I could smell it in the house when we came home.'

'I was at Lewis's school yesterday, making Easter bonnets.'

'Oh yeah. Must be my defective nose.' Anais slinks back into the living room and shuts the door.

Before Thea has the chance to analyse the strange conversation, a cherry tomato flies out of the kitchen door to splatter against the wall. Pulling the worst of the bobbles off her sleeve and pushing out her chest, she plasters a smile onto her face and goes into the large, airy room, where she finds her children's darling friends having a food fight, as the mums look on with indulgent smiles.

*

She keeps Lewis and Jade up late, to give Bruno the thank-you letters she made them draw before they were allowed to play with the presents. The letters are sweet, and characteristic of her children's different characters. Lewis has drawn a minutely detailed picture of a Transformer speech-bubbling the words THANK YOU FOR THE PARTY – the letters lightly pencilled by Thea, then gone over in shaky felt-tip. Jade has produced a colourful riot of hearts and rainbows, and footnoted the *Thank You* Thea spelled out for her with *I love you*. Thea can't wait to show Bruno – the progress Lewis has made since joining Hoare House is amazing. But when Bruno hasn't returned by ten, both children are carried up to bed, having fallen asleep on the sofa.

Thea pours herself a glass of the now flat champagne and sits down to watch *Strictly* on the kitchen TV. Bruno's children are watching the same thing on the one in the living room, but without the armour of Jade and Lewis, she can't quite bring herself to join them.

Five years together and it seems to get harder, not easier, with her would-be stepchildren. And it's not as if it started well.

After Bruno told them she would be moving in and Thea had assured them that she would never try to take the place of their mother, Socrates looked pointedly at her tits and said, 'I don't think we'll get you mixed up.' At the beginning, they took great glee in calling her by the names of his former flames – Suki and Joely and Keira and Sho – until Bruno had to step in. Anais had been told to apologise, which she did, before adding, 'Maybe it's fifteenth time lucky.'

Ho-ho.

The second sour glass goes down twice as fast. She is determined to say something to Bruno when he comes home. Tell him how disrespectful his kids are. But when the door does finally open, she chickens out and goes to meet him with a kiss and a smile.

He doesn't ask her how the party went, but she tells him anyway, and he grunts and says he's going for a shower before bed.

She washes her glass – Poonam has done the rest of the cleaning-up – turns the light off and follows him.

As she passes the open door of the living room, the teenagers stop talking, and she feels the flesh on her arms prickle. They really do hate her. Do they think she's going to marry their father and take him for all his money? She would never do that. She cares about Bruno. She's grateful to him. When they do get married and have children of their own, she will make sure there is a clause in her will, should she survive him, to cater for Socrates and Anais.

There's more than enough for everyone, she thinks as she climbs the walnut staircase and heads to her own bathroom.

To thank him for the party and the cake and the champagne, she puts on the sexy lace playsuit he bought her on their third anniversary. It's been coming on two years of trying and still her period arrives on the dot every month. She knew it would take a while – he's sixty and she's pushing forty – but if it carries on, she'll sneak off to her GP and check her hormone levels. *Think positive*, she tells herself, primping her honeyed curls over the rise of her breasts. She's mid cycle. Maybe tonight's the night.

But when she goes through the connecting door into the bedroom, he doesn't look up from the *Financial Times*.

'How was your day?' she says, slipping in beside him. He'll notice in a minute.

'Fine. How was yours?'

'The party was wonderful, thank you, so much.' She strokes his knuckle.

'That's what I'm here for.'

It takes a moment for the meaning of his words to sink in, and when they do, she stops stroking. 'Hey.'

He looks up at her and smiles over his glasses, but says nothing.

'That's not fair. We're a team.'

'Of course.' Back to the paper.

She experiences a flash of annoyance.

'Actually. There was something I wanted to mention to you.'

'Mmm.'

'Soc and Anais were quite rude to me today.'

'Oh?'

'They told me to clear the party mess up.'

'Ri-ight,' Bruno says slowly. 'And?'

'Don't you think that's rude? I'm your partner after all; they should treat me with respect.'

'You have to earn respect.'

She stares at him, frozen. 'I'm sorry?'

He turns the page of the newspaper.

'Bruno?'

He looks up, his face screwed in irritation. 'Oh for God's sake, it was a joke. I'm sorry they asked you to clear up the mess your kids made, okay?'

She opens her mouth and closes it again. If he'd been there, surely he would have told them off. Surely. Finally he's noticed what she's wearing. His eyes flick down to her breasts and she adjusts her position slightly to make them stick out. But now he's frowning.

'What's that?' He's pointing at the inner edge of her breast but doesn't seem to want to touch her.

'What?' she says, looking down.

'That funny lump.'

Her heart jumps into her mouth. She gets out of bed and hurries into her bathroom.

Peering into the mirror, her heart starts beating again. It's not a lump. The implant on the left side has slipped, that's all. It's probably just natural ageing, but there's now an indentation where the top of the implant stands proud of her natural breast tissue. Closing her eyes, she leans on the sink. Is this why he hasn't been interested in sex recently?

She pulls on her silk dressing gown and goes back into the bedroom. The light is off and he's lying on his side, facing away from her, but she can tell from his breathing that he's not asleep.

'It's just the implant,' she says softly. 'I guess it's going to cost a bit to fix. Sorry.'

31

He sighs. 'Can't you live with it?'

She tries to laugh – 'I can. It's whether you can' – and slides a hand over his hip. He twitches away from her and she snatches her hand back as if it's been burned.

'We'll talk about it in the morning,' he says.

But in the morning he leaves for work before she's got the children breakfasted and onto the school buses. The Hoare House one arrives first, purring up to the kerb, Mr Colin the driver tipping his liveried hat at her. The vehicle is so ridiculously flash, purple with gold calligraphy on the side, you would think it was a school for Saudi princes rather than children with learning and behavioural difficulties. The fees are eye-watering, but it's worth it: Lewis is much less aggressive towards Jade these days and is finally starting to learn to read and write.

Poonam comes in for an hour, but as usual she leaves the teenagers' bedrooms. The stink of unwashed feet and armpits will continue to waft under their doors to taint the entire landing.

Fuck it, she thinks: she will pay them back for what they said to her in a perfectly ironic way. She will clear up the *fucking mess* in their bedrooms.

She creeps up the stairs with Poonam's tray of cleaning products as if someone might still be in the house, and enters Anais's room.

Immediately she's assailed by the smell, as if something has crawled under the teenager's bed and died. Anais's curtains are drawn, so Thea turns on the light.

She wrinkles her nose and moves away from the bed. The sheet is stained with dried period blood. Scattered across the carpet are several pairs of dirty knickers, a grubby bra, and black tights whose toes retain the shape of human feet. Dust and hair balls gather under the bed like small, watchful rodents.

She forgot the hoover. But there's plenty to be getting on with.

The glass top of Anais's dressing table is opaque with dust and smears of cosmetics: a yellow-crusted cotton bud, a thread of dental floss with particles of food attached, greasy tweezers and blackhead-removal strips.

Thea smiles grimly. Perhaps Anais is learning just how hard it is to maintain the illusion of effortless beauty. *Just wait till you're pushing forty, sweetheart.*

She takes the bleach spray from the box but can't quite bring herself to pump it. Anais will be beside herself with fury. She will tell Bruno. Bruno will be angry.

A couple of months ago, this wouldn't have bothered Thea, but some nagging feeling – perhaps it's just the sex thing – tells her that her current position is not as strong as it was. As if the floor around her has turned from wood to glass and she must tread carefully or risk plunging through to the darkness beneath.

She will have to comfort herself with a stealthier victory. All posh kids take drugs. She'll find their stash and flush it down the toilet. As chilled out as Bruno is as a parent, he won't have much sympathy if they run to him complaining about lost pills.

Under the sneering gaze of the beautiful people who populate Anais's walls, she moves to the chest of drawers. It's a seething mass of tops and vests, all grubby and fetid-smelling, some with stains and holes. Thea can't understand how someone as rich as Anais – her allowance is a thousand pounds a month – would ever go out in these rags. Thea won't let Jade leave the house without brushing her hair and washing her hands. She wouldn't dream of allowing her to wear an item of clothing that wasn't good as new.

But Anais doesn't seem to care.

Is that the point? Thea wonders as she shuts the top drawer and opens the second one. That Anais doesn't need to prove anything to anyone? That she's so far above the matrix of shame that traps poorer girls, she can do whatever she likes.

Or is Thea overthinking it? Is Anais just a typical scabby teenager?

She opens the last drawer of the cabinet and recoils. It's full of underwear, but not the sort of clean white cotton knickers Thea

33

wore as a teenager, or even the pretty lacy stuff she would buy now. This stuff seems to be constructed mostly from metal mesh, rubber, leather and uncomfortable-looking buckles. Pulling her sleeve over her hand, she lifts up an item. How on earth would you go about putting something like that on? She drops it quickly: if Anais's lack of hygiene extends to this, then God knows what lurks in the crevices.

She pokes around squeamishly, but what she finds is not a wrap of weed or a baggie of pills.

At the back of Anais's drawer is a stack of Polaroid photographs fastened with an elastic band.

Thea takes them out, rolls off the band and goes through them.

The Polaroids all feature a naked and bound Anais dangling from various items of furniture by a belt around her throat. In one of the images, she has slumped forward as if she has fallen unconscious.

Thea's laugh is loud in the silence. So, pretty little trust-fund Anais is into bondage? But then a surge of bitterness makes the blood rush to her face.

It's not fair.

When Thea was a teenager her sexuality was a liability, something fragile to be protected from all who would seek to assail it. There was no question of her having actual *desires* of her own: all that mattered was that she wasn't a slag. Tony and his mates sneered at girls who enjoyed casual sex; though they were not above using them for just that, Tony would never have gone out with Thea unless her honour had been beyond reproach. She'd been a virgin when she went with him, for fuck's sake. A fucking virgin. And afterwards, after what happened, she'd had to trade sex carefully, to ensure its worth stayed high.

High enough to live in a house like this, with a man who pampers her with clothes and holidays and cosmetic surgery.

But still an interloper.

Anais belongs here. Girls like her can do whatever they like. Oral sex performed in just a string of pearls, lesbian flings,

34

multiple partners, bondage – it's all something to be proud of. Wild and liberated, not slutty.

Thea sits heavily on the dirty bed.

She can't remember the last time she enjoyed sex – if ever. She's always been far too concerned with what she looks like, how turned on Bruno is, when it's going to end. Imagine being able to tell someone you want to be choked while strapped to bits of furniture

She puts the photographs into her pocket, then takes them out again. She can't show Bruno without looking like a prurient snoop. Tucking them back under the bondage gear, she picks up the cleaning products and goes back out onto the landing.

Her appetite for provocation has vanished and she almost doesn't bother with Socrates' room, but she's got an hour or two before she's due to meet Adrienne for Pilates. Fuck it, maybe there's something worse in Socrates' drawers. At least it might give her something to laugh about with Lenny, Mel and Orly.

Socrates' room is completely different. The window is open, and the air smells minty fresh with deodorant. His bed is made and his surfaces are clear except for a neat arrangement of toiletries. Where Anais's walls are slathered with posters, Socrates has a single abstract art print that probably cost more than Thea and Tony's first flat.

Either the boy is a paragon of virtue and she will find absolutely nothing worthy of reproach, or he hides his misdemeanours well.

Half-heartedly she opens his top drawer. His T-shirts are stacked in neatly folded piles, the colours vibrant, the whites glowing. She slides it closed. His underwear drawer is equally Marie Kondo-esque, the socks paired perfectly and nestled together like pool balls. There's a slight rise in the middle of the top pair of underpants, like a lacklustre erection. She lifts a corner of the pile. Underneath is a Tupperware tub.

Bingo.

She smiles as she takes it out. But when she opens the lid, the smile fades.

Thanks to Tony's business activities, Thea knows what illegal drugs look like, and this is not cannabis or MDMA or coke. In fact it looks like a stack of gel foot plasters, the kind she uses to prevent new stilettos crippling her.

And yet – she peels a plaster from the stack – these wouldn't give you much in the way of protection. The gel pad is too thin.

There's some writing on the patch – white on white, so it's difficult to read against the adhesive backing. She takes it to the window and holds it up in the dusty sunlight lancing through the blind. Then she goes back to the chest, puts the plaster back into the Tupperware box and shuts the drawer.

Afterwards, she lets herself out of Socrates' bedroom and goes back downstairs.

Sitting at the kitchen island with a coffee from the Gaggia machine, she gazes out across the back garden, where a blackbird is pecking at the lawn.

The rich, spicy scent of the coffee brings back the conversation with Anais about the perfume. She pauses, the mug halfway to her mouth. Anais was obviously implying that another woman had been in the house when Thea was out.

She sips the coffee and sets the mug back down.

It's nothing to get stressed about. The little bitch was just trying to wind her up. Bruno was at work and wouldn't have time to nip home for a quickie with some new bit of stuff – although he did know that Thea would be out all day . . .

Oh, come on. There are better places to carry on an affair, like a work trip or . . . Bruno was away in Milan two weeks ago.

Oh no. No.

It would explain everything: the late nights, the lack of interest in sex, the lack of physical contact of any kind, in fact. Thea's still good-looking, she knows that, but as far as she can make out, since the divorce, apart from her, Bruno has only ever dated women in their twenties.

Tipping her head back, she breathes deeply, inhaling the scent of the single-origin Jamaican Blue, listening to the gentle lullaby of the dishwasher.

Don't panic. You've been in worse situations. You must not panic. Think. Think.

Eventually enough strength returns to her legs to allow her to stand up.

Firstly, she thinks, as she totters down the hallway, she may be imagining all of it. Building up simple work pressures into some ulterior motive that simply doesn't exist. Anais probably picked up the vibe and decided to try and sow seeds of doubt in Thea's mind, perhaps hoping for a showdown with Bruno. Because what Bruno hates more than anything else is an insecure woman. It was jealousy that ended his marriage (oh, and the four affairs) and he made it perfectly clear when they got together that he wouldn't have her checking up on him all the time, that a relationship should be based on trust, that it was okay not to be in each other's pockets. After Tony's possessiveness, it was one of the things she liked best about him.

Secondly, she thinks as she opens the door to his study, would Bruno really want to throw everything up in the air, their happy family life together, for a piece of tail? He's getting older now, and his main loves seem to be reading the paper and watching the cricket. Can he really be bothered with a new relationship with some energetic young thing who demands to be taken out and entertained?

Thirdly, she thinks as she opens the top drawer of his filing cabinet, they've been trying for a baby, and would a man do that if he was intending to break up with you?

Finally, she decides as she rifles through the files marked with the names of his investment portfolios, if the worst comes to the worst, there's always Si.

The bottom drawer is locked.

She sits back on the deep-pile carpet and drops her head between her knees. She really is scraping the barrel today. Snooping on all three of her quasi-family.

And for what reason? Paranoia? She, who has never been cheated on in her whole life, who has always been the object of men's desperate adoration? Tony begged her, literally on his knees and sobbing, not to leave him, to wait for him while he did his fourteen years.

It's the thought of that time – the time she nearly lost Lewis and Jade – that makes her jaw harden.

She wasn't Tony's girlfriend for twelve years without learning how to pick a lock. The drawer slides open with a sigh, as if it has been longing to tell her its secrets. It's filled with blue files, all neatly labelled.

There's nothing to alarm her in the *Financial* one at the front. The opposite, in fact. Bruno's stocks are performing incredibly. His savings bonds alone add up to seven figures. A letter from an estate agent informs him that a house similar to theirs – *his* – has just sold for six million.

Continuing to rifle through, she finds a folder marked *Will*, and holds her breath as she opens it. But it's dated 2001, back when he was still married, and before Socrates and Anais were born. She exhales, replacing the file and instinctively wiping it with the sleeve of her hoodie to remove any fingerprints.

Somehow, softly, softly, she will find a way to bring up the updating of wills without looking like she's hinting. Perhaps she could discuss the guardianship of Jade and Lewis in the event of her death, and whether he would be prepared to take them on. A pre-breast-op conversation, perhaps, in case of surgery complications. He certainly won't be told what to do with his finances by her, but perhaps she can make him think it's his idea.

Of course there's nothing here that might suggest an affair – no G-strings tucked between the papers, or dirty photographs – and she's about to close the drawer when her fingertips brush a folder marked *Medical*. She withdraws it. There are the usual insurance forms, the more recent ones with her and the children added. A receipt for the vaginal tightening surgery she had when they first got together. And then there are a couple of letters from his private doctor, Dr Tim with the scratch golf handicap. She skim-reads the most recent one, dated seven months previously.

Dear Bruno,
Thanks for coming in last week. You'll be pleased to know that all is well with your vasectomy. Your sperm count is still zero, so I won't need to see you again until next year.
Best wishes,
Tim

Half an hour later, she's still lying on her back, staring at the ceiling.

No Pilates with Adrienne now, no nothing for the rest of the day except meditation and alcohol, to make sure she can function as a convincing human being again once the children get home.

For two years they have been trying for a baby. For two years he has been lying to her.

She thought they were safe, she and the children, but they've been living in a house of cards. Like the magician's trick pack, it will stay up only until Bruno decides to click his fingers.

Eventually, somehow, she struggles to her knees. With a shaking hand she tucks the letter back into the file, replaces it, closes the drawer and locks it. Then, smoothing down the indents of her heels as she goes, she crawls backwards out of the room.

@GillingwaterFestival
2 months to go till #GillFest25 tickets go on sale and we can't wait!! Just confirming the line-up. Watch this space . . .

@WillTheCharcoalBurner
Replying to @GillingwaterFestival
It would be great to see some folk bands this year, to honour the solstice and the Goddess.

@MartyntheDaddyo
Replying to @GillingwaterFestival and @WillTheCharcoalBurner
Is this goddess hot then? Can I honour her with beer?

4

Lenny

Work has been an absolute bitch. Sitting in traffic, Lenny tries not to think about all those hours, the bedtimes and story-times, sacrificed to design the financial product that a rival released this morning, a single week before she was about to approach her clients with it.

She wants to vent at someone, to rant and rage and speculate bitterly that she has been robbed, that those bastards hacked the bank's IT systems and stole her idea. But she can't. Mainly because they probably didn't: creative minds come up with ideas simultaneously, it happens all the time, she should have been quicker. And also because no one outside the Square Mile really understands her job.

She turns the radio on, flicks it to a hard rock station, hoping all the jangling guitars and snarling will exorcise her own fury before she gets home. At least she'll be in time for a bedtime story tonight.

The song ends and she changes to a different station. She can feel the cortisol starting to subside, thank God. She doesn't want to be snappy with the kids. But it's replaced by a sinking of her mood as the first few drops of rain patter against the window. Ahead of her, brake lights shatter into shards of red. The traffic's no longer even moving. She won't be home for another hour at least.

What the fuck is she doing bringing up her kids in London? They deserve the sort of childhood she had, with fields and bicycles, friends who lived on the same street, not having to learn Latin when you're five years old.

Her phone rings: probably Jeanne. She's about to Bluetooth it to the speaker when she sees the caller ID.

Thea.

Her hand hovers over the screen, but she doesn't pick up.

It's probably some bullshit question about who's the best kitchen designer at Harrods, or does Lenny know any restaurant that does Wagyu beef. Back in the day she would have had an opinion on, and interest in, both of those topics, back when she and Thea hung out all the time, going for expensive lunches and shopping sprees paid for by Tony's nefarious deeds. But while Lenny's priorities have changed – she's more concerned with schools and piano lessons these days – Thea's haven't. If one morning she found she couldn't squeeze herself into her size eight kid leather trousers, Thea would probably kill herself.

Greta is in her pyjamas drinking hot milk by the time Lenny gets in, but Jackson's still in the bath, so after releasing Jeanne to go out and meet her boyfriend, Lenny takes off her boots and goes up to him.

He's washed his own hair, using far too much shampoo, and is scowling in concentration as he sculpts it into an impressive Mohican.

'Hello, Sid Vicious,' she says, and sits down on the toilet seat.

'Who's Sid Fishes?' he says, fixing her with his cornflower-blue eyes that she would have killed for as a teenager.

'Punk rock star.'

'What's punk rock?'

'Only the definitive musical genre of the last fifty years. How was your day?'

His Mohican is wilting and she reaches across to spike it up, but he jerks away, frowning.

'You okay?'

He shrugs.

'You and Greta been fighting?'

He shakes his head and bites his lip. He looks like he's about to cry, and Jackson never cries. She scans his body for signs of injury, but his skin is peachy and flawless.

She drops to her knees on the soggy bathmat. 'What's wrong?'

He draws in a shuddering breath.

'Come on,' she murmurs, a hand on his sudsy shoulder. 'Tell Mummy.'

'We had to say what our mummies and daddies did for work today, and I knew what you did, but when they asked me what my daddy did, I had to say I haven't got one.' The tears are falling now.

'Oh, baby.'

'The others said I had to have a daddy, everyone does.'

Lenny sighs and closes her eyes to prepare herself. 'I've told you this before, lovely. Lots of times. Mummy wanted you so very badly, she didn't want to wait to get a husband, so she chose the very cleverest, most wonderful man she could find and asked if he would make a baby with her.'

'And he said yes,' Jackson whispers.

'And he said yes, and gave me you two.'

He turns his shining blue eyes on her. 'Does he love me?'

She swallows. 'He would if he met you.'

'Doesn't he want to meet me?'

Downstairs she can hear the theme tune to Greta's programme. She'll be up in a minute to find out where Mummy is.

Lenny panics. She's thought this thing through so many times, and each question her imagined son asked her had a ready answer, but now that her real son is gazing at her with hopeful trust, she just can't think of one that won't inflict pain.

'All I asked him to do,' she says slowly, 'was help to make you.'

'You didn't tell him that I wanted a daddy?' His mouth has curved down at the edges, the sweet little lips pulled tight.

'That didn't come into it. When you ask if someone will help you make a baby, you—'

'Well you should have!' he cries. 'Because I do! I want a daddy like everybody else has! It's not fair.'

43

He starts beating the water with his fists, making troughs and swells that splash over the side of the bath and slop onto the tiles.

'Okay, time to get out.'

But after he's dried and dressed and is deliciously cuddleable in his fleecy dressing gown and sheepskin slippers, he refuses to come downstairs. She spends a desultory hour making a jigsaw with Greta, too distracted to have a proper conversation with her daughter, then sends her up to bed ten minutes early. Greta agrees to sit on Jackson's beanbag while Lenny reads the story, because Jackson won't come into her room, though it's her turn, and instead lies with his back to them both. After she's read about the tiger drinking all the water from the taps, and having sausages for tea, Lenny puts her daughter to bed and comes back to kiss her son.

Sulking she could take, or six-year-old rage with its predictable *I hate you*s, but Jackson is crying quietly into a pillow already damp with tears.

Lenny sinks onto the bed, a limp hand on his little back, and wonders what on earth she can do to make this better.

In the end, all she can think of is to punish herself.

She goes down to the basement and works out like she hasn't done in a decade, since the days when all she and Thea thought about was having a hard body and the clothes to show it off. Half an hour on the running machine, another twenty on the rower on max resistance, and then weights. She's nearly finished the last reps of her bicep curls when the asthma attack hits. The tightness of breath she thought was just stress from the shitty day at work followed by Jackson's meltdown becomes a coughing fit, and then a fist closes around her lungs.

She realises with panic that the closest blue inhaler is upstairs in her handbag on the kitchen island, along with her mobile. She's starting to see stars as she begins the long climb up from the basement. Halfway up, she is gasping for breath. Clinging to the banister at the top, she tries to call out, but her voice has been taken from her.

She drops to her knees and crawls along the cherrywood floor of the silent house. Her perfect furniture, her beautiful books and mirrors and vases and paintings all look on impassively as the life is squeezed out of her. She crawls onto the rug that cost her fourteen thousand pounds, and all it can do is ruck under her knees to slow her down. The kitchen door is a mile away. Ten miles. A light year.

Her lungs are like children refusing their supper. She must coax in each sip of air, pause to digest it, then scrape forward on the ounce of energy it gives her. Respiration happens in the cells, they always told her at school, not the lungs – they are just for gas exchange. So why can't her cells keep her alive as her lungs fold in on themselves like collapsing stars?

The inch-thick drop at the edge of the rug is enough to topple her over, and she rests her cheek on the floor and decides to give up.

A strand of cobweb connecting the brass legs of her hall stand glimmers in the lamplight. She wills the spider to come out and tip-tap over to her. Everything she has achieved in her life has been alone; she doesn't want to die alone too.

Her vision darkens.

Then her eyes widen. She didn't go into the kitchen tonight; she went straight upstairs to see Jackson. The bag is on the hall stand. She swivels her eyeballs and sees the thin tan handle dangling over the edge. If she can just . . . if she can just reach . . .

The bag falls. Items skitter across the floor like cockroaches fleeing a broom. The inhaler stays within reach. Her trembling fingers close on it. She raises it to her lips. She presses, sucks, and a single stitch holding her lungs together breaks.

She waits five seconds, repeats the procedure. Two more stitches break and a trickle of air enters the pocket of space. After ten more puffs she can breathe again, like any other human being on the fucking planet.

She bursts into tears.

Lying on her back on the hard wooden floor, she stares up at the blurry ceiling and thinks of her children. Ten more seconds and they would have been orphaned. Motherless as well as fatherless – both conditions inflicted upon them by her own selfishness. She must be more careful. Life is so fragile.

She crawls around repacking her handbag, then drapes it across her shoulder and pulls herself up on the hall stand. Leaning on the marble top, she gazes at her face in the mirror. A hollow-eyed corpse stares back at her, without enough breath even to mist the glass.

She needs a fucking drink.

It takes a bottle of Malbec before she's calm enough to try and sleep, but hobbling to the bottom of the stairs, she looks up at what might as well be the north face of the Eiger. She thought she was strong enough to raise her children alone, and now she hasn't even got the strength to climb the stairs to bed.

That night she beds down on the sofa with the babble of CNN for company, her brain dispelling any possibility of sleep as she imagines a life for her children that doesn't contain her.

From: The Staight Practice
To: Leonora Clarke

Your request for *4 x Ventolin 200 micrograms/dose Accuhalers (GlaxoSmithKline UK Ltd)* has been received and will be ready to collect from Walden Pharmacy, 24 Pelham Street, London, SW7 2ND in 3 working days.

5

Mel

Mel's fingernails make rapid plinking noises against her empty mug.

It's gone noon and that shit of a father still hasn't phoned to wish Billy a happy birthday. It's at times like these she hates herself for being so accommodating with Gary over the years, biting her tongue when Billy's upset with him, welcoming the latest girlfriend without wishing her the *best of luck*, making excuses for his puerile behaviour. When Billy was little, she'd even buy birthday presents herself and sign them 'Love, Daddy' – back when Billy was too young to be of any interest to Gary, before he got into Yeovil Town. Now they have father–son bromance excursions all around the country following the mediocre team whose season ticket, now that he's turned eighteen, will cost her three hundred quid a year.

She lights a fag, gazing moodily out at the garden that looks more like no-man's-land every year. She had plans when they moved in here. She would returf it, plant fruit trees and dig a vegetable patch. But life – and a little boy – got in the way. Still, at least you can kick a football across it.

Billy's coming down the stairs, so she grinds out the fag and bats away the smoke, hoping the onions she chopped earlier will mask it. *I don't want you to die, Mummy* – that's what he used to say. But she gets the feeling it wouldn't mean the end of his world any more.

He comes into the kitchen and helps himself to a handful from the bowl of grated cheese, phone tucked between chin and shoulder. 'Okay, Dad. Cheers. See you tomorrow.'

There. She's gone and got herself into a giant strop for nothing.

And then, as he's telling her what time Gary's coming to collect him tomorrow for their camping trip, just like that she bursts into tears.

Her huge son bounds across the room and scoops her up in his ridiculously massive arms and booms in his ridiculously deep voice, 'Mum, what's wrong?'

For a moment or two she can't speak for hiccuping sobs and bewildered laughter. What on earth *is* wrong?

Then, fool that she is, she realises.

You're eighteen, my darling, precious little boy. You're a man. And apart from the odd bit of financial advice, booze-and-lodging at Christmas and, God willing, babysitting duties in a few years, you don't need your mum any more. Your mum who lay awake with you while you twisted and screeched with colic. Who taught you to pee in the toilet, how to use a knife and fork, that dyslexia is a gift not a curse. Who marched round to the home of that bully Stevie Fletcher and rowed with his dad in the street. Who learned how to do long division and factorising algebra to help you with your maths. The mum you owe nothing to, because you deserved every single minute, every single ounce of love she could give you, and still do. Soon you will leave her to start your precious and wonderful life, and though her heart is breaking, she wouldn't have it any other way.

'Nothing,' she smiles. 'Just tired.'

'Go and sit down and I'll make you a cuppa.'

'I've got to get the food ready for tonight.'

'I'll do that, it's my party.'

'We'll do it together then.'

Mother and son. Hip to hip, breathing in rhythm as they chop cucumber at the window they've looked out of since Billy had to stand on a chair to reach the sink. *I'll wash and you dry. There's a good boy, you'll make someone a lovely husband.* Never believing the time would ever come, not really.

They start arriving at 6.30. Kieran first. Another booming giant masquerading as the best friend who used to cry at sleepovers and have to be driven home.

'Let me help you with that, Mel,' he says, and opens the jar of hot dogs with a flick of his wrist. 'You look nice. Off somewhere?'

'To a hotel for the night, so I don't have to deal with the neighbours complaining.'

'That's a shame.' Kieran leans on the kitchen counter and his sigh ripples his pectorals. 'I was looking forward to catching up.'

'Out of my way, I've got hot dogs to boil.'

The girls arrive in packs. Too old to giggle, but young enough still to need one another, exchanging loaded glances at every ingenuous comment from the boys. How frustrating it must be to have to waste your complexity and sophistication on the beautiful bouncing dummies that are teenage boys. Billy and Kieran are wrestling in the hall, barking oafish laughter.

There's one missing. They may not feel it any more, three years after the terrible event, but Mel does. She makes sure to think about Leylan every so often, to fix his memory to the earth, to stop him being carried away by the callous winds of time. If, God forbid, it happened to Billy, she would hope that his friends' mothers would do the same. It's not a thought to linger over on a day of celebration, and she pushes it away. There's no point torturing herself about what Billy will get up to when he goes to uni. Most kids try drugs at some point, but only a tiny handful die. Leylan was just very unlucky.

'I'm off, babes,' she says, pulling a sensible puffa over her green silk wrap dress. She knows he thinks she's meeting someone, but she's not. Tonight she will be toasting herself. A job well done.

Very well done, she thinks, as he leans in to kiss her, smelling of cheese and onion crisps. He's a gentle, kind, courageous and loyal young man, the spit of his handsome dad only without the shallow arrogance. She ruffles his sleek hair and kisses him.

'Goodnight, bunnikins. Have fun.'

She grins as the good-natured guffawing follows her out to the car, adding in her head: *Have sex, get drunk and make such a racket the neighbours call the police.*

The hotel is only eleven miles away, a conference place still offering the last of its cheap spring deals. It's got a pool and a sauna and steam room, and the restaurant is in the Michelin guide. She will treat herself to a decent bottle of wine and might even stretch to a starter.

Checking in, she books a table for one and hands over her credit card with another little burst of pride. After a lifetime of debt, this is the first year she's actually managed to pay off her overdraft and credit card bills in full every month. It's all thanks to the café: everybody's going mad for veggie/vegan stuff these days, so they all got a decent rise this year. Who'd have thought when she started waitressing there at fourteen that she'd end up as manager, with a proper manager's salary? Could this be counted as a career now? She smiles at the handsome boy behind the counter and he hands her the room card.

The bedroom is nice, all beige and white with tasteful prints on the walls and a packet of all-butter shortbread on a tray by the kettle. Probably no different to any other provincial hotel, but staying in a hotel at all is a luxury they very rarely stretched to when Billy was growing up. Tents and borrowed caravans were the holiday destinations of his childhood, and he never complained, making friends with the other children wherever they went, cheerfully throwing himself into karaoke and bingo and talent shows. His signature song was 'It's Not Unusual', because she used to dance round the kitchen whenever it came on the radio.

She has a bath because it's there and the hot water is free and the towels are soft, then regards herself critically in the mirror.

Breasts still relatively perky. A few fine stretch marks long faded to a light purple almost invisible on her dark skin. No wrinkles to speak of. No bingo wings yet.

She's thirty-nine. Some of her friends are only just thinking of having kids. But after all that criticism that she wasted her life getting pregnant at twenty – much of it from her mother – she's the one with a new and unencumbered future stretching out before her. She could take a college course. She's always fancied being a therapist. Billy's friends often used to come to her for advice, and she loved talking to them, helping them to see that their problems were not insurmountable, that they would, like everything else, pass and be forgotten. She's got the brains: well, she did at school. Top sets in everything, same as Lenny. And look what Lenny achieved.

She feels a swell of affection for her old friend. A single mum, through choice, at thirty-four. That was brave. Mel's mother immediately changed her tune, of course. Now it was Lenny who was to be criticised for her unnatural choice to maintain her career. *Why have kids if you don't want to be with them?*

But life's not as simple as that. The Polish nanny who comes to the café has a family back home that she sends money to. They're safe and warm and fed because of her, and love at a distance is no less powerful. When Billy goes, he will take half Mel's heart with him, torn and still dripping.

She smiles as she puts on her make-up.

So, what about a man?

Maybe. There seem to be a lot of divorces among the secondary school lot, plenty of free blokes. But maybe not. She won't be told what to do again, and she doesn't fancy making compromises. She's compromised herself for Billy all these years, and gladly: now maybe it's time for a bit of selfishness.

She heads downstairs. Picking up a magazine from the reception area, she makes for the bar and orders herself a vodka tonic.

It's a nice place; plush. Lots of that fake pink brass they make tables and picture frames out of these days. The low lights glinting off it are flattering, she sees, catching a glimpse of herself in the mirror behind the optics.

A man sitting alone on one of the banquettes looks up. Papers are spread out in front of him and his tie is loosened. A bit thick round the middle, a bit thin on top, but otherwise acceptable. He smiles, pretends to screw paper into a ball.

She has a second drink with him. The velvet is soft against her bare thighs, the glass tabletop cool under her wrists. It's a long time since she was aware of how her own body was feeling, as opposed to someone else's. He asks if she will have dinner with him. She wants to go halves, but he says it's on expenses.

They have olives and bread and starters and puddings, which she feeds him spoonfuls of, leaning across the table, not missing the glances he throws at her cleavage. They take the remainder of the second bottle of Sauvignon with them as they weave out of the restaurant and bundle into the lift. By the time it reaches his floor, her dress and his flies are already undone.

It's a hasty affair and none too satisfying, but the bed is comfortable and she sleeps brilliantly considering how stuffed and pissed she is.

She wakes to the stillness and silence of a watercolour dawn behind double-glazing. It's nice waking up with a man. He's not hairy or smelly. He didn't fart or snore or scratch.

She smiles. Kieran told her she'd pull in that dress.

He wakes up and turns over, stretching with a drawn-out groan.

'Good morning.'

'Morning.' She puts her hand on his chest, twisting the hair between her fingers. There's no point going home yet: the kids will still be flat out on every inch of floor space.

'Wait,' he says. 'Let me have a quick shower.'

He gets out of bed and half runs to the bathroom, evidently self-conscious about his wobbly white backside. She smiles again. It's sweet.

Then the phone on his bedside table lights up and a woman's face appears above the caller ID: *Home.*

Ah well, what did she expect?

He comes back from the bathroom with a towel around his sucked-in waist and his hair casually tousled. She nods at the phone, which lights up again with a message coming through.

Their eyes meet.

'Sorry,' he says. 'I should have said.'

'Do this all the time, do you?' she says. Not hostile – he's from Manchester, it was never going to be a thing – just rueful.

'No. But you were . . . you know, lovely.'

A good answer. They make love again, and afterwards she goes back to her room to pack and check out.

When she gets down to reception, he's standing by the revolving doors, muttering into the phone. Drawing level with him, she can hear him telling someone that he ran out of battery, that he's sorry, that she's always checking up on him.

She walks past him, but though his gaze moves over her, it's as if she's become invisible. Outside, she turns for one last glance back at him. He's gripping the front of his hair now, his expression stormy. It's not worth it, she wants to say: cheating. You'll lose everything. But it's his problem, not hers.

She walks to the car, puts on her favourite music station, and sets off for home.

As she parks, a bedraggled group of shivering teens emerges from her house, one missing a shoe. She keeps her head down, not wanting to shatter their illusion of grown-upness with her amused concern. After the door closes, she counts to a minute then gets out. Steeling herself for what she might be about to find behind that door, she takes a deep breath and lets herself in.

The hoover's going. That's a good sign.

'I'm home!'

The kitchen is almost clean, though the four black bin bags are overflowing. There's a smell of cigarette butts marinated in lager. A smashed glass has been scrupulously placed on the windowsill.

54

Putting the kettle on, she opens the window to let in the fresh morning air. As she lifts her arm to take down a mug from the cupboard, she gets a waft of the businessman's deodorant.

'Shit!' Billy says, coming into the kitchen and starting violently. 'Thought you weren't coming back till lunchtime.'

'I missed you,' she says. 'Thought I'd rather be with my boy before he abandons me for a week than sweating in some spa.'

'I'm nearly done, right, but please don't go upstairs, not until I say. It's not bad, but a load of people slept in the bathroom and—'

'Leave it,' she says.

'I just need to—'

'Leave it. If we need to pee, we'll use the downstairs toilet. Now, do you want some breakfast? I stopped off for bacon and bread.'

'Mum,' he says solemnly. 'You are my favourite person in the world.'

Not for much longer, she thinks.

They eat their sandwiches in front of a movie about a man abandoning his little girl to go off into space, which unexpectedly leaves both of them in tears. Afterwards Billy says he's going to clean the bathroom, but she turns on another film and he snuggles against her, smelling of bad breath and hair grease, and eventually he starts snoring. She kisses his forehead – still spotty – and squeezes his hand, the nails still bitten to the quick: breathing in every last precious scent and sight and touch of him before the doorbell rings and his father arrives to take him away from her.

It's only a week, but somehow it feels like the end of their time together. Or at least the beginning of the end.

She watches the car move slowly up the road. He doesn't look back. He won't when he leaves in September, because he'll be home again at weekends and in the holidays. He'll refer to this little house as *home* for years afterwards, but it won't be, not really, not ever again. Even if he fucks everything up and has to move back in while he looks for a job, or training, or another college course, everything will have changed. He'll be a resentful man-child getting in the way. She'll be the disappointed mother demanding rent. No, these are the last few months of his innocent, joyous childhood, where everything has gone according to the plan she mapped out for him and he accepted as his right and duty.

Goodbye, my darling, darling, darling boy, she thinks, as the Toyota turns the corner and gives a last cheery toot. An arm stretches from the window, impossibly long, the hand whose tiny fingernails she used to snip so carefully now the span of a dinner plate. And then he's gone.

She goes back inside, sinks down at the kitchen table and sobs.

@GillingwaterFestival
Tickets for #GillFest25 go on sale tomorrow from 8am at
gillfest@tickets.com. We're predicting huge demand, so tell
your boss you might be late in!

@ChoccyBiscuitFace
Replying to @GillingwaterFestival
Oh my god so excited!!!!!!!!!!!!!

6

Thea

The party is at a roof garden in central London. It's an amazing spot, looking out over the whole of Soho. Bruno's phone rings the minute they walk out of the lift, so Thea stands patiently beside him while he guffaws with the caller about a work skiing trip they both went on where someone broke their back.

More guests are arriving all the time. They pass her without a second glance, but that's only because she's standing in Bruno's shadow. She's been careful tonight. Perhaps over the last couple of years she's been guilty of letting herself go, as you do in a long-term relationship. She might have put on a few pounds – a snug ten now rather than a loose eight – and until last week she hadn't had Botox or a peel in months. But tonight she knows she looks her best: elegant, slim, as glowing and luscious as a forty-year-old can be.

Last Monday she went to Georgio for the works. Her face stung for days. The kids didn't like it: Lewis slapped her when she tried to kiss him. It was a timely reminder of exactly why she's doing all this.

He's made so much progress at Hoare House, is now completely unrecognisable from the boy who used to bang his head against the wall until it bled, or kick and punch his sister if she touched his food or toys. As a rule, she tries not to let her mind stray to those days, but now, as she sips her champagne waiting for Bruno to finish, she forces herself to remember.

They came at two in the morning, kicking the door down, bellowing. It was the most terrifying moment of her life. The children, still in their cots, started screaming: a terrible shrill sound she has never heard them make before or since.

Dazed as she was with sleep and dazzled by the flashing torches, the Tasers looked like guns. She thought Tony's clients had finally discovered he was cheating them, cutting the goods that he sold as pure. They were going to kill them all. She ran into the children's room, hauled them from their cots and lay across them on the floor. Lewis and Jade screamed and thrashed beneath her as she waited for the bullets to tear through her back.

Then she heard them shouting for Tony to get down. That he was under arrest.

They must have explained to her what was going on, but she has no recollection of what happened next, or over the next few days. Only that Tony never came home again. That all their furniture was seized. That she had no income to pay the mortgage.

They moved into a flat and she signed on. The benefits were nothing – haircuts were out of the question, let alone manicures. She started to look like a drug user herself – white-faced and hollow-eyed, nails bitten to the quick. She got a cleaning job to try and make ends meet.

Then someone dobbed her in for the cleaning. One of the other women in the block probably, jealous of her looks, as women often are. Thanks to that bitch, her benefits were stopped.

To get by, she started cooking in a local pub, putting the children to bed at half six so she could be at work for seven, returning after midnight. Sometimes they fought while she was away and Jade had injuries. Seeing them, the school alerted social services, who found that she was leaving the children alone at night. She begged the social worker not to take them from her. Promised she would get babysitters to cover her night shifts while she tried to get her benefits reinstated. The social worker agreed.

But they hadn't managed on benefits before, so how would they this time?

There was one way out. The way she had always relied upon. She stopped buying groceries, making do with the leftovers from the pub, and used the extra money to primp herself back to her best. Then, on her nights off from the bar, she went up to town, to bars where rich men hung out: Forge, Mahiki, Raffles. She would get Lenny to meet her so she didn't look like a prostitute.

The rich men circled her like flies, but she never let her desperation show. Not even as Lewis's behaviour worsened and Jade cried herself to sleep every night.

She would wait three days before returning texts. Told them she was busy when they asked her to dinner. When they did meet, she was playful and fun but never, ever keen.

Then one day the social worker asked how she could afford her new wardrobe and hair. The idiot cow thought she was doing it for herself, depriving her children so that she could look good. Not realising they were the reason she *had* to look good. The woman said she was considering a child protection enquiry.

That night, by the grace of God and Jesus and all the saints, Thea met Bruno.

Bingo. Three months later, she and the children moved in with him.

Bruno ends the call and his grin fades. 'You didn't have to wait for me. You know most of the people here.'

'Is Si coming?' she says, and smiles.

Normally Bruno would roll his eyes at this, but he's tapping into his phone again. 'No idea.'

They wander through the crowds and eventually join a group of couples Thea knows from other such dos. The women look a bit like her. Their clothes and make-up and hair are of identical quality, but no cosmetic procedure can alter the fact that Thea is naturally beautiful while they are just well polished. She gets into a deep conversation with one of the wives about the ideal thread count for Egyptian cotton, and when she looks up again, Bruno has gone.

Glancing around the room, she spots Si. As the woman burbles on about the woeful inadequacy of the Selfridges homeware department, Thea tries to catch his eye.

Si used to work in the same office as Bruno. She would see him regularly when she went to the work bar to meet them all. He was always kind, attentive, more interested in her life than Bruno has ever been. She told him the truth about Tony, and he got angry and thumped the table. *How could a man do that to a woman, leave her with nothing? If he was lucky enough to find a woman like Thea, he would never do anything to risk her happiness.* Once, when he was very drunk, he cried and told her he loved her. She held his hand and told him she was very fond of him too, while Bruno watched from the bar, smirking.

Perhaps Si would have been a better choice all along.

True, he's not quite as alpha. His salary is probably a quarter of Bruno's, but still more than enough to cover the Hoare House fees. A state school could never understand or cope with Lewis's educational needs. He would simply be labelled bad and stupid: fast-tracked to exclusion and a pupil referral unit. Hoare House, with its tiny class sizes and in-house counsellors, has taught him how to regulate his emotions, how to socialise, that life is not to be feared and fought. The fees are exorbitant but Thea would gladly pay ten times as much to keep him there.

Si's talking to an older man, and his conversation in mime is so different from Bruno's. Where Bruno declaims and gesticulates, leaning towards his companion as if to physically repel any attempt to contribute, Si is listening attentively to the older man's words. Occasionally he laughs.

Thea used to admire Bruno's arrogance, the remorselessness with which he dealt with those who underperformed: it felt like being on the winning team. Si is softer. He couldn't hack it with the big boys, according to Bruno; that's why he ended up running a hedge fund that barely breaks nine figures. But might they all have been happier with Si?

One drunken evening, she had promised him that if anything happened to Bruno, she would be with him. It seemed sweet at the time, and slightly pathetic.

Well, his ship just came in.

Excusing herself from the homeware conversation, she goes over to join the pair.

He turns when she touches his arm. 'Thea! How lovely to see you. This is Dietrich, from our Munich branch.'

Dietrich takes her hand and says, 'Delighted to meet you.'

'Thea is Bruno Haslett-Mowbray's partner.'

Dietrich raises his eyebrows. 'A very talented man.'

'Just like this guy,' she says, and snakes an arm around Si's waist. He's toned up since she last cuddled him, and he's wearing a delicious spicy aftershave.

She smiles up into his face. He's taller than Bruno – she has to crane her neck – and ten years younger. Plus, loads of men his age are bald, and acne scarring can be attractive: look at Richard Burton. *None of that matters*.

'Go on with what you were saying,' Si says to Dietrich. 'Bruno deals with those bonds, so I'm sure Thea will be interested.'

She's not. Of course she's not, and normally Si would be more considerate. Perhaps this Dietrich is important. Well, she won't get in the way of something that will enhance Si's career. While sipping her drink and nodding in all the right places, she surreptitiously glances round for Bruno. Still no sign of him. But there is a woman she's never seen before, striding towards their little group with a broad grin on her face.

Her dark hair is so tightly cropped most women would never be able to carry it off, and she's very young. Twenty-five, at most. Her muscular figure moves sinuously beneath a black bodycon dress. Despite the champagne, Thea's throat goes dry.

'Helloo,' Si says, opening his arms and enclosing the absurdly long and slim torso of the woman.

'Hey, egghead,' the woman murmurs into his ear.

As they embrace, Si slops his beer over Thea's shoes. To mention it would be gauche, but the beige suede might never recover. They're her sexiest and highest stilettos and go some way to offsetting the dress – high-necked so as not to show off the problem with the implant.

'This is Marla,' Si says, turning his body towards Thea but leaving an arm draped around the new arrival's waist. 'Marla, this is Thea.'

'Pleased to meet you, Thea,' Marla says in a ridiculously strong German accent. 'What do you do?'

Vot. Good grief.

'Just look after my kids.' Thea shrugs. 'Not very exciting.'

'Nuzzing vong wizzat.'

'No indeed,' Si says. 'The world can only take so many ball-breaking females.' He smiles into Marla's eyes.

Thea says, 'Si, can I borrow you for a moment?'

'Sure.' He turns to the other two. 'I'll be back. Don't go anywhere.'

She walks away, sliding between the enormous pot plants that enclose the main area, and up to the balcony that looks out over Soho Square. Far below, junkies are shambling across the grass in the dusk. Away from the heaters it's cold, and a chill wind has blown up, making the leaves of the plants behind her whisper.

'Hey, what's up?' Si leans on the balcony beside her, his beer bottle clinking against the railing.

Thea curls her hands around the cold metal. How to do this . . .

'Everything okay with Bruno?'

She was just going to simply call him out on his promise, admit her predicament, but now, here, stone-cold sober among these people, she chickens out.

'I just had a bone to pick with you.' She turns and pouts. 'How dare you tell that German guy I'd be happy to talk about Brazilian bonds?'

Si laughs. 'Sorry.'

'You're forgiven.' She holds his gaze, tilting her head so she's looking slightly up through her eyelashes.

'Seriously. You okay?'

'I've been better, but what the fuck. It's great to see you. It's been ages. Four months?'

Si shakes his head. 'Must be. Great place for a party, though, right?' He leans over the balcony.

She touches his back, warm under the pale pink cotton. 'Don't fall.'

He moves away. 'Christ, no. Can you imagine? All these pissed people. I hope they've got indemnity insurance.' He finishes his beer. 'Speaking of money, I should get back to Dietrich. He doesn't know many people.'

'He knows Marla.'

Si snorts, as if Marla's name is a private joke. 'Are you coming?'

Has he missed what she said about not being okay?

'I think I'll stay here for a bit.' She turns away. A cold breeze passes through the trees of the square and up the building to stir her hair.

The empty bottle clinks down beside her. 'Okay, see you later.'

And with that, he's gone, brushing back through the plants into the warmth and light.

Thea's gut convulses, making a noise like the twisting of a balloon animal. She grasps the railing, waiting for it to pass, and her foot topples Si's beer bottle, knocking it off the edge of the concrete. Fortunately no one is walking by below as it smashes into smithereens on the pavement. The noise makes one of the junkies in the square look up. Matted hair stands out from a skeletal face lit a lurid yellow by the park lighting. He raises his hand to her. She turns away. A moment later, she looks back to see that he has pulled out his cock and is masturbating.

Suddenly she's gasping for breath. Sinking to the floor with lights exploding in her vision, she wonders if she's having a stroke. The sounds of the party become echoey and distant, as if the guests are enclosed inside a bubble of air and she's alone on the outside, in a vacuum.

An image flashes into her mind, of the last time this happened to her. Then it was down to drink and a joint that Mel had somehow got hold of. It was at GillFest. They must have been eighteen. She staggered away from the crowds to throw up and collapsed in the piss-soaked grass, in the dark. Her friends came to find her. They walked her back to the tent, pausing to hold her hair as she threw up. Mel and Orly and Lenny. Two years before Mel became a mother, when Orly had a perm and Lenny was just a swotty schoolgirl instead of a financial high-flyer. Back when beautiful, young Thea was the desire and envy of all.

After a few minutes the attack passes. Her heart still pounds but she can breathe again. She hauls herself upright. She's been sitting in a puddle of Si's beer and the stain is spreading across the seat of her dress, like she's pissed herself. Still dizzy, she leans over the railing and sucks in the cold night air.

The shards of broken bottle glint up at her from the pavement. She imagines what it would feel like to walk back into the party and cut her wrists there in front of them; all those rich, beautiful people staring as the blood poured out of her to pool around stilettos and Italian calfskin, mingling with the spilled champagne.

Beneath her the junkies settle down under their cardboard blankets. No one comes to find her.

Deadly Traps Found on Festival Site

Spring-operated 'gin' traps have been discovered in woodland on the site of the Gillingwater Festival, due to take place next month. Illegal since 1958, the spring snaps on these devices are so powerful they can rip the feet off animals and even cause injuries to humans.

After increasingly vociferous calls to scrap the festival to protect the local ecosystem, there are fears villagers have taken the law into their own hands and are seeking to maim festival-goers who stray into the woods.

The Woollacott family, owners of the land, say all traps have been located and removed, and that the site is now safe.

7

Lenny

She's stuck in traffic on the way to work when Thea calls. She takes it on speaker.

'Thea, hi.'

'Hi, babes!'

'Everything okay?' The days when they would just ring for a chat are past.

'Yes, fine. Absolutely. All good. You?'

'Yup, great,' Lenny says.

'Fab. Because I need to talk to you about something extremely important. I don't know if you've noticed, but there's a very significant birthday coming up.'

Lenny groans.

'The big four-oh. Who'd believe it, right? Where did all that time go?'

Work, Lenny thinks. And then the wonderful slavery of the children.

'So I think that deserves a celebration, don't you?'

'Uh-oh. What did you have in mind?'

'Remember that mad summer at GillFest? You were with Rich, and me and Tony were just getting together, and Mel was screwing half the football team and Orly was, oh, stroking her cat and reading probably. It's the festival's twenty-fifth anniversary this year and the last day is . . . wait for it . . . your fortieth! If that isn't fate, I dunno what is!'

'A festival? Are you insane? At our age?'

'Get with the programme, Leonora. Forty is the new eighteen. And at least we won't have to climb over the barriers this time, and we might actually be able to afford to buy booze.'

'Does Bruno want to go?'

'Screw Bruno.'

Lenny raises her eyebrows at her reflection in the rear-view mirror.

'I thought we could do a girls thing. You, me, Orly and Mel. Get trashed, snog locals.'

Lenny starts to laugh. 'You, in a tent?'

'Why not? I still know how to let my hair down, and it's time we reconnected. We've all been far too distracted with men over the years. Mates before dates, right?'

Lenny laughs harder: this, from Thea.

'I know, I know,' Thea says ruefully. 'But maybe I've realised that the people who really matter, who'll be there for me whatever, are you guys.'

Lenny's laughter subsides. An asthma attack just made her reassess her priorities, so why shouldn't Thea be allowed to do the same? The rest of them always suspected she might have some existential crisis when she finally realised she wouldn't be beautiful for ever. Maybe this is it.

'Also,' Thea goes on, more sombrely, 'I think Orly could do with it. You know, spend some time with her friends, let her hair down, forget things for a while.'

She's right. It would be good for Orly.

'I don't know if I'd be able to get the time off work.'

'Thought you were the boss?'

'My clients are the bosses.'

'Okay, babes, well you make it happen. I really need to see you all.'

Lenny frowns. 'You okay?'

'Let me know, all right.' Thea hangs up.

Lenny shakes her head and smiles. Four middle-aged women

heading off to a festival to try and recapture their youth. Pathetic. But gazing out at the river flashing in the sunlight, she thinks of Rich.

It was only nine months, from the messy New Year's Eve party at the Red Lion to the day she left for university, and it's still her longest relationship. Funny, back then she never considered, not even for a moment, that she might stay for him – go to some local college and make a life down in the West Country, like Orly did with Harry. And throughout her twenties, climbing that greasy pole of finance with the tenacity of an alpha chimp, never once did she regret it.

If she'd stayed, she would certainly have missed out on the expensive houses and cars and holidays, the clothes, the restaurants, the job satisfaction.

But her children would have had a father.

The car in front moves, so she inches forward then comes to a halt again. The engine auto-stops. Outside the window the great worm of traffic stretches as far as she can see along the Embankment. It's a warm, high-pressure day and a shroud of brown pollution hangs over the city. She checks her handbag for her inhaler.

Imagine a weekend in the West Country, all that blue sky and clear air.

Growing up there always felt so dull and remote, stuck in the past while everything exciting happened elsewhere. Now she finds herself yearning for the quiet: clean air and birdsong instead of traffic noise, a horizon of trees and hills instead of high-rises.

Why shouldn't they go? Maybe Thea's right. Forty isn't that old, and so what if it was? Haven't they earned the right, at this age, not to care? The kids would manage with Jeanne for the weekend, and it would be good for Orly.

Yes, maybe all things considered, GillFest isn't such a bad idea.

She changes the station from Radio 4 to Absolute Eighties. 'Brass in Pocket' is playing. Whatever blockage was causing the traffic jam suddenly clears and the cars start moving again. Picking up speed, Lenny opens the window and lets the song spool out across the river. Her fingers tap on the steering wheel. Something that's been slumbering inside her has woken up and wants to dance.

@GillingwaterFestival

The line-up for #GillFest25 is confirmed and you can see the full programme here. We're super-excited. Hope you are too! Get the beers in! #GillFest25 #SummerSolstice_

@Minelathos

Replying to @GillingwaterFestival

The midsummer festival is not an excuse to get drunk and fornicate. It was initiated before the dawn of Christianity.

@Minelathos

Replying to @GillingwaterFestival

And the solstice is not the beginning of summer as the ignorant believe, but its end. Days get shorter. Winter is coming. Honour the goddess in the manner due to her or the months ahead will be harsh.

@Minelathos

Replying to @GillingwaterFestival

Light the sacred bonefires, keep vigil all night and welcome the rising goddess on your knees or she will avenge her dishonour with blood, and it will be on your hands.

@GillingwaterFestival

Sorry bout that everyone, we've reported that last tweeter (someone's been baying at the moon too long . . .) Threats and intimidation will not be tolerated, either here or at #GillFest See you soon!

8

Orly

She's lying on her bed, in her pyjamas. On her phone, images flicker: people running and hiding, vehicles thundering towards the camera. There's an explosion. She blinks as the light bounces off her retinas. Then the boom is cut off by tinkling music and the images vanish.

She almost lets the call go to voicemail, but the number that's come up on the screen isn't familiar. Maybe it's one of the local schools she emailed. Her heart sinks. The last thing she wants is an offer of an interview. She's put on five kilos in the last few weeks, her roots are down to her ears, and she hasn't even bothered waxing her moustache.

Eventually, prompted by guilt at what her mum would think if she didn't, she takes it.

'Orly?'

'Yes. Speaking.'

'It's Judy, from Henridge.'

Judy . . . 'Judy, oh hi! How are you?'

'I'm good. All good. I won't chat, because I've got someone here who's very keen to speak to you.'

In the background, she can hear the sounds of the school playground. It's always the same; just as every colour mixes up to brown, the complex desires and demands of each child meld into this hubbub of general shouting. It makes Orly's body go soft. Like she's listening to the voices of the dead.

There's a rustling, and then she can hear stertorous breathing close to the mic.

'Go on,' Judy says in the background.

A breath is taken and then a nasal voice says, 'I got into King Edward's.'

All the air in her lungs seems to fly up into her head.

'I got into King Edward's,' he says again.

She finds her voice. 'Jago! Oh my God!'

'Miss Sarpong went through those books you left with me, and the exam was really easy.'

'You got in! Oh my goodness, Jago, I'm so proud of—'

'Tell her about the . . .' Judy murmurs.

'I got a scholarship,' Jago says.

'An academic scholarship,' Judy says, close to the mic. 'A hundred per cent of the fees.'

Orly laughs in sheer amazement. A bursary was the best she had hoped for. 'A scholarship! Jago! You are amazing! You are an absolute superstar. Oh, I wish I was there so I could hug you!'

He laughs quietly.

In the background, the bell rings for the start of class. He and Judy will have to go.

'Will you get Miss Sarpong to send me a picture of you holding your letter?' Orly says quickly.

'Okay.'

'And another one of you in your new school uniform?'

'Okay. I have to go now.'

'I miss you, Jago.'

It's unfair to say that to him, inappropriate even, but just hearing his voice is like the gates of paradise opening up, just long enough for her to glimpse the colour, life and beauty beyond. Now they're closing again.

'Bye.'

'Bye, Jago.' Her throat has thickened and the words are pitched too low for him to hear beneath the roar of children pouring past. Then the roaring recedes: the doors into the main building must have closed.

Judy comes back on the line. 'There. How's that, then?'

'Amazing! Well done.'

'It wasn't me. He's so bright, and more importantly, thanks to all the time you spent with him, he knows how to work hard.'

Yes, Orly had value once.

'St Edward's loved him. I think he got the second highest mark in the whole cohort, and I bet he was the only one who didn't have a tutor.'

'What a hero. I don't suppose the parents said much.'

'Not really. Mum's unwell again, so . . .'

It's okay, Orly thinks. He's safe now. King Edward's will help him climb out of the oppressive hopelessness he was born into. He'll make something of himself. And he'll have stories about his time at school that will seem funny and poignant with the passing of time. Perhaps he'll even remember Mrs Goldstein.

'So, how are *you* doing?' Judy's voice has softened, for the invalid. 'Working anywhere?'

'Not yet.'

The last sparks of the firework are winking out one by one.

'Ah well, something will turn up.'

'Yeah, I'm sure. Thanks so much for the call, Judy. I hope he stays in touch with you all. If so, keep me posted with his progress, will you?' Putting it that way sounds like the normal objective interest of a dedicated professional. But what she really feels is utter desolation at losing him. Jago, who trusted and depended on her completely. Her child.

'Will do. Oh, and by the way, Miles is moving on. We think a group of parents went to the vicar about how unpredictable he was. He went off his head at 3BS the other day, yelling at them so loudly the whole school could hear.'

'Sorry, Judy, I'm getting another call. It might be from one of the schools I've applied to. I really should take it. Thanks so much.'

'Okay, speak soon, bye!'

The screen turns black and the hand holding the phone slumps onto the duvet. She can remember what it was like, being excited about the future, as Jago must be now. Looking forward to next month or next year, when a new chapter of your life would begin.

Life is going on everywhere else except for inside this room, her own personal bell jar of formaldehyde, Orly staring blank-eyed out through the glass walls.

A leggy spider tightrope-walks across the ceiling to the corner, casting a bouncing shadow.

Picking up the phone, she tries to find the thing she was watching. It's coming back to her now. The spy's cover has been blown and the only man who can save her is the one she was sent to eliminate. But before she can hit play, the phone rings again.

She smiles. Jago has remembered that they didn't utter the Vulcan blessing – *Live long and prosper*. He wouldn't be able to let that go.

Then she sees the name on the screen. Lenny. Again she thinks about sending it to voicemail, but of all the people she knows, Lenny is the one she could most bear to speak to.

'Len. Hi. How are you?'

'I caught you. Thought you might be in class.'

As good a friend as Lenny is, Orly has been too ashamed to admit the truth, even to her.

'No . . . I'm off today. Bit fluey.'

'Oh poor you.'

'Probably one of the kids. You know what they're like. Little bug hotels. It's amazing any teacher lives past thirty. You okay? How are the twins?'

'Good. They're great, yeah. Look, I won't keep you 'cos I'm on my way to a meeting, but I got a call from Thea this morning.'

'Is she okay?'

'She's fine, yeah. She was talking about my birthday and maybe – wait for it – having it at GillFest.'

Orly snorts, the closest she's come to a laugh in days.

'I know. We're old. But loads of people at work go to Glasto, so I thought, why not? Chill out, get back to nature. Drink copious amounts of alcohol . . .'

'I won't be able to get the time off.'

'I tried that one with Thea, but surely they can spare you for the Friday and Monday?'

'It's different with teaching.'

'You're off today; just say you're sick.'

It's not like Lenny to be so forceful.

'Really, I . . . I . . .' Orly sighs. 'Look, I'd only bring you guys down.'

'Not at all. I'm not doing it without you. Oh, and I'm paying – no arguments.'

'Maybe next year.'

'I won't be forty next year.'

'I have to go,' Orly says. 'I've got marking to catch up on. You guys go and have fun.'

She hangs up.

They're trying to take care of her. She should be grateful, and she is, but it doesn't fill the gaping hole in her heart. Because the thing you learn when you become an adult is that, astonishingly enough, the old adage that it's better to give than to receive is absolutely true. The pure, unalloyed euphoria she experienced at Jago's news – that wonderful knowledge that she has helped someone – is better than any drug. She needs to be looking after others, not vice versa.

Sighing, she goes back to the film.

She must have dozed off because, when she comes to, a completely different movie is on and the room has become suffused with the pink glow of the setting sun. She gets up and walks to the window, laying her palm on the cool glass.

People are coming home from work, their faces expectant as they let themselves into their houses to rejoin their families. Imagine your company being anticipated with pleasure rather than dread. All she does now is cause people grief. Every time she goes down for breakfast she can see it in her mum's eyes, that little spark of hope snuffed out at the sight of her expression, her unwashed hair and rumpled clothes. Another day of misery. And then there was the genuine disappointment in Lenny's voice when she refused the GillFest invitation.

Was it selfish of her? Lenny said they wouldn't go without her, so she's single-handedly ruined the birthday celebrations. Typical. What about the whole *better to give than to receive* thing then? If she's so keen to have someone to care for and nurture, why not her oldest friends? Why not give Lenny a birthday to remember? All she has to do is keep a smile on her face for four days. It'll be easier with a drink in her hand.

God, to be pissed again with her friends, rather than on the sofa in front of *QI* with her parents asleep either side of her.

She rests her head on the glass, and the happy scene of a mother and father swinging their toddler into the air on the pavement below disappears behind the mist of her breath.

@GillingwaterFestival
Tickets for this year's #GillFest25 are almost sold out. Returns will be available one month before the start of the festival.

@Sav550099
Replying to @GillingwaterFestival
Still waiting 2 hear if I can have the time off! If I miss out on a ticket gonna have to get someone to smuggle me in in their case!

@GillingwaterFestival
Replying to @Sav550099
Sorry, Sav, we'll be randomly searching cases for drugs – and stowaways!

9

Mel

She's in the bath when the phone rings, and almost breaks her neck running across the laminate floor of the landing to pick it up.

'Billy? What's happened?'

'Mel? It's Lenny.'

She exhales and sinks down on the bed. 'Hello, mate. How you doing?'

'Good, good. What are you up to?'

They chat about the party and Billy's camping trip with Gary. Mel bigs up the luxury of freedom, of having a clean house, of not having to watch trash on the TV, and doesn't mention the crushing loneliness bordering on fear at this foreshadowing of him leaving for uni. The emptiness continuing for the rest of her life.

'How's Orly?' Mel says. 'I mean to call her every week, but you know what it's like. I just haven't got round to it.'

'It was Orly I wanted to talk to you about actually. Oh, and my birthday. My fortieth. I thought we could have it at GillFest.'

Mel laughs. 'Shut up!'

'Why not? It's their twenty-fifth anniversary apparently. It'll be a big one. I thought it would be fun for all of us, and especially Orls. Take her out of herself for a while. Ply her with booze, get her dancing. What do you think?'

'Fuck, yeah!' Mel cries.

'One condition. I'm paying for everyone. It's my birthday, so I'm allowed.'

'No, no, you can't . . .'

But Lenny insists and Mel finally allows herself to concede, and they say goodbye.

Mel goes back to her bath and tops it up with hot water.

In the flotation tank of swirling steam, the sense of relief – that there might still be some fun to be had in a life without Billy – brings tears to her eyes. They mingle with the beads of perspiration on her cheeks and dribble into her mouth. She recognises the salt taste. Yes, it's the taste of unhappiness, of the father of your child screwing around and leaving you with nothing. But it's also the taste of dancing and fucking and wild, drink-fuelled fun.

She slides down and the water closes over her face. The only sound is the drumming of her heart pounding in her ears.

Melanie Court updated her profile picture

Polly P:
Is that GillFest?? You look so gorgeous! How old were you?

Melanie Court:
Eighteen. With my besties from school. We're going back this year!

Suzi Fiore:
So gorgeous!

Polly P:
OMG, have fun!!!

Glen Bailey:
I would delete this post, Mel. You don't want the local scumbags to know you won't be in the house that weekend. My cousin got burgled when he was at Glasto last yr.

Melanie Court:
Cheers, Glen, but I haven't got anything worth nicking!

Polly P:
At least we'll all know where to find you!

GILLFEST

DAY 1

10

Orly

Orly stares at her open wheelie case and wonders if it's too late to fake a serious illness. She's just started her period, so maybe she could claim cramps, but the days of being floored by those are long past. Nowadays she can get away with regular tampons instead of supers, and the others are probably the same – approaching perimenopausal. Too old for a festival, for God's sake.

Opening her chest of drawers, she contemplates the contents with despair.

After tucking into three solid meals a day for the past four months, everything is too tight, and the prospect of being surrounded by youthful festival babes swigging from beer bottles as they bounce on the shoulders of hot men, their sun-bleached hair blowing in the wind, makes her want to put her head in the oven. Worse than this, she'll be expected to behave like that herself. It's Lenny's birthday: she'll have to laugh and get drunk and dance barefoot.

Oh God.

In the end, she packs a second pair of shorts, a T-shirt and a hoodie. It's hot, so she'll travel in just shorts and a vest. A glance in the mirror reveals that she looks depressingly frumpy with her white bra strap showing. It doesn't really matter. No one will be looking at her with all the frolicking twenty-year-old hotties, but a little voice mutters something about self-respect, so she swaps the comfortable white one for a fuchsia-pink push-up with elaborate straps and underwire that will for certain feel like a torture device after three days. But at least it goes nicely with the red vest.

Bumping the case downstairs, she calls out that she's ready.

Her mum takes her to the station because her dad's leg is in plaster with the diabetes thing. Carol hates driving and spends the first ten minutes of the journey white-knuckled, leaning close to the steering wheel and randomly hammering on the brakes. Eventually she starts to relax and attempts some bright conversation with her daughter, as she has done for months. As usual Orly replies with grunts and sighs. She hates herself for it, but that's nothing new. Self-loathing, like grief, is a constant companion.

Harry played his role perfectly – the stoic sufferer, taking himself off to a hospice so as not to inconvenience them by dying messily at home. So why can't she be the dignified widow: sad, wistful, noble? Instead she's reverted to a whining morose teenager.

Going back to GillFest it really will be as if the intervening two decades never happened. After all, what has she achieved? Her marriage and career might as well never have been, and she's sailing past the point of no return for her fertility. Even if she met someone today who fell madly in love with her and wanted to have a baby straight away, she's too old to get IVF on the NHS. And the likelihood of her affording it on her own is nil.

Passing the car park of her old school, the years roll back and she can see all four of them standing on the gravel waiting for the bus: Mel smoking a crafty one, Orly eating Maltesers, Thea doing her make-up, Lenny trying to learn her music theory. What did Thea and Lenny do so right? Yes, Thea was prettier, and Lenny was cleverer, but the gulf between them was not so vast that their lives should end up so vastly different.

There she goes again with the whining self-pity that will ruin everyone's weekend.

'Here we are.' Her mum pulls into the station car park. 'The train doesn't leave till eleven ten, so you've got fifteen minutes. I'll wait with you.'

'No, it's okay.'

'Well . . . if you're sure . . . Say hello to the girls for me. I do sometimes bump into Mel at the supermarket. She's kept her looks, hasn't she?'

Orly nods wanly as she watches backpack-laden teenagers stream into the station entrance.

'And Lenny's done marvellously,' her mum goes on relentlessly. 'I was talking to her at the . . .' She breaks off and stares into the middle distance, and for a moment looks twenty years older than her sixty-two years.

Funeral.

Orly feels a rush of filial guilt for what she has put her parents through. What she's *still* putting them through.

'Yes, she's done really well,' she says. 'And bringing up the twins alone. They're such lovely kids too. She deserves it all, though, she's always worked so hard.'

Her mum turns and lays a hand on hers. '*You* deserve it all.'

Orly swallows. The last time her mother looked at her like that was on the morning of her wedding.

'Now, you go off and have a wonderful time, okay? Promise me.'

'I promise,' Orly whispers, and gets out of the car before she starts crying.

The train has come all the way from London and is rammed.

Slim, beautiful girls drape tanned, waxed legs, adorned with ankle chains and tasteful tattoos, over the laps of their equally beautiful boyfriends. The last time Orly was dating, this was the age of her dates, but they do not even glance at her as she squeezes past them, only shuffle in politely as they would for a geriatric.

She manages to find a seat by the window and, after stowing her case in the luggage rack above, sits gazing out at the countryside, all gold and green and just coming into bloom, as the train pulls away with a jolly whistle. She tries to zone out the music and laughter and sheer fucking happiness that surrounds her, dense and fragrant as the smoke from the joints that the train operator has clearly decided to turn a blind eye to. Some obstacle under the table means she can't move her legs, and her right foot is beginning to tingle with pins and needles. The train rounds the long bend of Cuckoo Hill and then picks up speed on the straight track that cuts across the flood plain.

Someone shouts, 'Listen!' and a hush descends.

Now they can all hear it. The distant throb of the festival's heartbeat.

There's a group intake of breath and then the carriage erupts into whoops and applause. Someone's speaker is turned up impossibly loud, and from the corner of her eye Orly sees the girls waving their arms above their heads as the boys punch the air.

She sinks lower into her seat. This is going to be hell.

'Don't worry, it might never happen.'

A man is smiling at her across the table, wedged into a nest of rucksacks and blue laundry bags. The wheelie case between his feet is the reason she can't move her legs. He's handsome in a craggy way, thin and tanned, with deep lines etched around his bright blue eyes and his wide mouth. He must be well over forty but seems to have a full head of hair under his flat cap, which is a plus. His obvious dishevelment and the slight smell of cannabis that wafts from his camo jacket as he leans towards her are not. She smiles tightly and looks away.

'Looking forward to it?' he persists.

'Mmm.'

'I been going every year since ninety-four. Is it your first time?'

'No.'

'Yeah?'

She doesn't reply and he gets the message, sitting back in his seat and rolling a joint.

The doors open at the penultimate station before Gillingwater, and in the few seconds before they close again, the carriage is filled with pounding music and the roar of helicopters. A ballooning sense of anticipation charges the ions in the air.

Someone enters the carriage and starts picking their way between rucksacks and tents and legs.

'Orly?'

Her heart sinks down to her flip-flops and she closes her eyes for a second – *give me strength* – before turning to see who has recognised her. This is a local train, after all, and half the people she went to school with never left the area. Then her heart bounces back up again.

'Mel!'

'Oh my God, what are you doing on this train? I thought you'd be coming from Bath!'

'I went to see Mum and Dad first,' Orly says, the lie tainting the genuine pleasure of seeing her friend.

'Cool! Shove up!'

There's no space for another person, but the guy next to her gamely gets up and Mel flings herself down, dropping her backpack in the aisle. They hug. Her mum was right, Mel looks amazing, in a tight vest and jeans shorts, the pockets hanging beneath the cut-offs, like something a girl half her age would wear. Her dark hair coils in glossy ringlets, her neck and hands and slim arms are draped with silver chains and rings. Even the ham-fisted tattoo of a dolphin she got on her shoulder when they were sixteen, which spread and blurred to an unidentifiable green blob almost immediately, looks cool.

'How are you?'

'Fine.' Orly smiles and nods, hoping the desperation will shine through her eyes – *don't ask any more*.

'Cool, cool, cool. Now, am I your best friend . . .' Mel dives a hand inside the rucksack she has swung onto her lap and draws out two cans of gin and tonic, 'or not?'

'You are.' Orly grins, opening one and swigging it. At this time of the morning the contents just taste like warm chemicals, but perhaps they will do the trick and ease her anxiety.

On an empty stomach the alcohol takes effect immediately, softening her thoughts, drawing them away from herself and towards the beautiful landscape drifting by. Midsummer. When everyone in the northern hemisphere is out having fun with their friends, not moping in their bedrooms. She must make an effort to enjoy herself, if only for Lenny's sake.

'You'll never guess who popped up on my Facebook suggestions the other day,' Mel says.

Orly swallows. 'Who?'

'Pandora Rankin.'

Somewhere a champagne cork pops, to the sound of cheering.

'You must remember Pan. That girl who came in year four and left because of the thing with Mr Whatshisname. We hung out with her loads.'

'Yes. I remember.'

'She's been all over the place, but she's back living round here now.'

'Yeah?'

'I told her we were going to GillFest for Lenny's birthday, said she should come along, get the old gang back together.'

The group with the champagne is now bellowing, 'I get knocked down, but I get up again'. They used to go and see Chumbawamba in Bristol when they were teenagers. The rousing anthem thumps through her brain like a migraine.

'Orly?'

'Cool, yeah, we should look out for her.'

'She's got my number, so she's going to give us a call.'

'Great.'

Orly turns back to the window and concentrates on her breathing. *Could this fucking weekend possibly get any worse? Pandora Rankin. Oh God.*

'Cheers,' says the man opposite, holding out his own can of cider. 'Happy days.'

'Let's hope so,' Mel grins, rubbing her hands.

'Never missed a year,' the man says. 'What about you?'

90

'We haven't been since school. Right?' She turns to Orly, and Orly smiles and nods. The shock of Pandora Rankin is starting to subside. Pan was always a flake. She probably won't turn up, and even if she does, she'll be with other people and might not bother to call. And if she *does* call and wants to have a drink with them, Orly will just pretend to be sick.

'I bet it's so different now,' Mel is saying. 'In the internet age.'

'Ah, still the same vibe really, y'know?' The man grins, revealing brownish teeth. 'Chilled out, friendly, just the way it should be.'

'That's what I'm here for,' Mel says, drinking deep.

The man introduces himself as Trey and asks what bands they hope to see, and Orly lets Mel do the talking while she returns to gazing out of the window. The track runs parallel to the road now, and traffic stretches off as far as the eye can see, each car roof radiating heat shimmer like a thousand little shiny barbecues. At least she's not in a car, she thinks; that's something.

Her eye follows the road snaking off into the distance, and there it is, imprinted on the hill like one of the magic eye posters that were all the rage last time they made this journey. The festival. In amongst the seething mass she can pick out the huge eye of the Litha Stage and the bright splodges of the marquees; a yellow crane, the big wheel and the helter skelter, towers of scaffolding, all enclosed by a wall of grey metal: like a concentration camp of enforced fun. She rests her head on the cool glass.

'Lemme have your number,' Trey is saying. 'Maybe we can hook up for a beer and a boogie.'

'Sure, yeah.' From the corner of her eye, Orly sees her friend's smile falter slightly. Mel never could distinguish friendliness from being hit on. It resulted in several near misses at school where she'd had to be rescued from boys who'd got the wrong idea. These days they'd have been done for sexual assault.

'Where you camping?' Trey says, and Mel gives a non-committal answer. Before he can say anything else the train's brakes squeal and a cheer erupts from the carriage.

Trey grins, exposing his sharp stained teeth. 'Here we are. Later, ladies!'

As the train shudders to a halt and the tannoy announces that they have reached their final destination, he leaps to his feet and, laden with bags, begins hopping and ducking towards the doors. The other passengers stir more slowly, almost reluctantly. Perhaps they're feeling a hint of what Orly is – the pressure of having a *fucking awesome* time that makes you just want to crawl into bed and pull the covers over your head. Or maybe they're simply being sensible. The doors have opened but no one in the rammed carriage will be moving for a while yet.

'He's left his case,' Mel says.

She's right. The battered black wheelie case is still crushing Orly's legs. But Trey has already disembarked and is picking his way through the crowd, laden down like a packhorse, offering high-fives as he goes. Mel leans across and hammers on the window.

It's no use. The air throbs with shouting and singing. He doesn't turn, and before the crush in the carriage has subsided enough for them to go after him, he has vanished into the station building.

'We should take it for him,' she says.

Orly peers down at the case. There's something seedy about it: the stains on the front, the fraying cords, the rusting padlock. A phone number is scrawled on a luggage label dangling from the handle.

'I don't know. What if it's . . . a bomb or something?'

Mel laughs. 'I don't think he would have forgotten it.'

'He might have meant to leave it on the train.'

She slides the case out from beneath the table. 'He's got my number; he can come and get it.'

'He probably left it deliberately,' Orly grumbles as she hefts her own case down from the luggage rack. 'So you'd have to see him.'

'Win-win,' Mel says, shouldering her pack. 'I fully intend to get laid this weekend, and if it's with an indie has-been, so be it. The skinnier they are, the bigger their dicks look. Come on.'

They join the throng on the platform and shuffle forward, inch by agonising inch, eventually passing through the station building and out into the jam-packed car park to await the shuttle buses. Seven arrive, scoop up their loads and depart and the next train is just pulling in when Mel and Orly finally get on one. The doors close, shutting them into a sauna of body smells, and they're off.

The three-mile journey takes an hour in the unending crocodile of traffic, but finally they're dropped at the edge of a mass of people trying to get through the ticket barriers. By now Orly is too exhausted even to cry. If she really believed Trey's case contained a bomb, she would throw herself on it.

The sun has passed overhead and is shining directly into her eyes. The music pounds. The sixth person in ten minutes stomps on her foot, leaving more black marks on her polished toenails. A few metres from the turnstiles, they come to a dead halt as people fumble for their phones or paper tickets, but at last it's their turn.

This is it. Her last chance to turn around and go home. But looking back, she sees that chance is long past. The tide of people behind her will not let her through even if she wants to.

She holds the barcode of her ticket against the scanner, then enters the cage of the turnstile and passes through to the next circle of hell — the queue for bag checks. Her pelvis drags from the weight of her period. She hasn't changed her tampon since nine o'clock and she's probably gone through her knickers, but she doesn't care. Her world has reduced to a single point, a prison formed by Mel's hair, the bare shoulder of the guy to the left of her, the hat brim of the girl to her right.

And then suddenly the crowd parts.

The people she has been conjoined to for the last two hours peel away as the track widens out. A patch of sky appears, the royal blue of a raspberry slushie.

She stops and breathes for the first time in what feels like hours. The air is scented with sugared peanuts and beer. Flags flutter. Above the hedge that lines the track she can make out the tips of the standing stones, glittering in the sunlight. An elderly woman with cascading grey hair, a monochrome pre-Raphaelite, hands her a scarlet tissue-paper flower and a map.

Mel drops her bag and raises her arms to the sun winking between flags and towers. She arches her back and exhales like she's having an orgasm.

Orly thinks of her mother, of her promise. She turns her face up to the cloudless blue sky, closes her eyes and smiles.

Perhaps this won't be so bad after all.

@GillingwaterFestival
Welcome to all of you who've just arrived! It's a beautiful
day and we can't wait to see the musical legend that is Paul
McCartney starting his set on the Litha Stage at 3pm.

@00StringTastic
Replying to @GillingwaterFestival
Is he still going? Isnt it time he was put down humanely? LOL

@Lollo777
Replying to @GillingwaterFestival and @00StringTastic
Mark Chapman had the right idea LOL.

@StringTastic
Replying to @GillingwaterFestival and @Lollo777
Not funny mate.

11

Orly

Lenny has booked them into a quiet field on the edge of the campsite, the furthest they could possibly be from the Litha Stage, where the main acts will play. It's almost peaceful, Orly thinks as she picks her way across the tussocks of grass, brushing away the butterflies that bob around her head.

A scream makes her look up.

She smiles and holds up her palm.

Thea is tottering towards them in slip-on sandals. In one hand is a glass of champagne, in the other a tent peg. She has definitely already taken a selfie of this ensemble.

'You're here!' she squeals, hugging them with her wiry arms.

'We are!' squeals Mel in good-natured mockery.

Thea has aged since Orly was last paying attention. The skin of her neck crumples to fine wrinkles as she moves her head, and her cheekbones look all the sharper for the deep hollows beneath. Only her hair seems to be immune to the passing years and is still a luscious waterfall of caramel and gold, whereas Orly's thinned so much during Harry's illness that she has to blow-dry it carefully to give it any body at all.

'You're right on time!' Thea leads them to the hedgerow at the edge of the field. 'We've just pegged out the ground sheet.'

Lenny is frowning so hard at the instructions that she barely registers their approach. Orly has time to study her best friend and marvel afresh at how unrecognisable she is from when they were last here. Gone is the long curtain of hair they all worked so hard for at school, to flick from one side to the other in class. Now she has a boxy crop, and her features have taken on an almost graphic angularity. If she didn't know Lenny, Orly would be intimidated by her. Especially the way she is scowling at whatever diagram has the temerity to thwart her huge intelligence.

'Helloo,' Mel calls. 'Earth to birthday girl! Are we having fun?'

'This bloody thing makes no sense whatsoever,' Lenny says, waggling the offending paper as she stomps over to hug them both.

'Give it here,' Mel says. 'I've put up more tents than Thea's had hot waxes. Your first mistake was trying to follow the instructions. Now, stand back and let the professionals sort it.'

After opening her case and retrieving a spare pair of knickers, Orly excuses herself to go and find a toilet. Tramping through the field towards the gateway, she tries to make sense of the map. There's a crescent of campsites at this end of the site, buttressed by woodland on their side and fields on the other. The main track then runs like a spinal column through the festival to the cranium of the Litha Stage, with limbs branching off it leading to the other areas – Earthfields, the standing stones, the fairground and various niche-themed pockets Orly suspects she will never visit. There are a couple more patches of woodland, and the toilet and refuse areas.

Branching off to the right a few metres from the gateway is one of these. Pristine and gleaming on this first day, the green Portaloos are laid out in a sweeping arc around at least a hundred oil drum bins arranged like a spiral galaxy.

Gingerly Orly opens the door of the nearest toilet.

It's not nearly as bad as she feared. Unlike the last time she came, she does not have to perch over a hole above a fly-infested pit, haunted by the possibility that she might drop something down there, or worse, fall through and be left praying for death rather than rescue.

She pulls down her shorts. Sure enough, her period has triumphed over her tampon and the blood is on the verge of seeping through her knickers onto the denim. She changes the tampon and the knickers, balling the dirty ones into her pocket, then depresses the flush. Blue liquid sloshes into the bowl and a hatch slides open: for the briefest moment the pit of hell is revealed to her, before it slides shut. Hiding her bloody finger as best she can, she opens the door and steps back into the sunlight.

Fortunately, close by there are some aluminium sinks set in wooden frames and fed by hoses, and when she turns the tap on with her clean hand, crystal-clear water flows.

The sun is strong on her back as she walks back down the main track, past beautiful people in straw hats and bangles who are positively thrumming with anticipation. The heat seeps into her pores, spreading like syrup across the knotted muscles of her shoulders, loosening them. She finds she can breathe more easily – dusty air sweetened with the scent of hay.

By the time she gets back, the tent is upright and pegged down, and Mel is mopping the sweat from her face and neck with her T-shirt. They all stand back to admire it. There is a large central area formed by the inner tent, and a space at the front, between the inner and outer tents, which Orly will bag. Lying awake half the night, she can never quite shift the sensation of needing a wee, and can be up four or five times.

Tucking the stained pants into a pocket of her case, she stows it just inside the inner door.

'Fancy giving me a hand now you're free?' says an Irish voice.

Standing beside a semi-erected tent the same size and shape as theirs, but red rather than green, is a tallish, good-looking bloke of about thirty.

'The fellas said they were going for beers about two hours ago, but I think they might have got distracted.'

Orly looks at the others hopefully. The thought of another delay to the commencement of the *fun* appeals.

'Nah, you're all right,' Mel calls over good-naturedly. 'We've got drinking to be getting on with.'

'Fair enough,' the man says. 'I'm Ben, by the way. If you need anything, give me a shout.'

'Thanks. I'm Mel. This is Orly, Thea and Lenny.' She points them out one by one.

'Good to meet you.' He returns to his attempts to get the end of his pole plugged into its hole.

'Right then.' Mel turns and grins at them. 'Let's get this party started. Where shall we head first?'

'Who's on the Litha Stage?' Thea says.

'Paul McCartney.' Mel grimaces.

Lenny says, 'I like Paul McCartney.'

'Me too,' Thea says.

'That's because your kids are too young to have dragged you into the modern world,' Mel snorts.

'Maccy P, Maccy P!' Thea chants, clapping her hands.

'Yes, definitely,' Lenny says. 'Boring Paul gets my vote. *Mull of Kintyre*,' she croons. '*Oh mist rolling in from the sea, my desire . . .*'

Thea joins in. '*. . . is always to be here, oh Mull of Kintyyyyyyyyyrrrrrre.*'

'Orly?' Mel pleads. 'Help me!'

Orly smiles. 'It's Lenny's birthday weekend, so it has to be Paul.'

Mel's theatrics are cut off by her phone ringing.

Orly's smile fades as Mel answers and listens.

'You dick!' she says finally, laughing. 'And you're in luck, we did take it off the train for you.'

Not Pandora then. Orly exhales.

'Yes, you bloody do owe us! . . . I'm not telling you, you might be an axe murderer! We're about to head out, so I'll bring it with us and call you to arrange a handover . . . No, I certainly won't open it. I have no desire to see your dirty kecks!'

Orly explains to the other two what happened.

'Fine. I'll call you in a minute . . . Yes, pinkie promise!' Mel ends the call, laughing.

'You're so going to shag him, aren't you?' Orly says.

Mel grins. 'Depends how drunk I get.' She turns to Lenny. 'Maybe I'm not the only one. I don't think Rich ever moved away. We might bump into him . . .'

Lenny snorts. 'I'm not sure he'd fancy me now.'

'Bollocks! He fucking worshipped you.'

Lenny smiles. 'We'll see.'

They leave the tent, Mel hauling Trey's case, and make their way across the campsite. After so many days without rain, the ground is hard and uneven. They have to watch their step so as not to turn an ankle in one of the tractor ruts that have set like concrete.

'So how was your journey from London?' Mel says. 'The road looked hideous from the train.'

'It was okay,' Lenny says. 'We set off really early and took turns driving and sleeping. Thea did more than her share, actually, and she paid for petrol, which wasn't fair!' She shakes a playful fist at Thea, and Orly feels a prick of jealousy. She pushes it down firmly.

'I was only—' Thea begins, but the sentence is cut off as she suddenly lurches sideways. Mel tries to catch her but misses, and Thea crashes down on the case, then rolls onto the mud, where she sits, nursing her ankle under the straps of her woefully inappropriate sandal. The others stare down at the case in silence. The black plastic lid has snapped and a triangular section has pushed in. Through this gap they can see the contents.

Bags of white powder, coloured pills and rolls of marijuana.

'Shit,' Lenny breathes.

'Oh my God.' Thea gets to her feet.

Mel looks up at them with anxious eyes. 'I didn't know. Honestly. I would never have brought it in.'

'He used you as a mule,' Thea says quietly. 'What a cunt.'

It's odd to hear the nasty word from Thea's lips, as if time has rolled back, plucking her out of her affluent middle-class life and dropping her back into the criminal underworld.

100

'What do we do?' Orly says. 'Call the police?'

'No,' Thea says sharply. 'That would be the end of Lenny's birthday.'

'That doesn't matter . . .' Lenny murmurs.

'They might suspect we were involved,' Thea says.

Mel's eyes are uncharacteristically wide and fearful.

'But what else do we do with it?' Orly says. She wonders if any of the others are thinking what she is. That this case represents thousands of pounds. A scene opens up in her mind's eye – four women clinking cocktails glasses on a Monaco beach – and then winks out. This is not *Ocean's 8*, and they are not master criminals.

Mel tugs the broken shard of plastic back into place, then lifts the case into her arms. 'Right.'

'What are you doing?' Thea says.

'Gonna dump it. Nothing to do with us. There are some bins just over there, right?'

'Umm . . .' Thea says. 'Do you really—'

'You guys don't have to come. It's my fault. I'm not having this shit getting into the hands of all those kids out there.'

'What about Trey?' Orly says. 'He's a drug dealer. He's probably dangerous.'

'He's seen you and me once, so he probably wouldn't even recognise us, and I never told him where we were camped. He's only got my number.' She sets off, grim-faced, towards the gate.

The others exchange glances, then follow.

Fortunately the refuse area is deserted, though even on this first day the bins are almost full. Oil drums painted in Caribbean colours, artfully rusted in patches, spew their contents onto the grass. The case should be easy to overlook in all that mess.

Muttering curses, Mel dumps it beside a drum. Then she walks back to them rubbing her hands and attempting a grin. It falters at the sound of an engine.

A tractor and trailer is trundling through a gateway leading to the arable field beyond. It bounces over the ruts in the dried mud, then pauses for a figure to get out and close the gate. A thickset man in jeans and T-shirt, he has the sort of full brown beard London hipsters sport, only this one looks authentic and is paired not with mankles but a flat cap.

He gets back into the cab and the vehicle trundles over and stops by the bins. The windscreen is opaque, reflecting the sky, but Orly feels like he's watching them. Her eyes flick to the bin.

'Why is he just sitting there?' she murmurs.

'It's nothing to do with us,' Thea says softly. 'There aren't any cameras, right?'

The cab door creaks open and the man climbs out again, his head turned in their direction. With his eyes shadowed by the cap, it's impossible to make out which one of them he's looking at: it must be Thea. It's always Thea the men notice. But Orly's not sure. It could be Lenny, standing at the end of the group, or Mel beside her. Lenny is returning his gaze with a little crease of her brow. Then the moment's hesitation is over. He heads round to the trailer and starts unloading empty drums onto the grass. When this is done, he moves on to the full ones, picking each one up as if it's no heavier than a coffee cup and throwing it onto the trailer. Without another glance at them, he picks up the case.

They watch him hurl it in with the rest of the rubbish and move on to the next bin.

'Come on,' Thea says in a low voice. 'Let's go.'

The further they get from the bins, the greater the sense of elation. Adrenaline courses through Orly's veins. They have just got away with something pretty big. And performed a good deed too: that's a considerable amount of drugs that won't be getting onto the market. She might have saved a child's life!

'You know what, I'm actually looking forward to a bit of Macca,' Mel says, as if the case incident never occurred.

It was always like that with Mel. Anything bad that happened to her – getting dumped (which she rarely was) or bitched about, or failing an exam – was all just water off a duck's back. Orly envies her.

'Did you know that guy?' Thea says to Lenny as they step back onto the main track. 'He was looking at you.'

'I don't think so,' Lenny says. 'He probably just fancied me, right?' She grins.

'I wouldn't mind doing it with a farmer,' Mel says. 'Those rough hands all over you.'

'Smelling of cow dung,' Lenny says.

'All under his fingernails,' Thea adds.

'Eww!' Orly laughs.

They walk on, past the movie zone, the standing stones, the fairground, numerous bars and some food stalls that Orly gazes wistfully at. For her it was never about the music. Last time they were here, she and Thea would sit out the acts the others flocked to, drinking from bottles of the cheapest alcohol they could get their hands on. They didn't care about germs then, or taste. If it got you pissed it did its job. They would loll on benches surrounded by the fragrance of fresh sawdust and frying burgers and discuss their plans for the future. Thea's only dream seemed to be not to end up like her mother. Abandoned by Thea's father just after Thea was born, her mum had scraped by on benefits, falling into the arms of the next man who looked like a rescuer – and never was.

On these occasions, when it was her turn to share her dreams, Orly would just make something up – air stewardess or local journalist, something that sounded respectably ambitious. Because she had no particular passions or talents, and the only thing she dreamed of was getting married and having children. She'd expected to grow out of it when the dollies and princess era ended, but never did. Wanting to have a baby when you're seven is cute, but by the time you're seventeen it's pretty tragic. And a kick in the stomach for the parents who had such hopes for you. In the end she said she wanted to be a teacher. Slightly disappointing for her dad, who had visions of a lawyer or doctor daughter, but respectable enough. It turned out, more by chance than design, that teaching was Orly's vocation. She had a lovely

103

career, and then a lovely husband, but when it was time for the lovely babies, they got cancer instead.

The eye-shaped Litha Stage is in sight now and feedback drifts over the dusty air. It's been done up since they were last here. Before, the eye was constructed from plywood – the stage a ragged circle cut from the white-painted sclera – and swayed in the slightest breeze. Now it's considerably more impressive. Instead of a painted blue background for the artists, there is now a huge screen: filaments of iridescence stream from a central point, like the living iris of some enormous god.

Thea marches ahead, her arm linked with Lenny's, her fist punching the air in time to the pre-set music pumping from the stage. Mel's singing along too. No doubt it's a famous track – Kanye or Rihanna or something – and Orly ought to know it, but she doesn't. Their progress slows as more and more people fall into step with them, like rats summoned by the piper.

By the time the flow oozes to a halt, the stage is still hundreds of metres away. Squeezing into a slot between two very tall men, Orly thinks of all the people who watch festival sets from the comfort of their own sofas, their view of the artists unimpeded, the music delivered clear and perfect through their TV speakers, not drowned out by screaming.

They wait for long minutes under a merciless sun, until finally a figure appears onstage. The noise becomes deafening, like the roar of warplanes. The figure stands for a moment, presumably in bewilderment from the sheer insanity of this adulation. It says something unintelligible, and then the first chords begin.

Propelled forward in a rib-shattering crush that takes her breath away, Orly is, for a moment, suspended, held up by the press of the bodies around her. She takes a gasp of air, warm and damp with the sweat and excitement of fifty thousand people.

When you were young and your heart was an open book.

Orly closes her eyes against the sting of tears. It still is, she thinks. Her heart is just the same as it was the last time she stood here, two decades ago. Despite everything, age and misfortune have not made her bitter or resentful. She still wants the best for all her friends. She harbours no ill feelings towards her in-laws, or Miles for firing her, or even the GP who misdiagnosed Harry's cancer as haemorrhoids. All she wants, with a bone-deep longing, is to give something, some part of her, the best part, to someone. And the only people she has left now are her parents and these three wonderful, loyal friends.

She opens her eyes to reach for Lenny, but her friend is nowhere to be seen, carried off by the longshore drift of the crowd.

The song ends, and Orly is crushed and elbowed and shunted all over again until the next one begins. A new piece that no one knows. The excitement subsides as the crowd waits politely for it to finish.

She cranes her neck to peer over the heads that surround her. Thea is ahead and to the left, flicking her hair and pursing her lips, as if she is the sole object of the crowd's attention. Mel stands a little way from her – Orly only spots her by the flash of the jewelled clips in her hair. Her eyes are closed and she's swaying to this new piece, giving it all the generosity of her attention.

It takes her a moment to spot Lenny, just behind her and away to the right. Feeling Orly's gaze, Lenny turns and smiles, but the smile is strained. Perhaps she has been hurt in the crush.

Orly is about to mouth to her, ask if everything is okay, when the song ends and is succeeded by the opening chords of the classic everyone has been waiting for.

There's a roar and she's propelled forward on the human tsunami. This song speaks even to her philistine heart. She knows it so well, rides along with the melody in a kind of ecstasy as it builds to the soaring crescendo. People are screaming along. She raises her own arms and abandons herself to it.

Laa la la LALALALAAAAAHH, LALALALAAAAAHHHH . . .

She turns to grin at Lenny.

Her friend's eyes are wide with panic. She is sucking on her blue inhaler, sucking and sucking, the tendons on her neck taut as guy ropes. But the device is not doing what it should, because Lenny's eyes are getting wider and there's a blue tinge to her pallor.

'Excuse me!' Orly starts pushing against the bodies. 'Excuse me. I need to get to my friend!'

Her voice is lost in the noise. She squeezes through a gap and around a man who clearly has no intention of moving. After at least a minute of polite manoeuvring, she has gained barely a metre.

Lenny's eyes are half closed now, and she hangs limply in the cage of limbs surrounding her. Abandoning politeness, Orly thrusts her shoulder into her nearest neighbour. He stumbles out of her path. She does this again and again. The girls don't like it, they call aggressively after her, but she doesn't stop. She has momentum now. She's nearing Lenny. But Lenny is not where she was. Orly stops, jerks her head round and back again.

Lenny *is* there. She has slipped down, falling between the legs of the oblivious crowd.

Orly dives forward and pulls her up, strapping her friend's limp arm over her shoulder.

The song ends, and in the momentary lull of screaming, Orly bellows in her bossiest teacher voice, 'Out of my way!'

Dazzled eyes come back into focus. This time people do as she commands, shuffling aside as she staggers towards where she thinks the edge of the crowd must be. Lenny's breath in her ear wheezes like fingernails down a blackboard. Her legs drag. The hand Orly is clutching to retain her grip is cold.

After a few minutes, the pack of human bodies starts to thin out.

'Bad trip?' someone calls.

'One too many?'

Orly's vision jumps with the strain of Lenny's weight. Her feet catch on each tussock of grass, slide on each crushed can.

'Medic tent's over there,' someone shouts.

Orly hasn't got the breath to thank him, but pivots in the direction he points. Lenny's breaths are now just shallow squeals.

106

The ribcage wedged against Orly's neither rises nor falls. She's going to die.

And then a man in a fluorescent jacket is running towards them. He takes Lenny's other arm and their pace immediately increases tenfold.

A tent comes into view, with a little four-by-four ambulance parked outside it.

'What's she taken?'

'Nothing . . .' Orly pants. 'Asthma . . .'

'What's her name?'

'Lenny.'

'All right, Lenny, we're going to get you sorted.' They bundle through the doorway. 'Squeeze my hand if you can hear me . . . there's a good girl. That's it, up on the bed. Lie back for me.'

Lenny squeezed his hand. She is still alive. Orly sinks against the metal tent pole.

'I'm just going to give you some medication through a nebuliser.' He straps a device to Lenny's head, moving the clear mask down over her nose and mouth. 'There . . . that's better, right?'

Lenny's eyes are fixed on his with the intensity of a newborn baby gazing at its mother. Her hand is clamped over the mask and her cheeks are sucking against her teeth at every breath. But at least the breaths are going in. Orly can see her chest rising and falling.

'There you go,' the medic says, his voice so soothing it's almost hypnotic. 'That's all you needed. Now you just rest here for a few minutes, breathing normally, and let the steroids get to work. I'll be just over here if you want me.'

As he walks away, Orly sinks onto the grass and drops her head into her hands, feeling nauseous. She can't lose someone else. She'll have no one left.

In the distance she can hear the first bars of another song, one that Harry used to play on the guitar when they first moved in together. He didn't like her to hear his stammering chords, but she would listen at the door, fantasising about him teaching their child to play. *Take these broken wings and learn to fly.* Checking

107

Lenny's view of her is blocked from up on the bed, Orly allows herself to cry. It was a trick she learned when he was ill – not to show how she felt until she was alone, to keep up the pretence they both conspired in, that he would get better.

A hand touches her shoulder and she looks up into the medic's brown eyes.

'You okay?'

She nods.

'That must have been scary.'

She nods again and wishes he would keep that steadying hand on her for ever.

'Don't worry. She's going to be fine.'

The hand is removed, and the warmed patch cools as he turns to Lenny.

'Better? Can you speak to me yet?'

'Better,' Lenny says, her voice muffled by the mask.

Orly wipes her eyes and gets to her feet. The colour has returned to her friend's face.

'That your inhaler?'

Lenny holds out the cylinder of blue plastic she must have been clutching the whole time. He pumps it. Nothing happens. He pumps again, then raises it to his nose. Then he frowns.

'This is empty.'

Lenny pushes herself upright and tips the mask away from her mouth. 'I only got it . . . last week.'

She has enough breath for a full sentence. Thank fuck.

'How many times have you used it?'

'Once or twice. Maybe it's faulty.'

The medic is turning it over in his hand. 'You've only used it a couple of times?'

Lenny nods.

'Look here.' He shows them the nozzle. 'See all that powder residue? This has been used many times without being cleaned.'

'No,' she says. 'No way. I test them, you know, seeing if they float,' the sentence is punctuated with staccato breaths, 'every week, chuck them as soon as they start to bob up. And this one was brand new, in its box when I packed it.'

'Do you have kids? Maybe they were playing around with—'

'They would never do that!' Lenny snaps. 'They know it keeps me alive. It must have been a faulty batch. Jesus.' She tears off the mask. Her cheeks are now darkening from healthy pink to angry red.

'Hey. Calm down, or you're going to have another attack. Now, I don't work for the NHS so it's nothing to do with me, okay? Have you got more inhalers with you?'

Lenny shakes her head.

'Right, I'll get you a couple.' The medic walks away and Orly goes over to the bed. Lenny's hands are shaking and she presses her lips together as her eyes well up. Orly's mouth opens but she doesn't know what to say. She's never seen Lenny cry before.

'The kids,' Lenny mutters. 'They would have been all alone.'

'Never,' Orly says. 'We would never let that happen.'

Lenny sniffs and her voice cracks. 'Thanks.'

Orly bends to hug her friend. It's a terrible thing to admit, but there's something, not exactly pleasurable, just somehow *rewarding*, in seeing Lenny brought low and being able to do something to help her. It's always been the other way around. As if reading her mind, Lenny says into her ear, 'You just saved my life.'

'Here.' The medic comes back holding a blue disc-shaped device. 'This is the new kind. See, it's full.' He pumps and a fine spray mists the air between them. Catching the low sunlight coming through the tent flaps, it turns to glitter.

Lenny sits up and swings her legs off the bed. She makes a show of inhaling deeply. 'Thank you so much, sorry I'm such a grouchy patient.'

'Ha, don't worry, I've had worse.'

They shake hands briskly – a satisfactory outcome to their meeting – and the two women walk back out into the sunlight.

'Shitty death,' Lenny mutters.

'Don't do that again,' Orly says.

12

Lenny

Lenny tramps along in silence beside Orly, who has always been an expert at knowing when to keep quiet. She's scared and shaken, but it seems to be manifesting itself in pure rage that makes her want to punch the smiling faces coming in the other direction. Instead she makes do with issuing vicious kicks to whatever item of litter drifts into her path.

She hates it. Having this weakness, this mortal vulnerability that she can do absolutely nothing about. On occasion, when she was young, she would deliberately provoke an attack, just to try and force her body to subdue it without intervention, but it never worked. She always ended up gaping like a fish in the bottom of a boat, grasping for her inhaler.

To think that something as stupid as a faulty plastic pump could be the end of her, the pathetic whimpering conclusion to all that drive and hard work; the end of her children's happiness.

Her legs are still wobbly and it feels like there are tiny moths fluttering in her lungs, but at least she's alive. Though it was touch-and-go for a moment. As she drifted in and out of consciousness she had that tunnel-vision thing that's supposed be due to oxygen depletion in the brain, and a warm cosy sensation that was close to happiness. Atheist that she is, she wonders whether, if the attack had gone on for longer, she might have seen her parents beckoning to her from the bright light. Her mood softens a little more. She wouldn't mind seeing her old mum again.

It must have looked pretty bad to Orly. After all she's been through, her poor friend could do with a break. Lenny sneaks a glance at Orly trudging beside her, pasty and exhausted. She's almost unrecognisable from the bright, self-contained girl at school.

It had taken a while for Lenny to notice Orly among all the strutting drama queens and bitches. She wasn't fake or show-offy. She threw no tantrums, there were no squealing melodramas about *he said/she said* (or more usually *she said/she said*). In some ways they were opposites – Orly hated competition and conflict as much as Lenny thrived on it – and perhaps that was why their bond was so close back then. Over the years that followed, Lenny thought they had grown apart. In her pre-kids days it was Thea that Lenny seemed to have more in common with: they shopped and lunched and drank together at the best boutiques and bars, and she still likes Thea a great deal, but having kids has given her a different perspective. If it ever came down to the wire – bankruptcy, terminal disease, something happening to one of the twins, God forbid – it would be Orly who would stay by her side to the end.

An image flashes into her mind, then, of the four of them walking down this same track twenty-two years ago. Their rucksacks had been woefully under-packed, and they only possessed one jumper between them. It got passed around until they met up with Rich, who willingly gave up his hoodie and spent the rest of the weekend shivering and goosebumped.

Lovely Rich.

Mel said they might bump into him, and Lenny knows what she and Orly would think if they did. A chance to rectify the mistake Lenny made by leaving him. A father for the children. Companionship, security. All the things you valued when you didn't have the cushion of wealth.

He was so good-looking, stupidly so. Blonde and blue-eyed, with a footballer's thighs and a rower's torso. The biceps did little for her, but the fact that he laughed at her jokes did: the interest he showed in her conversation where other boys just wanted you to parrot their opinions and giggle at their stupid pranks. Oh, and open your legs, of course. She was intelligent enough to understand that she liked him because he reinforced her own opinion of herself. She also liked him for the patience and care he took in arousing her. Once or twice before him she'd allowed herself to be dry-humped against the wall of the school or local pub, but had always got bored and pushed the boy in question off, rebuffing his sneers that she must be frigid by offering him another try once he'd had more practice. Some of them were scared of her after that, but not Rich. That scored him even more points, until eventually she kidded herself that she loved him.

She stops dead.

'Len? Are you okay?'

Lenny wonders for a terrible moment if she's having a stroke or an aneurysm. Something that's making her hallucinate the fact that her ex-boyfriend, her first love, the person she has given barely a thought to for twenty years until this very moment, is standing in front of her in a yellow jacket handing out fabric bags to passers-by.

'Oh wow,' Orly murmurs. 'Rich.'

Lenny says nothing as the vague sense of disappointment sinks in. Of course he's older, and he probably has the sort of job that doesn't encourage golden curls or allow the time for gym-honed pecs. His prettiness has coarsened, swallowed up by stodgy cheeks and a flaccid jawline.

'He hasn't seen us,' Orly says softly. 'If you want to . . .'

Piqued by the implication that she is somehow scared of an encounter, Lenny sets a smile on her lips and strides forward. 'Thought I might see you here.'

Rich looks up. He blinks, and there is a terrible moment when she thinks he's not going to recognise her. The capillaries in her cheeks begin to dilate as she realises how much she has changed from the girls-school clone of twenty years ago. But he

113

isn't looking at her figure, or her lopped hair, he's looking into her eyes, and as she looks back, she sees the moment recognition flares, a bright flame that makes her heart throb.

'Oh, hey, hi, wow. Len.' He runs his hand through his hair, then leans forward, and they kiss – on one cheek: Lenny's careful not to make a poncey London two-cheek mistake now she's back in Somerset.

'This isn't my job,' he says, holding up the bags. 'I work at Foster-Piggot – I'm a solicitor. I'm just handing these out for fun. The firm paid for our tickets.' He nods at his colleagues, a spotty youth and a petite woman who's almost disposed of her bags.

'Great,' Lenny says. 'A solicitor. Brilliant.' Is that nervous babbling because of her, or because he wouldn't want *anyone* to think he's just a free-bag-hander-outer?

There's a pause.

'You remember Orly,' Lenny says. 'My bestie.'

'Yeah, of course,' he says, staring at her. 'You look so . . .'

'Different?' Orly says. 'You're probably thinking of Thea.'

'Oh no, no way.' Rich is flustered. 'Of course I remember you! We used to hang out at the Oak, right?'

Lenny wants to roll her eyes at his woeful backpedalling. *Everyone* used to hang out at the Oak.

'You were seeing Timmo Browning for a while.'

'Not me.' Orly smiles and glances at Lenny. Timmo Browning was a total prick, and only Mel would lower herself to getting off with him.

'It's so great to see you! Both! Let's get out of the sun a minute.' Rich, a forty-year-old man, is actually blushing as he ushers them into the shade of the nearest tent. 'What have you been up to all these years? I looked for you on social media, but I guess you aren't the Facebook type.'

'No, sorry.'

Standing just inside the awning, Lenny can see Rich's female colleague looking around, perhaps for him.

'I work in banking. All very boring.'

'Banking?' His eyebrows lift. 'What, like, NatWest or . . .?'

'Investment. Hedge funds. That kind of thing. Very dull.'

He inhales and blows the breath out. 'Well, I always knew you were going places. Out of this dump anyway.'

And there it is, the bitterness she always knew would come for him. He had his chance. For a while he talked of joining her at the same university – she didn't mind either way – but then his dad got him an interview at a local firm, very possibly the place whose name is on the bags. She has nothing against the people who stayed in their home town – Mel did, and is perfectly satisfied with her choices – but those who stayed and then resented everyone who left and made more money than them get up her nose.

'We should probably go. The others are waiting for us. It was great to—'

'Ah, don't go yet.' His hand is on her arm. 'It's been so long. Remember the last time we were here? It was tiny compared to this, right?'

'Farmer Woollacott used to come round with his tractor and trailer,' Orly says, 'collecting the full Portaloos. Remember when that one fell on the girl in the year above us?'

Lenny and Rich splutter with laughter. It was truly horrific at the time. She was knocked unconscious and lay on the grass covered in lumpy blue slime.

'He didn't even apologise, as I recall,' Lenny says.

'His son just sat there laughing like a nutcase,' Rich says. '"She's got poo on her!" he mimicked.

'That kid with the hare lip?' Lenny says. 'Remember he caught us in the barn and we paid him off in sweets not to tell his dad?'

'Was that the summer of the knicker thief?' Rich says. '"They seek him here, they seek him there . . ."'

'"But they'll never find your underwear",' Lenny finishes, and they laugh again. The sun haloes the back of his hair, and with his face in shadow, he might almost be the beautiful boy she knew.

The barn was in a field between the two schools – the girls' and the boys'. Owned by Woollacott, the field was further away from the main farm and had been left fallow for years. She remembers the smell of the sun-warmed fir trees that lined the playing field as she crept through to the lane behind the hockey pitch, the scratch of rusted metal on her thighs as she vaulted the gate into the field, the sensuous thoughts that unspooled as she waded through the long meadow grass to ensure she was turned on and ready by the time she got to the barn. They only had an hour for lunch. She would start undressing as soon as she stepped into the cool, straw-scented darkness, leaving her uniform wherever it fell.

It was a rickety old building that had once been red, but by then most of the paint was peeling off, the walls were missing panels and the roof was open to the sky in parts.

From this distance there's a magical romanticism about the scene – the sunlight lying in bars across Rich's pale body on his gym towel, the dust motes like spinning specks of gold, the butterflies and dragonflies that drifted in and out, birdsong, the summer wind in the grasses – but the main thing she remembers is the sweating urgency to be done before the bell went for the end of lunch. They could hear it across the fields and sometimes they were too slow – at the beginning, when they were still tender and shy. It was one of these times that she lost her underwear. The rest of her clothes, and Rich's, were where they had dropped them, but her knickers had gone. They didn't waste much time looking. It wasn't as if she'd tossed them wildly into the air, and the barn was empty apart from piles of ancient straw and bits of blue plastic rope. They were gone, and there was no helping it. She'd been careful to keep her legs together and her skirt rolled down during art.

'My money was on a badger,' Rich says. 'Lining its burrow.'

'Probably one of your pervy mates,' Lenny snorts.

'I bet that creepy teacher loved it,' Rich laughs. 'The one who got fired.'

'Mr Newman,' Orly says quietly.

'I wonder what happened to him after it all blew over,' Lenny says.

Rich shrugs. 'Probably topped himself. I would after that. Everyone thinking you're a nonce.'

Orly flinches.

'We should go,' Lenny says quickly, to move the subject away from untimely death. 'The others are waiting for us at Earthfields.' Her heart sinks, just a fraction, and she can tell Rich feels the same. The pleasure of reminiscence and the accompanying images in her mind were over too quickly.

She hugs him, and now, after all that remembering, she realises he smells exactly the same. An indescribable *Rich* smell, savoury and soothingly familiar.

'Maybe we'll catch up with each other again,' she says, and then pauses, waiting for him to ask for her number, like a proper unwoke nineties teenager. She could ask for his, and yet somehow she can't bring herself to. At school, Thea always warned them about being too forward, that boys didn't like it. And even Lenny, of the 143 IQ and the MBA from the London Business School, listened.

He doesn't ask. He just smiles wistfully and murmurs, 'It was so great to see you.'

They walk out of the tent and then speed up their pace, until finally they're running over the dry grass, giggling like teenagers.

Earthfields is exactly as Lenny remembers. Walking under the enormous sign made from scrap metal, they pass teepees exhaling the strong smell of weed, caravans and stalls selling vegan food, a withy pot-making workshop and a meditation class. In the centre is a large bonfire, the flames flickering on the exposed flesh of those dancing around it to the music of a fiddler in a top hat cascading ribbons. Behind it the sky has turned a deeper blue. The afternoon has tipped into evening without them noticing.

They spot the other two standing by a trestle table advertising *vegan Buddha bowls*. This will surely be Thea's idea. Now that she's put on a fitted jumper over her flowing top, Lenny realises for the first time how emaciated her friend has become.

117

And something in the way she is carrying herself makes Lenny wonder if she's in pain.

'It's *alive*!' Mel shrieks over the bongo drums being played by an entirely naked man with a joint hanging out of his mouth. 'What the fuck, dude!'

Lenny's guess that Mel is drunk is confirmed as her friend wobbles over and encloses her in a lager-scented embrace. When she extricates herself, Thea is there, her cheeks pinched, her eyes sunk deep in their hollows.

'Don't do that again,' she says. 'We were so worried.'

'Sorry.'

'Yeah,' Mel slurs. 'Really fucking worried. So worried we had to get smashed to deal with it! Fnar!'

Fnar. That's one Lenny hasn't heard since school.

'We're having some rabbit shit – which is like rabbit food only with brown lumps in it – if you wanna join us. Not my idea, I might add. Fatso here insisted.'

'If we're going to poison ourselves with booze for the next three days,' Thea says, 'I thought we should get some wholesome nutrition.'

'Good plan,' says Orly. 'I'd go vegetarian, but my mother would never—' She stops, but before Lenny can ask what she was about to say, they are back at the stall and Thea is ordering.

The canopy and a banner staked to the ground beside it feature an image of a crudely drawn female figure with a gaping cavity between her legs. She's pulling it even wider with her hands. It makes Lenny feel queasy to look at and surely can't do much for the food sales.

'Who's that on your flags?' she asks the tattooed stallholder.

The girl looks up from her task of loading purple sludge into a cardboard box. 'Sheela Na Gig. Mother goddess of fertility.'

Lenny smiles. Just as her parents feared the first time she came, the festival is a nest of heathens.

'I know you!' Mel bellows at the stallholder as she takes their money. 'You were in the year below us at school!'

The woman's eyes flick from face to face, her expression neutral. 'Yeah.'

'Wow. Cool. And now you're doing this!'

'Yep. Left at sixteen. Had enough of all the bitches.'

'Fuck yeah,' Mel says, waving her arm. 'That place was bitch queen heaven. I left at sixteen too.'

'So what are you doing?'

'Oh, massive disappointment on all levels. Single mother, work in a café.'

'Happy?'

'As a fucking sandgirl!'

The woman laughs. It transforms her face, and now Lenny recognises her as the undersized urchin who always smelled unwashed. Now she has tattoos on her neck. A point well made: she isn't going to be a victim any more.

Taking her box of sludge, Lenny moves away, to be joined by Thea and Orly, while Mel continues chatting to the girl, leaning unsteadily on the counter.

'Do you remember we used to call her Baldric, because she always looked so rough?' Thea whispers.

Orly nods, grimacing.

It wasn't like Orly to be cruel, but then again, they all were as teenagers. Empathy, and the resulting mortification at the things you did and said, the pain you caused, came later.

The opportunity to extricate Mel comes when the phone clumsily tucked into her back pocket lights up. Thea pulls her away, reminding her that it might be Billy, and Mel snatches it out. But looking at the screen, she swears.

'It's him.'

'Don't pick up,' Orly mutters, and Mel ends the call. Then she composes a text, letting them all read it over her shoulder.

Dumped your drugs. You were lucky I didn't call the police. Now fuck off and leave me alone.

Before Lenny can stop her, she presses *send*. Then she tucks the phone back into her pocket, apparently without a care.

Wandering over to the fire, she starts dancing with a semi-naked man whose body is completely tattooed but whose face, framed by fair ringlets, is angelic. He seems delighted by Mel's gyrating in front of him, her black hair flashing in the firelight, though his grin might well be chemically enhanced.

Lenny spots a stall with a banner advertising organic beer and heads over to it.

Five bottles later, she's caught up with Mel. She's not used to drinking these days. Her thirty-fifth birthday present was the onset of hangovers, so she very rarely goes beyond a single glass of red wine at dinner. It's just not worth it for the suffering at work the next day.

But GillFest is her big chance for a blowout without having to worry about either work or children, and she's going to take it. She'd forgotten how good it feels to be three sheets to the wind, she thinks, as she crouches for a pee in a dark area behind the teepees where the woodland begins. Halfway through, she topples over, managing to wet her shorts in the process, but it's dark now, so no one will notice.

She stays where she is, lying on her back on the cool grass, gazing up at a sky rippling with the seas of coloured lights from below. The children would love this sight. She wonders what they are doing. Fed, bathed, read to and in bed, no doubt, as per her instructions. Jeanne is a good au pair: reliable, unflappable and patient. She likes the children well enough, especially Greta, who is entranced by her, but they will never be more than a professional responsibility to the French girl. This is something Lenny never considered before she had children, or even when they were babies. She just wanted someone who would keep them clean and fed, like material possessions that needed to be serviced and maintained. Now she would take them dirty, hungry, wild and naughty if it meant spending their time with someone who actually loved them.

Orly calls her name and she hauls herself to her feet with a grunt and staggers out from between the teepees.

Rich is there.

She runs to hug him. 'I don't see you in twenty years and now it's twice in one day!' At least that's what she intends to say, but it comes out a little bit tangled and Rich laughs.

'You ladies enjoying yourselves?'

'Yup!'

'Clearly.' He turns and she follows his gaze to where Mel and the tattooed angel are sitting close together on a hay bale, talking intensely.

'Thea's on her own,' Orly says. 'I'll go and keep her company.'

Lenny knows her friend is just being tactful, but when she finally picks out Thea, standing staring into the flames, she does look lonely. Or if not lonely, then lost. Thin and tired and too old for her clothes. The lines that bracket her mouth are not laughter lines, but the simian marks of emaciation. Is she ill?

'Another beer?' Rich says, and she turns her attention back to him. In the firelit dusk he looks like his old self again – or perhaps it's just the drink – and she has a strong urge to push her tongue into his mouth.

She glances down at the hand holding his bottle. No wedding ring. Not that that means much. But maybe he never married because he never got over her. The thought is outrageously arrogant, and the sensible part of her brain tells her not to be so stupid, but the drunk part drowns it out – *see the way he's looking at me?*

'Or would you prefer . . .' With a flourish, he draws from his pocket a bottle of white rum. 'I take it it's still your favourite?'

'Fuck yeah!'

'I couldn't seem to find any Coke, though, so how would you feel about dandelion cordial?'

'Delighted.'

They start off on a hay bale, but as the bottles are slowly drained, they sink down to lean against it, little blades of straw jabbing their backs. Orly and Thea are laughing at Mel, who is now being taught to juggle by the Adonis.

121

'I can't believe she's pulled already,' Lenny says, but her tongue is definitely no longer receiving all the messages sent from her brain. 'I guess she was always the sexy one.'

A split second after she says it, she realises what she was after, and sure enough, Rich delivers.

'*You* were the sexy one.' He takes her hand and it feels so good, so right and comfortable, that she closes her eyes and lets her head fall back against the bale. Almost immediately the world starts to spin and she opens them again. She turns her head and Rich's face is there, so close his features are out of focus.

And then they are kissing, and the years fall away.

She has to keep stopping as the dizziness becomes unbearable, and though she's really enjoying the kiss, she's too pissed to be properly aroused. But Rich isn't. He's moved his lips to her neck and collarbone and his breathing is ragged. They could do it right here, she thinks, and no one would care. In fact it would be right and appropriate. A good GillFest story to tell your mates – I saw a couple fucking by the bonfire – but as his hands move to her breasts, some sense of decorum cuts through the fug of alcohol.

Pulling herself to her feet with the help of the hay bale, she drags him after her – 'Come on' – and they weave through supine revellers to the line of teepees.

In the cool darkness beyond, she sinks onto the grass and lies down on her back. She's way too pissed to feel like taking much of an active part, but Rich doesn't seem to mind doing most of the work. Lifting her top, he tugs down her bra straps and runs his tongue over her nipples. She taught him that – she remembers telling him very sternly how to do it – and either he has never forgotten or else all women like it being done the same way. It's a shame really; if she was sober, she'd be really aroused, but the ache between her thighs is weak and distant, as if the body parts involved are further away than usual.

He starts undoing her shorts but can't manage it one-handed – the other is supporting his bodyweight – so she helps him, then unbuttons his jeans.

Oh yes, she thinks as more of his body is revealed to her. A little hairier, a little flabbier, but the construction of bone and joint and muscle is as familiar as her own body, as if that nine-month period hard-wired something in her brain. Perhaps she was always meant to be with him.

'It wasn't a coincidence me coming here,' he pants as he shuffles his hips into position. 'I had to see you.' He groans almost alarmingly as he enters her. She gasps, more through surprise at the unfamiliar sensation of penetration than anything else, but he misconstrues it as sexual ecstasy.

'Oh God, Len. I fucking love you. I fucking love you. I've never stopped.'

It's not going to happen, she can feel it at once. Like the epidural she had with the twins, drink has numbed her below the waist, and she'll just have to ride this out until he comes, which will be ages because he's drunk too.

She'll just try and enjoy it for what it is, a moment of adult intimacy – no, more than that; of tenderness. Something that is vanishingly rare in her work- and child-dominated life. She puts her arms around him, her palms against his slightly tacky back. Beneath her fingertips she can feel the raised mole whose contours she knows as well as the one on her own stomach.

Has he got children? she wonders as the stars tremble in her vision. Does he take them to Shawley Rec on a Saturday afternoon to feed the ducks and eat cake? Is there a bitter ex, or a sad one: someone who could never quite live up to the memory of his first true love?

There she goes again. Who does she think she is? Presumably not the solitary middle-aged woman who lies awake worrying about her life choices and her poor fatherless babies. Rich is still an attractive man, and he was always a kind one. She could do a lot worse and he could probably do a lot better.

He pants into her ear, tickling it with breath that smells of Bacardi. She bites his shoulder. It has just come back to her how he liked to be bitten, hard enough to bruise, to the extent that his

123

mother thought he was being bullied. It's like flicking a switch. He gives a prolonged groan, shudders, and slumps onto her.

She laughs.

'Oh my God.' He raises himself onto his elbows and looks into her face. 'Did you?'

'Nah, too pissed.'

'Oh, wait, well hang on, let me . . .'

'No, don't. It was nice. It really was.' Her back is starting to ache. It was never like this when she was seventeen, lying on ridged concrete with boys who thought the harder they thrust, the better girls liked it.

'Good. I love it when you come. You always make that face.'

She smiles, but he's starting to annoy her. Those doe eyes gazing sloppily into hers.

She twitches her hips. 'Now where are my knickers?'

She's only joking – they're in the shorts wrapped around her knees – but Rich gets off her and starts to look around. She pulls up her shorts and sits up, pressing her fists into the small of her back and wincing.

'Hey!'

She freezes.

'Hey, mate, what you doing?' Rich scrambles up, fumbling with his jeans, and runs towards the wood that abuts the teepee area. A moment later he has been swallowed by the shadows of the trees.

The night air is cold on her exposed body, and all around her the tents boom softly in the wind.

'Rich?'

Suddenly it feels like she's in a horror movie. Like a man in a leather mask is about to swim out of the gloom with a bladed weapon and punish her for the moral transgression of having sex. Lenny's view of sex as something to be enjoyed, like a pizza or a good crap, is probably a reaction against her parents' Christianity, but she has never quite shifted the notion that it's a sin that deserves punishment.

But the pale figure that steps out of the trees a moment later is only Rich.

'Fucking peeping Tom!'

'Really?' She pulls up her bra straps and tugs down her T-shirt. 'Are you sure?'

'Tall guy with a beard. Didn't you see him?' It sounds like an accusation.

'No.' Irritated, she gets to her feet. At least all the heavy breathing has cleared her head a bit.

'Come on, let's go back.' He takes her arm, as if she's his possession now. She pulls away from him, stepping between the guy ropes towards the lights of the bonfire.

Thea, Mel and Orly are on the other side of the flames. Thea and Orly look bored. Mel is still on the hay bale with the tattooed guy.

Rich tugs on her arm again and she turns sharply. She doesn't feel like being pawed. But his expression is one of wincing regret.

'I should go,' he says. 'My friends are waiting for me. When can I see you again?'

'Oh.' So he never intended to spend the evening with her. She doesn't care. Well, she didn't, until he said that. 'Um, tomorrow night?'

'Meet me at the art-house cinema at seven, yeah?'

'Sure, okay.' Her tone is casual, but she's rather distracted by the fact that he's off already. She wouldn't have wanted to spend her whole evening with him, but still.

He kisses her, then walks away towards the entrance arch. She watches him for a minute and can't quite imagine how a few moments ago he was naked on top of her. That strange juxtaposition of tender intimacy followed by indifference that casual sex always brings. Though she didn't expect it to be quite so casual.

She marches across the grass towards her friends.

'So?' Orly says, her face brightening at Lenny's approach.

Lenny shrugs and grins and takes Orly's beer.

'That mouth had better not have been around Rich's cock!' Orly says, pretending to snatch it back. Her cheeks are flushed and she looks better than she has in long months. If nothing else, this birthday trip has been worth it just for that.

Thea clinks her bottle, but Mel is apparently too mesmerised by the tattooed boy even to register her arrival.

'Is she in again?' Lenny laughs.

'Looks like it,' Orly says wistfully. 'How does she do it?'

'Because she's happy,' Thea says.

'*Men will want her, 'cos life don't haunt her*,' Orly murmurs. 'Who sang that?'

They are throwing suggestions in – Donna Summer, Roberta Flack – when a shadow falls across the pair on the hay bale.

'Heads up,' Thea murmurs. 'It's Balders.'

The woman is now minus her apron, revealing an exposed midriff and tanned thighs of stunning muscularity. She walks past them and up to the tattooed boy, bending to ruffle his dreadlocks. His attention immediately snaps away from Mel. Turning his head, he kisses Baldric's stomach.

'Damn,' murmurs Orly. Mel's shoulders slump and she prepares to get up, but instead of taking the boy away, Baldric sits down on the grass and starts up a conversation. The other three wander over in time to hear the boy declare that Mel feels exactly as they do about the influence of Wicca on the modern eco movement.

Lenny raises her eyebrow at Mel who shrugs. *Worth a try.*

'You're Wiccans, are you?' Thea says, just about courteously.

'We believe in the power and wisdom of nature,' the woman says.

'Thea believes in enhancing nature,' Mel says, sweeping her bottle in an arc that encompasses Thea's rickety frame.

Lenny's pelvic floor tightens sharply. Mel is too drunk to remember that you do not draw attention to Thea's surgery, ever. But tonight Thea doesn't appear to mind.

'Can you tell fortunes?' she says, and Lenny winces. Her friend has gone too far this time and insulted the pair. But glancing across in warning, she sees that Thea's gaze is serious and intense.

The woman looks at her steadily, then a corner of her mouth twists up. 'Cross my palm with silver and I'll give it a go.'

Thea fumbles in her pocket and draws out a ten-pound note. 'For that I'll do all of you.'

Thea sits meekly on the patch of grass the woman has patted. The woman turns Thea's hand over and peers down at the lines that net her palm. 'So, what do you want to know?'

Thea's chest is rising and falling quickly, making those stick-on breasts bulge and droop. 'The future.'

For a moment there is silence. Even the bongo drummer seems to have run out of energy. The flames make dark shadows flicker across Thea's white skin.

'Okay.' The woman drops her hand.

'What did you see?' Thea is trying to smile, but her eyes bulge from their sockets.

'I said I'd do all of you. You now.'

Mel shuffles over to her and stares off into the distance as the woman reads her palm. What would Mel be wishing for? Lenny wonders. A new man now that Billy's leaving home? Or something more exciting. Travel, perhaps, a new career, a move abroad. There's a certain freedom in having your kids young. You may not have much money when they're grown and gone, but you have something infinitely more precious – youth and time. Lenny will be pushing sixty by the time hers leave.

When it's her turn, Lenny succumbs because it's easier than not to. The woman's grip is strong and cold, like metal. Lenny looks away, but she can still feel the eyes moving across her skin. When her hand is released, it's a relief. She stands up, plucks at her shorts: beneath them her damp knickers have turned uncomfortably cold.

'You.'

'No,' Orly says. 'I don't want to know.'

Mel reaches up and yanks her onto the grass. 'Come on!'

As the woman grasps Orly's hand and twists it, Orly winces in pain. It's all nonsense, of course, but the way those watery

127

eyes skitter left to right, and up and down, like spiders running along the lines of Orly's palm, makes Lenny's flesh crawl. The girl finishes, drops Orly's hand and leans back against the inked skin of the dreadlocked boy.

'C'mon then,' Mel slurs. 'Are we going to win the lottery?'

'Will we meet tall handsome strangers?' Thea is trying to smile, but a nerve in her cheek is twitching.

The girl's clear eyes meet theirs and her lips twist into a smile. 'You're all going to end up alone.'

Lenny pauses in the act of adjusting her underwear.

Orly laughs uncertainly.

'Your relationships are worthless and even your friendship is a lie. You'd do anything to see each other fuck up, but you're too scared to let go because then you'll have nothing.'

'Oh fuck off,' Mel slurs. 'Tell us what we're lying about then if you're so fucking . . .' she stalls, then finishes lamely, 'magic.'

'They're not my lies to tell.' The girl's smile passes like a disease from face to face.

'Okay,' Lenny says. 'That's enough. I think we'll have our money back, please.'

The woman dips her hand into her pocket, pulls out the note and tosses it up into the night air. It flips and begins to fall, see-sawing erratically through the sparks of the bonfire.

Mel goes after it, but she's too drunk. As she throws her arm up and forward, her body follows. Lenny can see she's going to topple into the bonfire, but is too far away to prevent it. Then suddenly Thea shoulder-barges her out of the air, and Mel rolls safely onto the cool grass. Thea, however, crashes down into the embers that spread out from the pyre, and before she can scramble away, the tips of her hair catch light.

The tattooed boy leaps up and hauls her clear, clapping the hair between his palms until the flames extinguish, leaving thin snakes of smoke.

'For fuck's sake!' Lenny yells at the girl, who's laughing as she rolls what looks like a joint. 'You could have killed her!'

'It wasn't my fault,' the girl snorts. 'She just couldn't keep her hands off that.' She points the roll-up at the ten-pound note, lying in the embers a little further in from where Thea fell. For a second there's still a chance to rescue it, but then the edge of the note catches. A flame leaps high and orange, licking the Queen's face and then eating it, and a moment later the note has disintegrated to grey ash.

'Thea, oh my God, are you okay?' Mel crawls over and throws her arms around Thea, now tugging at the charred ends of her hair to try and inspect the damage.

'I'm fine, honestly. I could have done with a trim anyway, my ends were so split.' Her tone is light, but her shoulders are trembling.

'You saved me! Oh my God.'

'I was going for the tenner!' Thea laughs.

Lenny says, 'You need to wear more sensible shoes.'

'Come on, Suke,' the tattooed boy says. 'Let's go fuck.'

Suki. Of course, that was her name. Not Baldric.

'Bye, ladies,' she says. 'Enjoy yourselves.'

Watching the couple saunter off towards one of the teepees, Lenny feels unnerved. School is such a distant memory, she had forgotten how cruel women can be. It seems a distinctly female thing to hurt for no reason other than to enjoy the spectacle, but that might just be her age. In the more equal world that Greta will grow up in, rivalry can be directed towards more productive ends.

She helps Thea and then Mel to their feet and tries not to stare at Thea's ruined hair. Presumably there's a hairdresser on site. Perhaps they can sort something out in the morning. At the moment, all Lenny wants to do is sleep. It's been an eventful evening.

'Shall we head back to the tent?'

'Hell no,' Thea says, her eyes glittering. 'It's still early!'

She's brave, Lenny thinks, as she watches Thea picking the black tips off her hair. Her appearance, which seems to scream insecurity, might fool you into thinking she's fragile, but she's not.

She's a survivor. She survived Tony's incarceration, leaving her with two young children. She got back on her feet, slapped a smile on her face, pulled on some heels and landed herself a new man. Lenny has always admired her for that.

'Where's Orly?' Mel says.

They look around.

'There!' Thea points.

Orly is passing under the entrance arch, walking so quickly she keeps tripping.

'Fuck's the matter with her?' Mel slurs.

@GillingwaterFestival
We try to keep #GillFest drug-free, but if you do buy illegal drugs, please be careful. Today a woman was taken to hospital after an overdose.

@Cleb88
Replying to @GillingwaterFestival
I saw her! Seriously thought she was dead. Foaming at the mouth eyes rolled back like a fucking zombie!

@Pughpughbarneymcgrew
Replying to @Clebb88 and @GillingwaterFestival
Drug free my arse. You dont even try. I saw a guy by the Litha Stage openly selling. If she dies its on your conscience.

13

Orly

The music pounds like artillery. Smoke rolls across the ground, people emerging from it to blunder into her path. A girl is screaming and pointing at nothing while her boyfriend tries to restrain her. Someone else is howling like a wolf. Every eye that catches hers is white-rimmed and wild, and she looks away before whatever drug these people have taken prompts them to come after her. It's as if the fun-loving, chilled-out festival-goers of the daytime have been replaced by dark doppelgängers with sinister intent.

She thinks she's back on the main track, but nothing looks the same in the firelit dark. Stumbling along close to the hedgerow to avoid the revellers, she tries to push down the panic that is threatening to close her throat.

Could that malicious woman really have read her palm? Because she was right. Orly is a liar.

The fact is, she isn't sure her friendships could withstand the truth: that by the end she had wished Harry dead, and now she's jobless and living with her parents. The truth would make her into the type of friend magazines warn you about – *draining, negative, avoid at all costs*. Better to pretend everything's fine.

The grass beneath her feet has changed colour. She looks up.

She is almost at the entrance to the fairground. Its mauve and acid-yellow lights give every face a cast of madness. Carousel music vies with the wailing of the ghost train and the ringing of the test-your-strength machine.

132

She's gone the wrong way. But behind her the track forks in three directions, not the two she was expecting. Which way is the campsite?

Suddenly a man is blocking her path.

'Hey.'

'Go away!' Panic tightens her vocal cords, making her voice shrill.

'Sorry, I didn't mean . . .' He reaches for her and she strikes out at him and stumbles away.

She can see what's going to happen before it does. The bottle is lying on the ground exactly where her right foot is descending, and though her brain has plenty of time to scroll through all the painful outcomes when the two meet, it seems not to have the time to send a message to sidestep. Her foot lands, the bottle rolls, and she is falling backwards.

But before she can jar her coccyx on the baked earth, strong arms catch her and lift her to her feet. Wrenching free, she spins around and screams loudly enough, she hopes, that people will hear over the music. 'Fuck off!'

The cry is immediately lost in the jangling noise of the fair, but the man steps back and holds up his hand.

'Ben,' he says. 'It's Ben, from the tent next door to you.'

She stares, then the muscles that were tensed for fight-or-flight fall slack.

'Are you okay?'

'I . . . I'm lost. I was trying to get back to the campsite.'

'It's not far,' he says. 'Just down there.' He points, and now she sees that the track running left to right is the main one. The smaller path opposite must just lead to bins and toilets.

'I could take you . . . Actually, why don't I just show you. Look, you see that flag?'

He's afraid of her, she realises as he explains the route. Afraid to be alone in her company in case she flips out again. His friends are standing by a hot-dog van, smirking.

'Got it?'

133

'Think so.'

'Okay, cool, well . . . If you've got a problem, just—'

'I'll be fine, honestly.' She walks quickly away in the direction he described, and within twenty minutes she is back at the gateway that leads to the campsite.

The tents crouch silently, ghosts in the gloom, their guy ropes whispering. Coolness radiates from the ground and through her sandals to her sore heels. There's the tent, outlined against the black trees, small and somehow vulnerable against the looming shadows.

Picking her way across to it, she climbs inside and zips it up behind her. Though the walls are only thin membranes of nylon, she feels safer at once. She crawls deeper, unzipping and rezipping the inner tent and clambering across the cases and holdalls to the nest of sleeping bags.

Alone in the cool darkness and rapidly sobering up, she realises she has been foolish. The woman, Baldric, was winding them up. Perhaps as revenge for Mel chatting up her boyfriend, or to get back at them for the treatment she received at school. Orly can't imagine holding a grudge for so long, but perhaps people do. Baldric said they were all lying, and presumably all of them have a few secrets – it's not as if there's a big flashing arrow above Orly's head. At least there wasn't before she ran away.

She curls up on the bag that, from the strong smell of perfume, must be Thea's and wishes she hadn't been so stupid.

It's very quiet.

Is it midnight yet? How much longer will the others last? Did Lenny shag Rich? If so, they might get back together. Orly tries to be happy for her friend, but fails miserably. Lenny will leave to join the ranks of the coupled, only attending formal gatherings and always with her partner in tow. Late-night calls and impromptu visits will be no more.

There are rustling footsteps outside, very close.

She freezes. If it was the others returning, there would be voices and laughter. Has someone watched her come back here alone? Ben or one of his friends? Or a stranger lying in wait for vulnerable females?

She reaches for the nearest case for something she can defend herself with. Perhaps there are nail scissors in Thea's washbag. She opens the clasp and rifles through. Could she use Thea's spray-on deodorant and the cigarette lighter tucked into the side pocket as a flame-thrower?

Too late.

The outer zip of the tent is pulled up, followed by the inner one. 'Jesus!'

'Sorry.' Lenny grins, ducking in. 'Were you expecting someone else?'

'Oh, you know, only murderers.'

Lenny crawls over to sit beside her. 'How come you ran off?'

Orly sighs. She can't remember any more why she was trying to keep it a secret. These are her friends. They've seen her crying and puking and leaking period blood through her school skirt.

'What that woman said. It's me, I'm the liar.'

'Really?' Lenny sounds amused. 'What have you done?'

Orly tips her head back and blinks away tears. 'I lost my job. I've moved back in with Mum and Dad. I didn't want you to know in case you . . . felt sorry for me, I suppose. I just can't take any more pity. I'm fed up with being Orly the drag.'

'When did it happen?'

'Four months ago.'

'Nice timing. Fire the new widow.'

'It wasn't their fault. Miles had to make cuts and I was constantly off.'

'Because you were sick.'

'Mental health problems are different. For all he knew, my depression would keep coming back.'

'Is there anything I can do? Do you need money?'

'No! Please, Len.' Orly's voice cracks. 'I hate being like this. Having everyone feel they need to look after me. That used to be *my* role with Harry. I hate being on the receiving end of it.

135

And now, without even the kids at school, I feel like I haven't really got a purpose any more. Like my whole life is pointless.'

She asked not to be pitied and now here she is whining like a brat. She scrubs the tears from her eyes with her sleeve.

'It won't always be like this, you know that,' Lenny says softly. 'You'll meet someone else, have kids. And you'll be a great mum.'

'I'm running out of time, Len. It's not easy to find someone to be with. I'm not even ready to start looking yet. And even if I did meet someone, they're not going to want to jump in and have kids straight away. It'll take a couple of years of getting to know each other, and then I'll be well past forty. My mum went through the menopause at forty-seven. It's too late. I had my chance and it didn't work out.'

She lies back on Thea's sleeping bag. She did everything just as she was supposed to. Not like Mel, a teen mum, or Thea, getting herself knocked up by a criminal, or Lenny with her scandalous sperm donation. She got married to a nice boy and sensibly put off trying for kids to establish herself in a career. And it was all for nothing.

Lenny lies down next to her. 'I fucked Rich.'

'Never. How was it?'

'Same. Bit boring. He went off straight afterwards, so clearly he wasn't that impressed either.'

A flame of hope springs up in Orly's heart. So they might not get back together after all. She quashes it guiltily. Too possessive by half. A true friend would want the best for Lenny.

'You're not a drag,' Lenny says quietly, slipping an arm around Orly's waist.

'Thanks,' Orly murmurs.

'I mean it. You're my best friend.'

Orly feels a little glow of warmth spread out from her chest. They lie in one another's arms, the awkwardness of the situation gradually wearing off, to be replaced with peace.

A while later, they hear the others crashing across the campsite, squawking and laughing.

'Look who we found!' Mel announces, crawling into their warm cocoon, bringing cold air and booze smells and fag smoke. She presses the switch of the torch hanging and the tent is bleached in light.

A woman crawls in after her but Orly's sideways view of her doesn't ring any bells. She sits up.

'Helloooooo!' the woman cries. 'Long time no see!' She is glossy and young, with pixie-cut highlights that spark in the torchlight.

'Doesn't she look amazing?' Thea says, following her in. 'And look what she did to my hair!'

Then Orly realises. It's Pandora Rankin.

'I'm a hairdresser.' Pandora shrugs. 'Had to get my artistic side out somehow.'

The charred ends of Thea's hair have been cut off and the whole thing is styled into a pretty layered bob.

Orly shuffles back into the most shadowy part of the tent.

'How are you guys? Orly, I heard about Harry. So sorry.'

'Thanks,' she murmurs.

'Wow, so great to see you,' Lenny says. 'So, what have you been up to all these years?'

'How long have you got?' Pandora laughs. 'I've lived in Thailand, Singapore, Dubai, Tehran. You can do hairdressing anywhere.'

Mel's phone rings.

'Sorry,' she says, grimacing at the screen. 'That's the fifteenth time tonight. I'll turn it off.'

'Wow, that guy *really* likes you!' Pandora laughs, showing perfectly even, perfectly white teeth. Orly glances at Thea, who is watching Pandora with a sort of hungry misery. Despite Thea's expensive efforts, Pandora looks ten years younger than all of them.

'So how come you're here,' Mel says, 'and not shacked up with some Saudi prince?'

'Oh, you know. It got boring working for other people, so I came back to the UK a couple of years ago and set up my own salon.' She names a smart market town about thirty miles away. 'Got myself a twenty-five-year-old boyfriend and here I am!'

'Twenty-five!' whistles Mel. 'How did you manage that?'

'It's not hard. We're *cougars*, grrrrl. They love it that we're sexually liberated. Although you do have to send them to Pornaholics Anonymous. First time we did it, Jay tried to choke me and was *super*-shocked when I complained. Apparently modern girls love it!'

Mel splutters delightedly. A bright new energy has entered the group. Pan always did have charisma. That was what allowed her to fit seamlessly into the school mid year and gain entry into any friendship group she set her sights on. It happened to be theirs.

'Lucky bitch.' Mel's shaking her head. 'Twenty-five. All the guys our age are fat and bald.'

'Ahh, it's not all that.' Pan leans on Thea's open case, making the side fold inwards, and from the corner of her eye Orly sees her friend stiffen. 'His conversation ain't up to much, and as for his mates . . . Jesus. It's like being back at school, only without the pervy teachers!'

They all laugh, except Orly.

'Ooh, posh goodies!' Pandora has dived into the washbag Orly left open in her hunt for a weapon, and draws out a small glass bottle. 'La Fleur Rouge serum. Whose is this?'

She's about to unscrew the cap when Thea lunges over and snatches it out of her hand. 'It's mine,' she snaps. 'And it's very expensive.'

Orly is secretly pleased by Pandora's surprise, rapidly concealed. Thea thrusts the bottle back into the washbag and pushes the whole thing under her clothes.

'Woo, it's that good, huh? I gave up on all that shit years ago. All you need is a decent sunscreen. You ever seen the damage on a UV photograph? Terrifying.'

They all start talking about skin products they have tried and abandoned, facials that have promised and not delivered,

138

the sag of boobs, and finally, of course, the inevitable struggle with weight. No one has asked Orly where she ran off to after the palm-reading. Presumably they thought she was upset about Harry – grief has its uses – and no one presses her to stay when she says she's tired and might hit the sack. Pandora hugs her warmly as she crawls past and promises not to disturb her when she eventually goes back to Jay.

Orly slithers into her sleeping bag in the outer tent and shuffles as far as she can from the conversation going on next door. It soon moves on to the defining moment of Pandora's time at Summer Hall.

'They wouldn't let me retake the exam, so I was royally fucked. Wouldn't happen now, of course. The cunt would have gone to prison.'

Orly gathers the sleeping bag over her head and presses it to her ears, so that soon all she can hear is the white noise of polyester and nylon.

An hour or so later, Pandora clambers over her and lets herself out of the tent, zipping it quietly behind her.

Orly exhales, but Pan's departure doesn't ease the crushing guilt that settled on her at the sight of her old classmate, as strong as it was all those years ago.

Even your friendship is a lie.

Pandora thought Orly was her friend. That's why she never suspected.

GILLFEST DAY 2:

MIDSUMMER'S EVE

14

Orly

Over the course of the night, Orly attempts every trick they taught her in counselling – mindfulness, the 4-7-8 breathing method, visualisation – but each time she's dozing off, her bladder forces her up and out of the tent. Crouching at the edge of the wood, her senses spring to alertness and she's back to square one.

Finally, at around four, the sun rises above the line of trees and ignites the tent like a flare. She sighs and sits up, rubbing her gritty eyes and running her tongue around her dry mouth. She needs a drink and another wee.

Crawling out, she almost puts her hand down on a pair of damp knickers and recoils in disgust. Did Lenny leave them here after the shag? More likely Mel pulled, or peed her pants. They are small and raggedy-looking. Nothing like the lace and satin delicacies she glimpsed when she opened Thea's case. Or maybe they belong to a perfect stranger and are riddled with God knows what. Getting to her feet, she toes them away from the tent, then heads into the woods for more privacy now the sun's up.

She's about to pull down her pyjama bottoms and crouch when someone clears their throat.

'Morning.'

She spins round to find Ben, doing up his fly.

'This is just a coincidence, I swear. I'm not stalking you.'

143

'Oh, I'm sure you'd be able to find more glamorous people to stalk,' she says, smoothing her hair, then kicks herself. There's nothing less attractive than low self-esteem.

'I dunno. Who doesn't look their best pissing in the woods at dawn after a heavy night?' He runs a hand through his own hair. It catches on something and he takes it away, looks at his fingers, wipes them on his jeans and murmurs, 'I really hope that's mayonnaise.'

Pressing her legs together – she really needs the loo – she says, 'Did you have a good night?'

'Not bad. I just couldn't get pissed, you know? I was full of hot dog and then I couldn't drink any more and then I got bored. If you're not a music nut or a drug fiend,' he lowers his voice to a whisper, 'these things can get a bit dull. To me anyway, but I'm boring.'

'Oh, me too.'

Gah. Shut up!

'Well, I'll leave you in peace to contaminate the local watercourse. My mate had a go at me about peeing in non-designated areas. These woke festival types, eh? See you later.'

'Hope so,' she says.

He doesn't acknowledge the flirtatious comment, but it doesn't matter. The fact is, Orly said it. She had the guts and the inclination, because she actually quite fancies Ben. Is that a betrayal of Harry? No. Harry's dead: it's not her fault that she's still alive. For a while she didn't feel it – she felt numb and cold as a corpse. But the encounter with Ben has left her warm and tingly.

Perhaps this trip is going to be good for her after all.

Back in the tent, she scrolls through the news feed on her phone until the others wake.

'Which of you sluts left your knickers outside?' she says, unzipping the inner tent, determined to start the day on a fun note.

'Eww,' says Thea. 'Really?'

'Not me,' Mel says, yawning. 'Mine are still on. I think they might have fused with my body.'

144

'Maybe one of the lads next door pulled,' Lenny says, and a string of Orly's heart gives a little twang.

Later, as they're outside blinking and stretching and drinking tea warmed on the stove Mel brought, Orly points out the knickers, curled in the grass like a question mark.

'Seriously,' Thea says. 'What grown woman wears days-of-the-week pants?'

'I used to,' Lenny laughs. 'But they were always the wrong day.'

'Good luck to whoever it was,' Mel says, from behind her sunglasses. 'I really thought I was in with that tattooed guy.'

'Boy,' Thea corrects. 'Child.'

'Ha, he was at least twenty-one! Back me up, Len!'

But Lenny is bending over the knickers and now she picks up a twig from the ground and lifts them into the air.

'Fuck me,' she breathes.

'What?'

'My mum could never be bothered to sew name tags on, so she always biroed my name. See the initials on the label?'

They gather round and peer at the faded writing. *LC*. Leonora Clarke.

Thea whistles.

For a long moment no one seems to know what to say.

'Could they be the ones you lost at the barn?' Orly ventures. 'The ones Rich was talking about? Could he have left them here as a joke?'

Lenny turns to her. 'So, what, he's been carrying them around with him for twenty years just waiting for the opportunity to pull this prank?' She's smiling, but there's tension around her eyes.

'I always thought he was weird,' Mel says, swaying. She's obviously still pissed from last night.

'You bloody liar,' Lenny laughs. 'You tried to pull him before we got together!'

Mel snorts, pours away the dregs of her tea. 'Right, I'm going to turn my phone on and call Billy.' She crawls unsteadily back into the tent, followed by Thea, who's saying something about a yoga class. Lenny and Orly look at one another. Lenny grimaces.

'What should I do with them?' she says doubtfully.

'Dump them in the woods?'

After a brief hesitation, she flicks the stick and the knickers fly off into the undergrowth to land among the other pieces of litter.

When they get back inside, Thea and Mel are staring at Mel's phone, which is sitting on the groundsheet, buzzing and whining every few seconds as message after message comes through.

When it eventually falls silent, there are twenty-three missed calls and seven voicemail messages.

'Don't listen to them,' Orly says.

'I have to, to delete them.'

Mel's face is grim as she holds the phone to her ear. They hear the first few seconds of each message. The earlier ones are accompanied by snatches of background music and conversation, but the last is just a low voice, pressed close to the mic. Mel punches the key to delete it.

'He can't track your phone, can he?' Orly murmurs. 'Find us here?'

They look at Thea: thanks to Tony's nefarious activities, she knows about this sort of thing.

'It's possible.'

'I'll take the battery out,' Mel says. 'I'll message Billy first, tell him that my phone's on the blink and to call you, Len, if he needs to talk to me.'

She unlocks the phone with the same simple pattern Orly uses, brings up her contacts and finds Billy, then makes the call. 'Billy, it's Mum. My phone's on the blink, so if you need to speak to me you'll have to call one of the others. I'm messaging the contacts to you now. Love you, babes.'

She ends the call, but as she composes the message, her phone springs into life and she jumps hard enough to drop it. The thing skitters across the groundsheet like a cockroach, and they all shrink away from it. Eventually it falls silent, and a moment later a text comes through. They can all read it.

Call me back or u will be sorry.

Mel swears. Snatching up the phone, she wrenches off the back, levers out the battery and hurls all the pieces into the corner.

'Right. That's that. Now, let's go. I said we'd hook up with Pan later.'

They trudge desultorily round the stalls and watch a few bands on the smaller stages. The minute the time clicks from 11.59 to 12.00, they make for the nearest beer stall and lounge in the sun, as people who have seriously partied drift in, yawning and wretched, and set about drinking away their hangovers. No one says much, and Orly wonders if the others are feeling as she is: that the reappearance of the knickers and Trey's messages have killed the fun. One is creepy, the other properly threatening. Orly glances round uneasily as she drinks, scanning the faces in the crowd.

Two beers down, they wander to the cinema and manage ten minutes of some art-house film, set in a grim London tenement, before stumbling back into the sunshine. It's too bright after the darkness of the movie tent and there are groans all round. With all the events of this morning, only Thea thought to bring her sunglasses.

'Why don't we go back for a snooze?' someone says.

This is unanimously agreed upon and they troop back down the track as the drumbeats start up.

The early-afternoon sun is a tin disc, its unrelenting glare coaxing melanomas from fair scalps like Orly's as she tiptoes between broken glass and splashes of vomit. The snooze is a bad idea. It'll be drunk sleep, heavy and unrefreshing. She'll jerk awake with a pounding headache and a mouth as dry as bone dust. And then they'll have to set to it again. Pouring alcohol down their throats in a desperate attempt to keep up the festival spirit. With Pan. The prospect is depressing, and makes Orly vaguely resentful. She spent years hiding her feelings, trying

147

to be strong for Harry. Hasn't she earned the right to be true to herself? Well, all her true self wants to do now is go home.

A man staggers past, vomits copiously in the ditch, then spins round and punches the air with both fists as his friends cheer.

In whose universe can this possibly be described as fun?

Yes, they enjoyed it when they were eighteen, but they enjoyed everything back then. Everything was so very, very funny. The pranks they played, the cruelties they devised for the spectacle of a reaction. The world was there to entertain them. Making teachers cry, shoplifting, lying. Nothing had consequences. They were always forgiven, indulged for their youth. Even their own emotional catastrophes were juicy titbits to be relished, because nothing mattered. Each knew their teenage years were a thrilling interlude between the boring stability of childhood and adulthood.

They tramp across the field in silence, as if each of them is experiencing the same sinking feeling at the prospect of another forty-eight hours of this.

'Hi.'

Orly looks up. Ben is standing at the entrance to his tent.

'I was waiting for you.'

Her heart swells, but immediately deflates again as she registers his expression.

'Some guy was here when we got back. In your tent. We got rid of him by saying we were gonna call the police, but I don't know if you ladies wanna move. Take a look inside.'

As they crawl through the opening, they are hit by the powerful smell of perfume.

The tent has been trashed: clothes strewn from cases, washbags emptied out. It must have taken a degree of force to smash Thea's perfume bottle. Their sleeping bags are wet. Too wet for one small bottle of Chanel.

'Oh my God,' Mel says. 'He's pissed on them.'

Thea dives inside and starts going through her things, picking up the bottles and jars and checking their contents before stowing them carefully back in her washbag.

The others stand there aghast, nobody seeming to know what to do but blink away the acrid fumes.

'Drag them outside to dry,' Lenny says finally.

'I'm not sleeping in a pissy sleeping bag,' Thea snaps, zipping up her case, but she follows the others as they pull the bags out into the fresh air.

'He knew you,' Ben says. 'Described you two.' He nods at Mel and Orly, whose pelvic floor contracts sharply. 'Said you'd stolen something from him. I told him he'd made a mistake and that the tent belonged to a bunch of young girls.'

'Thanks,' Mel says.

'Did he take anything?'

They check. There doesn't seem to be anything missing. Somehow that seems worse: sheer malice with no financial gain.

'Should we move the tent?' Mel says.

'You know what,' Ben says. 'If you go nearer to the main areas it would be hard to hear if . . . if something happened. At least out here it's quiet. If someone . . . you know . . . at night . . . everybody in the field would hear. I'm a pretty light sleeper. I'll listen out for . . .'

Screams.

'Let me know if I can do anything to help, yeah?' He retreats to his own tent, head bent. Does he feel guilty for not stopping this? He should do. Orly feels a flash of anger. Isn't that what men are for? To stop things like this happening? Look after you, protect you, provide for you? Not fucking die.

'I'm so sorry.' Mel looks like she's about to cry. 'It's my fault.'

'No,' Lenny says. 'You did nothing wrong. It was just common decency not to leave his case on the train. You can't live your life expecting people to screw you over.'

'We should go home,' Orly says.

All eyes turn to her.

'I mean, this guy is dangerous, right? He's been threatening Mel on the phone, and now this. What if he comes back later when it's dark?'

'No way,' Thea snaps. 'I for one am not going to let this arse-hole spoil our weekend. Even though I may smell of eau de piss for the next two days, I say we stay.'

'Me too,' Lenny says. 'Honestly, Orly. Don't worry. If he really meant to hurt us, he'd have waited for us to come back. He just wanted to pay us back, and now he has.'

'Mel?' Thea says. 'You're not going to pussy out on us, are you?'

Mel smiles gratefully at her. 'Hell no.'

They spend the rest of the afternoon clearing up the mess. Going for a pee in the woods, Mel finds a stream that is still remarkably clean and they decide to give the sleeping bags a rinse. Crouching in the sparkling water, barefoot, swishing the brightly coloured fabrics like Indian washerwomen, Orly tries to tell herself that it was just a nasty prank, that's all. And she of all people should know that nasty pranks don't necessarily make you evil. But there's no getting away from the uneasy feeling that they are being watched, from the shadows between the trees, by someone who wishes them harm.

They wring out the bags, twisting each between two pairs of hands, and lay them on the scorched grass around the tent. After the coolness of the wood, the temperature out here is unbearable. Pinning the tent flaps open to air the place they lie down in the shade of the trees.

Orly looks at her watch. Two p.m. Eight more hours of daylight. Her face is tight with sunburn. She completely forgot to bring lotion. The dead grass is sharp beneath her, scratching and jabbing her flesh. Behind her the wood whispers.

'That was thirsty work,' Mel says. 'Anyone for beer?'

'Me,' Thea says.

'I might just stay here for a bit,' Orly says as casually as possible.

'Ah come on,' Mel says, a note of irritation in her voice. 'Don't let that cunt ruin our fun.'

'No, no, it's fine,' Orly says, willing them to leave. 'I'm just going to call my mum. She wanted me to check in now and again.'

'I'll wait for you,' Lenny says.

'No, no, you guys go. I'll text to find out where you are.'

She waits until they are out of earshot, then goes back into the tent. After scrolling to her mum's number in her phone and pressing 'call', she tucks it under her shoulder and starts packing her case. It was a mistake to come here in the first place, and now fear has added to the toxic mix of emotions swirling in her bloodstream. She won't tell the others she's going; just text later to say she had to leave because her dad was unwell or something.

'Hi, Mum.'

'Orly, hi,' her mum says quickly. 'I can't stay on long. Your dad's got a doctor's appointment in Dorchester. Are you having a good time?'

Of course. The foot thing. She'd forgotten. Dorchester hospital is a good forty-five minutes from Newton Collard; added to the waiting time and then the appointment itself, her parents won't be home for hours. It's not fair to make her mum get back in the car again to pick her up. But worse than the inconvenience, she realises now at the sound of her mum's bright voice, will be her disappointment when Orly tells her she wants to come home. The wilting of her hopes that her daughter was getting better.

'Yes,' she says bleakly. 'It's great.'

'Good to see the girls again, I bet.'

'Yeah, really nice. And the weather's been—'

From the background comes her dad's crotchety voice, *We need to leave, Carol*, and her mum answers him, flustered and snappy. *I know. Just wait.*

'Are you sure you're all right?'

'Yes, fine,' Orly says. 'Just checking in to make sure you guys are okay.'

'Oh, I'm so glad. Better dash then. See you soon.'

'Hope the appointment goes well.'

The screen goes dark as she hangs up. And then the tent rustles. Orly wipes her eyes to see that Lenny has come back in.

151

'Sorry,' Lenny says. 'I hung around because I was worried about you.' Her eyes move to the half-packed case. 'Do you want to go home? I'll take you.'

'No, no,' Orly sniffs. 'It's your birthday. I'm just being silly.'

'You're not. That was a shitty thing to have happened. I don't like it either, and I can totally understand why you want to go. Look, this trip was as much about you as it was me.' She sits down. 'I wanted you to have a good time, and you're not. Why not have a night at home, in a comfortable bed, without having to worry about a psychotic drug dealer urinating on you in the night? If you want to come back tomorrow, I'll come and pick you up.'

Orly wants to say no, that it's too much trouble, but she can't bring herself to. She lowers her eyes, thanks Lenny and starts to pack again. She won't be coming back tomorrow.

They walk quickly down the track, as much in fear of bumping into the other two as seeing Trey. Mel will relentlessly josh her to stay for *just one more night* until she surrenders. Thea, whose idea this whole thing was, will be silently offended. She can imagine them talking about her behind her back. *How can she expect to get better if she won't help herself?*

But they make it to the entrance, and as they walk down the quiet track to the gates, the case trundling on the gravel, Orly feels her stomach muscles relax. Perhaps she can just pretend to her parents that she got food poisoning. That would be perfectly plausible – her mum warned her about buying dodgy snacks from vans last time they came. She might even be pleased to have been proved right.

Behind the hedge Orly can see the tips of the standing stones. They haven't visited them this time, but twenty years ago she remembers leaning against their cool flanks while they drank cheap cider, pretending they could feel vibrations down their spines.

The gates are still being manned by security guards, who wave them through, and they cross the gravelled queuing area, now unrecognisably deserted, into the car park. The temperature soars as they pass between the glinting metal hulks. The heat radiating from them distorts the air, making the whole scene ripple like a dream or some alternate reality. Perhaps it is the standing stones after all, pulsing their ancient power.

The festival hubbub recedes, and soon the only sounds are the rustle of the dead grass beneath the case's wheels. It's too hot out here even for the birds. There is not the merest whisper of cloud to interrupt the burnished blue of the sky.

After a few minutes Orly's head is pounding, and ahead of her Lenny pauses, hands resting on her knees. Is she trying to catch her breath? Even Orly is struggling, the hot, dry air catching in her throat.

She should never have agreed to Lenny's offer. She should have just grinned and borne it, like a grown-up. Now her friend is clearly suffering. She tries to hurry over, but her bones have turned molten. Lenny straightens up and carries on, and Orly staggers after her.

'Over here!' Lenny calls.

Orly joins her by the silver Range Rover, squinting at the glare from its mirrored surface. Lenny takes a key fob from her pocket and points it at the car.

Nothing happens.

She tries again, and Orly listens for the *thunk* of the central locking, but it's hard to hear anything with the blood pulsing in her ears.

'It won't open,' Lenny says.

She shakes the fob, wipes it on her shorts, turns it over and tries again. Still nothing.

'The battery must have gone.'

'Could it have shorted out,' Orly says, 'because of the pee?'

'I guess so, though it was tucked away inside my sponge bag. Maybe it's not the key at all, maybe it's the heat.' She squints up at the sun, a merciless white eye glaring down at them. 'The car might have overheated and cut out. We could try again later.'

You could phone a garage, Orly is about to say, but stops herself. Why should her friend have to go through the hassle and expense and waste of time just so that Orly can go home a day early?

'I could walk to the station. It only took ages on the bus because of the festival traffic.'

'It's three miles, and in this heat . . .' Lenny's hand is shielding her eyes. Orly follows her gaze.

Beyond the car park it's just field after field, a patchwork of yellow and green and the occasional dark copse, as far as the eye can see. They're in the middle of nowhere.

'It's fine,' Orly hears herself say. 'Let's go back. I was overreacting.'

'No you weren't. That was horrible. But . . .' Lenny slips the key fob back in her pocket, 'there are some real arseholes out there. If you're still worried later, we can come back when the sun's gone down. Come on. Let's go back in.'

And suddenly, despite the blistering heat, Orly shivers.

As they trudge back through the cars, the helter skelter comes into view, and then the big wheel. Orly's heart sinks even more. They'll have to hit the fairground at some point. Mel will insist, and Thea will want to buy one of those sugar dummies so she can suck it provocatively for attention. No, of course she won't. That was twenty years ago. And Orly doesn't have to pretend not to be scared of the rides any more. If she doesn't want to go on them, she can just say. They're not going to tease and jeer at her.

Behind them, someone's vehicle has started and gives a merry toot as it accelerates out of the car park.

Not too hot for that car, then. So why would a high-end Range Rover suffer such a fault?

Her eyes slide across to Lenny's to see if she's noticed, and Lenny looks at her.

'First the inhaler,' she says. 'And now this. Somebody up there doesn't like me.' She smiles.

Orly doesn't reply. She couldn't trust herself not to sound shrill with panic. Because overreaction or not, the voice in her head is telling her to turn around and start walking, get away from this place as quickly as she can. Lenny is right, someone doesn't like them, and now that same someone has managed to stop them from leaving.

They pass back through the gates and the roar of the festival engulfs them.

As Lenny pauses to tap a message to the others, Orly concentrates on her breathing, telling herself to keep calm, take it easy: she just has to get through one more day and then she can go home.

Until then, they are trapped here.

WhatsApp Group: Lenny's Birthday Fest

4 participants
Lenny (group admin), Orly, Thea, Mel

Thea
Len, Orls, where are you two?
15.12

Lenny
Sorry we were just chatting. Lost track of time.
15.47

Thea
We're at the fairground. Guess who we found?
16.08

Mel
Guess who we found?
16.08

Lenny
Who?
16.09

Thea D'Agnelli added Pandora

Pandora
Whasupp bitches!!!!!!!!!!!!!!
16.14

15

Orly

They trudge back to the tent – untouched, thankfully – to deposit Orly's case, then head to meet the others. But as they approach the fairground, Orly finds that she can't face them, not yet. Not Pandora.

'Shall we go and see the standing stones?' she says. She has the urge to touch them, to rest her forehead on the cool stone.

'Sure.'

They go back the way they came. To the left of the festival entrance a little wooden gate is set back from the track, and they pass through into a small grassy area enclosed by willows. The branches hang so low that, at first, all Orly can see are the bases of the nearest two stones. Despite the fact that this sacred monument is the whole reason the festival was established here, the place is completely deserted.

Under the shade of the willows the grass is blessedly cool and lush, and Orly kicks off her flip-flops. The blades pushing up between her toes give her a burst of childlike pleasure, as do the leaves that brush her face as she pushes through them and out into the clearing.

'What's that?' she says.

In the centre of the five pillars of Welsh bluestone, tall and solemn as the high priests who erected them, someone has piled more stones. No, they're not stones.

'Bones,' Lenny says.

Orly recoils. The knobbled sticks are perfectly white, without a scrap of hair or skin.

'Why the hell would someone build a mound of bones in here?'

'Let's go,' Orly says.

But Lenny takes a step closer. 'I suppose they must be animal. Maybe cow? Or horse.'

'Please. Lenny.'

'Sure, sure, let's go and meet the others.'

Orly turns and walks quickly towards the trees. Lenny's footsteps swish through the grass behind her. But then there is another sound.

A clacking.

She stops and turns slowly, dread lifting every hair on her body, and freezes to the spot.

Children are dancing on the pile of bones. No, not children; tiny but fully grown people with white, mask-like faces and emotionless slanting eyes. Their gossamer garments drift in the still air as their tiny feet tap-tap, light enough not to disturb a single bone from its place.

'What the fuck . . .' Lenny murmurs.

Orly can't breathe. Is she having some kind of delusion? But if so, Lenny is too.

A man steps out from behind the stones, bearded, in a green, wide-brimmed hat. He is moving his hands in an odd way.

Lenny laughs. 'Puppets. They're just puppets.'

'Not *just* puppets, my love,' he calls in a strong West Country accent. 'These are my little ones, my darlings. They dance on Midsummer's Eve, as we all should, to stop the evil spirits from catching our souls.'

'And are those bones, inside the stones?'

'They are.' The puppets stop moving; their arms hang limply by their sides, but their faces remain alert, and some subtle movement of the man's hand keeps their attention directed towards Orly and Lenny.

'Why?'

'For the Midsummer bonefire, of course. You think a bonefire is for wood? Where do you think the word comes from, my loves?' He grins and his little ones do a jig. Clickety-clack.

'People say it's a medieval thing, that when the churchyards got full, they'd burn the bones to make space, but that's just a cleaned-up version of the truth. Bonefires began in Druid times, to ward off evil. There were animal bones, and human bones: people who'd died from disease or old age, as well as . . .'

He pauses and looks at the puppets, who look back at him. 'Do you think these sweet little ladies should hear this?' he stage-whispers. The puppets nod solemnly.

He looks back at Lenny and Orly. 'Human sacrifice.'

'Thanks for the history lesson,' Lenny says sharply. Perhaps she doesn't like being referred to as a 'little lady'. 'But we've got some-where to be. Incidentally, I hope this is legal. If there are human bones in there, I imagine the police will want to be informed.'

'These ones is so old they don't even got a headstone no more,' the man says. 'Police ain't interested in that. But off you go then, trit-trot. We'll be lighting the great fire on Midsummer's Night, so come back and see how prettily they burn.'

They are already walking away, passing under the willow leaves and through the gate to the sound of little heels dancing on bones.

Out in the noise and commotion of the festival, the two friends look at one another.

'Trit-trot,' Lenny says, and they both start to laugh. Once she starts, Orly can't stop. The tension pours out of her in gasps and hiccups until finally, exhausted, she leans on Lenny's shoulder and takes one last shuddering inhalation.

'I needed that.'

'Come on,' Lenny says, squeezing her. 'Let's go and get wasted.'

'Hey hey!' Mel weaves over to meet them, her hair flashing with the lurid lights of the fair. 'Finally! Where you been? We missed you!'

As she spins Orly round in a beer-smelling hug, Orly is almost glad that she stayed. Lenny's right about Trey: he's punished them and now he'll leave them alone. Otherwise he'd be risking them calling the police, and he wouldn't want his nefarious activities coming under that sort of scrutiny.

They walk with Mel past the hook-a-duck and test-your-strength stalls. Thea is leaning against the side of a pink double-decker bus, talking to someone with their back to them. Spotting them, she waves and her companion turns.

Pandora.

'Come on!' Mel calls, before they can join the pair, 'The dodgems are stopping!'

Taking Orly's hand, she pulls her over to the queue for the nearby ride, which has just started to filter down as the empty cars fill up. Pandora and Thea come over, shamelessly pushing in front of a group of lads who have just joined the queue, as pretty girls can.

Pandora is drunk. The way she's whooping and waving her arms to the music blaring from the dodgems brings out the teenage bitch in Orly. *Stupid cow.* Pan was always like this. It's why Orly did what she did. Not for a prank, like she pretended to herself afterwards, but because Pan was a massive fake. To get away from her, Orly leaves the queue for the dodgems and heads back to the beer bus. There's an open hatch at the side where you order, and she waits for her turn.

'She's a bit of a pain, isn't she?'

To her surprise, it's Thea who joins her, leaning close. Without the perfume, Thea smells slightly unpleasant. It might be her breath. She has the breath of a sick person. Orly hasn't seen her eat anything since the Buddha bowls yesterday.

The thought – always that echo of Harry – notches down her mood. And why did they have to meet at the bloody funfair? Even back in the days when she was young enough to feel immortal, Orly didn't trust the mechanical skills of the macho grunts parading round in their vests. Now, after limb-severings

160

and drownings at even the most respectable amusement parks, there's no way she's risking a ride.

The dodgems wind down, the drivers disembark and the cars refill, Lenny and Pandora climbing into the last free one, leaving Mel at the front of the line. The air-raid siren that's supposed to indicate the beginning of the fun sounds. Their car isn't working properly, or more likely its occupants have forgotten how to operate one: they shriek as it spins uncontrollably. Finally another car punches them out of their orbit and they run aground at the buffers, laughing hysterically.

Orly turns away.

Above her, the Ferris wheel is a circle of stars picked out against the sky. It's the most Mickey Mouse construction she's ever seen, like something you might hire for a school fete. Little gondolas swing from metal threads. You can see the rust from here. A woman right at the very top is leaning so far out, the whole car is tipping. If the impulse suddenly came upon her, she could simply hurl herself out into the air. A few seconds of blissful freedom before smashing down onto the metal gantry.

Orly jumps as Thea grips her arm. 'Shall we?'

'No way. You know full well I hate this sort of thing.'

'Ah, go on. You can have one to yourself if you're scared.'

'Why would that make me less scared?'

"Cos tipping them is half the fun!'

A shrill scream makes Orly's head snap up. The woman clings to the car's frame whilst berating the man beside her. Did he pretend to throw her out? Could there be anything less funny?

'Len!' Thea yells over the music. The ride has finished and Lenny is climbing down the steps of the dodgems, but Pandora has remained in the car and is gesturing for Mel to join her. Lenny ambles over.

'Are we going on?' Thea says.

Orly shakes her head. 'Not me.'

'Just you and me then, Len,' Thea says. 'Come on, it's stopping.'

The car that draws level with the platform is swinging in a breath of breeze, as if it's made from paper, not sheet metal, and as the two women climb in, something groans. They close the safety barrier and the car is sweeping on to the end of the platform, to allow others to alight, when suddenly Orly wants to be up there in the stillness and silence.

She leaves the beer queue, runs over and vaults the barrier just as the paper boat launches into the air.

Lenny helps her inside and she sits down breathlessly, already regretting her decision as they start to rise. Her hand tightens on the frame, the rust crackling beneath her fingers.

The wheel turns and their little boat moves further and further from the ground. The people dancing and drinking below shrink away so fast. When it reaches a certain height, it starts to swing.

Orly's breath catches when she remembers Thea's threat to tip it. But Thea is firmly in her seat, staring out across the undulating landscape beyond the festival's splash of colour. The sun is low in the sky and shadows have cut through all that cosmetic plumping to reveal the skull beneath her skin.

'Amazing view,' Lenny says. 'Doesn't it tempt you, Thea?'

Thea looks round. 'What?'

'To come and live in the country, all this beauty and peace.'

'Oh, yes. Well, maybe when I'm old.'

'You'll never be old,' Lenny says, and Thea laughs.

The gondola keeps on rising, over the roofs of the stalls, to the level of the treetops and then up into the deep blue.

Orly squeezes her eyes shut, but she can feel the breeze cold on her cheek, sense the air thinning, hear the receding music of the rides, the man telling people to scream if they want to go faster.

So, there must be people who do want to go faster, who relish the exhilaration of danger, who don't shrink into the deceptive solidity of a rusted seat back, waiting for the ride to end. Isn't that what she's done for years, ever since Harry was diagnosed? Just squeezed her eyes shut and waited for it all to end?

The wheel judders to a halt.

Peeling open an eye, she gasps, and every muscle in her body tenses. They're right at the top. The highest they can possibly go. And look, she's still alive. The gondola has not disintegrated, the mechanism of the wheel has not exploded into its constituent fixings and sent them plummeting to earth. She's alive, up here in the fragrant air. She breathes it in. The smells of cooking meat and popcorn are so faint that she can pick out the musty scent of a midsummer cornfield.

Testing the limits of her courage, she peers over the rail. Scattered across the ground below, the stalls are like sweets wrapped in bright cellophane. The festival's layout is a jolly skeleton waving up at her. She can even see the campsite. Is that their tent, just by the treeline? Her breath catches. The wood is so close: a furtive hand that has curled around them, waiting for the right moment to close into a fist.

She turns her attention back to the fair below, trying to pick out Mel and Pandora.

People stream in and out of the rides, in groups or duos, rarely alone. Some move with more confidence than the others, a sort of swagger that displays their ease with the world. One in particular catches her eye. He is alone, but his movements are exaggerated, as if he knows everyone. He doffs his flat cap to a group of passing women with a little bow.

Her knuckles whiten on the rail. 'Trey.'

'Are you sure?' Lenny says doubtfully, leaning out and following her gaze. 'Loads of guys wear flat caps.'

The gondola yaws alarmingly. But Orly is sure, not just from the cap, but by the way he walks. He wants people to see him, to register what he is, to buy from him.

'Shit. Where are the others?'

'I can't see them.'

'We need to get down and find them.' Without thinking, Orly shouts down to the vest-grunt, 'Can you let us off, please?'

Faces look up. A cap tilts. Orly shrinks back inside the car. It rocks gently in time to the Wurlitzer music.

Then there is a mechanical squeal and the wheel starts to move again. The descent is breathtakingly swift, and the lights and smells and noise surge back over them. When the car comes level with the platform, the vest-grunt hurries over and yanks the bar up. 'One of you been sick or what?'

'No,' Lenny says. 'No, we're fine. Thanks.'

'Then why the fuck did you—'

But they don't catch the end of his sentence as they hurry away in the direction of the dodgems.

There's no sign of Trey down here in the forest of full-size people. Then the crowd splits and Orly spots Mel and Pandora descending the steps of the arcade. Mel's dark curls are throwing off coloured sparks from the lights of the one-armed bandits. She is unmistakable.

Orly is about to call out to her when Lenny grips her arm and pulls her behind the burger van.

In the shadows behind the helter skelter, between the arcade and where they are now concealed, two dark figures are talking closely. Orly can just about make out what might be the sharp beak of a cap.

The two women are walking straight towards the helter skelter.

'Mel hasn't got her phone, has she?' Lenny mutters.

One of the figures steps out from behind it into the light and slaps the shoulder or back of the one still in the shadows.

'What about Pandora?' Thea whispers.

The other figure steps out, head bent as he tucks something into his pocket. His features are shadowed by the cap, but Orly recognises that tanned, creased neck.

Opening the WhatsApp group, she hits Pandora's number.

The Wurlitzer pauses, and in the sudden silence, everyone in the fairground must be able to hear the ringtone. In what seems like slow motion, Pandora's hand delves in her pocket and draws out the glowing screen; she says something to Mel and then brings the phone to her ear.

164

'Tell Mel,' Orly says as clearly and evenly as her taut vocal cords will allow, 'that Trey is right there, by the helter skelter.'

The movements are simultaneous. As Trey steps back out into the light, the two women slide around the other side of the ride. Like figures on an antique clock they circle one another, the huge striped slide between them, and then wheel off like planets falling out of orbit: Trey to join the throng by the arcade machines, Pandora and Mel to slip behind the van. Without a word, the five friends turn and walk out of the lollipop glow of the fairground and into the shadows of the late afternoon.

They hurry past the outlying stages, with their neglected acts singing to empty fields and turned backs, and eventually reach the Village Green, a quiet spot peopled by middle-aged men sipping craft beer. Instinctively sensing that this place is safe, their pace slows, then stops. They sink down onto the hay bales strewn outside the large beer marquee, look at one another round-eyed, then burst into laughter. Their faces are flushed by the light of the sun sitting atop the marquee like a cherry on a cake.

As the terror subsides, Orly feels almost high.

That night, she dances.

She can't even remember the last time she did that. Her wedding? The staff Christmas party the year before Harry was diagnosed? Who knows? Who cares? She was never very good at it. Her body isn't fluid like Mel's, she can't keep to the beat like Thea or throw herself into it without inhibition like Lenny, but the mere sensation of bodily abandonment, to music loud enough to drown out all thought, is as intoxicating and liberating as any drug.

Eventually she has to be pulled away. They have literally danced the night away. The eastern horizon is pale as they weave their way back to the tent. Somehow Pandora is still with them. So much for the hot young boyfriend. He can't be all that if she'd rather spend her festival with four middle-aged women.

165

Orly's legs are heavy as they tramp down the track. It's a novel sensation. She can't remember the last time she was physically tired. Was that all it took? All these years of insomnia, and all she needed was a night's dancing. It's not as easy as that, of course. Most days she never had the energy for exercise. It's being here that's done it. She feels a surge of love for her friends. They have saved her. The idea of cuddling up in her sleeping bag is delicious. And with a bit of luck, she's sweated so much she won't need to get up in the night for a wee.

But all her gratitude drains away as they come parallel with Earthfields and Pandora bolts for the bar, screeching, 'Nightcap in the tent!'

So she's coming back with them again. While they wait for her return, Orly turns away so the others don't see her expression. She's back soon enough, wobbling towards them with a bottle of wine and no glasses. They'll have to swig it like teenagers.

They walk on, to the end of the track. Beyond it the tents are aglow, like bioluminescent insects. Someone has hung a man's waxed jacket on the gate. It slouches from the top rung and seems to cast a proprietorial gaze over the campsite.

Only as they get to the tent do they realise they left the sleeping bags out. They're damp with dew and it seems to take an age of giggling clumsiness to get them back in.

Orly remains outside a moment, holding her bag, no longer in the mood to join the fun. With Pandora here, no one even notices: they just crawl back inside, chatting and laughing. Funny how quickly your sense of belonging vanishes: half an hour ago, she loved her friends with all the ardour of a teenager; now she feels like walking off into the night. But that sort of attention-seeking behaviour belongs firmly in the playground, and with a sigh, she follows them inside.

Her little patch of grass looks inviting, but as she lays out the bag, she thinks of Trey. Lying by the door, she'll be in the first line of attack if he comes back.

As if reading her mind, Lenny pokes her head out of the inner tent. 'Come in with us. We can all snuggle up.'

'I'll need a pee in the night, though.'

'Come next to me. I sleep like the dead.'

With the extra body, they have to huddle close, and personal space goes out of the window. Thea sits on Orly's other side, and their arms are pressed uncomfortably together until Thea raises hers and wraps it around Orly. Orly lets her head fall on Thea's shoulder, just like when they were kids.

She'd forgotten what a good friend Thea was in the days before her transition to beautiful butterfly. Thea's passion for her friends was fierce in its intensity. With horrible Elaine as a mother, perhaps she was looking for a receptacle to pour all that love into, and they were the lucky ones. Orly remembers when Mrs Finch called her *a dull-witted child* and Thea keyed the old bag's car. When it looked like Mel was to be dropped a set in maths, Thea marked her test too high and ended up getting a detention for it.

Orly's forehead rocks on the sharp point of Thea's clavicle and she feels a sudden plunge of unease.

Thea is so thin.

Ill-smelling and ill-thin.

In the maelstrom of self-pity that has been revolving around her for the past couple of years, has Orly missed something important?

While Pandora is holding forth about Buddhist meditation, Orly lifts her head from Thea's shoulder and whispers in her ear, 'Are you okay?'

Thea looks at her, and for a moment, by some flicker of her eyelids, it seems as though she might be about to tell Orly something. The truth, as opposed to the perfect social-media version of her life. The glossy lips part and Thea breathes in, but then there's a lull in conversation as Pandora swigs the wine. The silence is enough to destroy the fragile moment.

'Fine, why?'

'Oh, nothing. You've just . . . you've got so thin.'

Thea grins. 'Thank you!' She waggles a hand at the wine. 'My turn!'

Orly is next. The liquid tastes like warm urine and the rim of the bottle is slimy with spit, but if she drinks enough, she might fall asleep and not have to listen to another of Pandora's anecdotes. She's currently describing how she was asked to cut the hair of an Iranian warlord while his tiger patrolled the living room.

The story is cut short when her phone rings. Glancing at the screen, she grimaces and gives a savage swipe to accept the call.

'What?' she snaps.

There are rueful exchanged glances. *Remember what a bitch she could be?* At least that's what Orly's glance means.

'I'm with my *friends*.'

They shuffle around, adjusting their positions on the thin groundsheet.

'We *are* here *together*.' Her lips twist at the word. 'It's just that I have better things to talk about than Swindon Town football club.'

They smile, but nervously. Pandora's eyes flash with something like hatred.

'Like what? I'm not being like *anything* . . . No I'm not, you're just pissed . . . Yeah, whatever.'

She hangs up. The circle of smiles falter when her grim expression does not lighten.

'Twat,' she spits, pocketing the phone.

Mel makes a sympathetic noise.

'I'm serious. It's not that he's thick. It's just that he left school at sixteen to do an apprenticeship, and now he hangs around with all these drongos and I think his IQ has just *gone* . . .' She makes a whistling sound and traces her finger down into the mess of sleeping bags by her feet. 'I used to think I could help him get up to the place he deserved to be, you know? *Educate* him in art and books and stuff, but he just doesn't *care*.'

Mel shakes her head. 'You can't change people.'

Pandora snatches the wine bottle from Orly and the liquid inside sloshes up and over the rim. 'It should never have been like this for me, right?' She casts a fierce gaze around the group and seems satisfied by the shaken heads. Orly's armpits prickle.

'We all had plans, right? Except maybe you, Mel.' The bottle waggles in Mel's direction and Mel's smile tightens.

'I was gonna go to art college. Meet some sexy intellectual. Live the hippie dream, travelling the world, creating our *art*.'

'You've worked all over the world,' Mel says.

'Oh yeah. I've cut hair all over the *fucking planet*.'

Lenny becomes preoccupied with unlacing her trainers. Thea is examining her fingernails.

'And why is my life so fucking shit? Who did this?'

They all know what she wants to hear. In the end it's Lenny who says, 'Newman.'

Pandora explodes. 'No!' She's panting through flared nostrils, like a bull. 'That arsehole was *nothing*. I could have dealt with him.'

'The school let you down,' Lenny says.

'Fuck the school. Somebody set me up. Somebody I thought was my *friend*. Some fucking . . . fucking . . .' she's spitting now, '*bitch* set out to ruin my life and she . . . she fucking did.'

'I'm sure whoever it was didn't mean—'

'Bullshit!' Pandora snarls. 'She knew *exactly* what she was doing.'

Silence descends.

Mel and Orly exchange glances. Thea's face is devoid of expression, as if the person inside has gone off somewhere, leaving a painted shell. Lenny just looks bored.

'Going for a wee,' Orly mutters, and crawls out into the chill air. It's colder than last night, and the soporific effects of booze and physical exhaustion are immediately swept away, springing her back to alertness.

Behind her, in the tent, someone says something and there is loud laughter tinged with relief. *Everyone's allowed to have a meltdown now and again*, Mel will say in the morning. *It's fine. She was just pissed.*

So Pandora is unhappy with her relationship. Does that mean she will latch onto them, not only for the duration of the festival, but afterwards? Will she become part of the group, invited to all the get-togethers?

The conversation is continuing now as if nothing's happened, as if this interloper hasn't just put a downer on the whole night. Orly feels like crying. It's her own fault, she knows. This is only what she deserves. In fact, maybe all of it – Harry's death, her shit life and bleak future – is only what she deserves. A ruined life for a ruined life.

She pushes the thought out of her mind. She's drunk. It's late. In the morning she will feel better, and there's only one day left now. Just have a wee and go to bed.

She would just do it round the back of the tent, but it's conceivable that people might still be returning for bed, so she makes for the wood. At least she changed her tampon earlier on so she can be nice and quick.

She crouches at the edge of the treeline and the urine patters into the undergrowth. The festival is hidden by the hedge bordering the northern edge of the wood, but the sky to the east is lightening. It will soon be dawn: the beginning of their last day.

People are still partying, but the voices and music are muted and distant. She longs for her bed. The one she shared with Harry. They spent so much money on the mattress. It had fifteen hundred pocket springs, and memory foam, and when you lay on it you might have been completely alone. Pointless. As Harry's weight fell away, he barely made a dent. That was before he became incontinent. The council came and collected the mattress before she left the flat.

There's a rustle behind her.

She topples backwards into the wet leaves and sits perfectly still.

An animal of some kind creeping up behind her? Has she strayed into a fox's territory?

170

The rustling comes again, but quieter now, almost furtive. Her head snaps in the direction of the sound. A little way off there's a shape, low to the ground. A mound that might be a rubbish heap, or just the topography of the wood. Or a crouched figure.

She stares at it until stars pop in her vision, but it doesn't move. Slowly she rises to a crouch. Still no movement.

The tent is a frail glow at the edge of the field, the women's figures picked out in the torchlight. She had felt safe inside, like they were enclosed by real walls, but it was an illusion. They're totally exposed out here. In the blink of an eye a blade could slash through that thin fabric and the bodies inside. She regards the tent with a predator's gaze. Women are so easy to harm.

This evil thought scares her more than the shape in the undergrowth, and she goes scurrying back.

But as she steps out of the line of trees, the glow of the tent winks out. They must have turned off the torch ready to sleep, thank God.

It's darker than she thought. The light on the horizon wasn't the dawn, but the rising moon. It has crept over the hedge to stare at her.

She picks up her pace, viscerally aware of the darkness pouring from the trees at her back. But soon she is among the little village of tents again and drops gratefully to her knees in front of the door. She unzips it and ducks inside.

Crawling through, she puts a hand down, expecting it to land on grass or sleeping bag, but it doesn't. It lands on a body.

The body jerks into life. Strong arms grab her and a huge shape rises up in the gloom. A man has been lying in wait for her – the figure from the woods? She screams and lashes out with feet and elbows. There's a grunt as she makes contact with a jaw.

Where are the others? Why aren't they coming to help her? What has he done to them?

'Lenny!' she screams. 'Thea! Mel!'

'It's okay.'

171

'FUCK OFFFFFF!'

'Orly! You're in the wrong tent!'

She stops thrashing.

A phone lights up, revealing a blinking face.

'Orly!' a voice shouts from some distance away. 'Where are you? What's going on?'

The face belongs to Ben.

'Oh my God, Ben, I'm so sorry.' She calls out to the others, 'I'm okay! I . . . I just got the tents mixed up.'

Ben adds, 'Only us murderers over here.'

'What the fuck, man?' says a bleary voice from the back of the tent.

'It's okay, Danny,' Ben says. 'Just some girl trying to take advantage of me.'

'I'm so sorry,' Orly repeats, backing out through the tent flaps.

He follows her out and they both stand up. The moonlight falls on his face, framed by a bouncing kiss curl he must spend ages flattening.

'It's fine, really. I wasn't asleep anyway. I don't drink as much as the others, so I don't hit the wall. I was kind of bored, so some pretty girl crawling over me was actually very welcome.'

'Oh.' *Pretty girl.*

'Easy mistake. Green and red are interchangeable at night.'

In which case, maybe her face looks bright green. The moon has risen higher and is surrounded by a misty halo. The sky is so clear she can make out the spilled sugar of the Milky Way.

'Beautiful, isn't it?' Ben tips his head back and his dark skin is instantly gilded with silver.

'I used to know loads of the constellations, back when I was teaching,' she says. 'I can only remember Orion now.'

'You're a teacher?'

'Was. In between jobs at the moment. Living with my parents. They're so proud.'

'Tell me about it. I only moved out six months ago. My flat's just a wee bit bigger than my laptop. They spend all that money

172

on ads telling us how important teachers are, then pay us in chocolate buttons.'

'You teach too? Primary or secondary?'

'Senior. Maths. I love tormenting teenagers.'

'Where?'

He names a local comprehensive. 'So where do your parents live?'

'Not far actually. Newton Collard?'

'Oh yeah, I know,' he says. 'Cool.'

Silence settles like snow, gentle and soft. The air is perfectly still. There's not enough breeze even to rustle a leaf in the wood, and the sounds of the festival are muted, like a hyperactive child who has finally whirled itself into exhaustion. Now that her eyes are used to the depth of the sky, Orly can see it is not black but the deepest blue. More stars appear wherever she looks, infinities of them, nestling together, as if they are close to one another instead of millions of light years apart and getting further by the moment. Perspective can be very soothing.

'It's at times like this I really wish I smoked,' Ben says. 'Then I wouldn't look like such a wet twat, just staring up at the stars.'

She laughs.

There's a rustle from the tent she can now see is green. As opposed to the one that, even in the leaching moonlight, is clearly bright red.

Mel appears, the snakes of her hair rising up around her as if tasting the air. 'Ah, so you're alive.'

'Sorry. I thought I saw someone in the wood and it set my nerves on edge.'

'Really?' Mel's head turns to the dark shadow of the trees.

'Oh, it was nothing. My imagination.'

'Right,' Ben says. 'Thanks for the little home invasion, Orly. It was fun. Sweet dreams, all.'

Orly can't help cursing Mel's appearance as he crouches and crawls back into his tent.

Mel's eyes are widened theatrically when Orly turns to her. *You've pulled!* she mouths.

173

Orly smiles and puts a finger to her lips. Champagne bubbles are rising in her blood. A moment later, Lenny comes out, and then Thea.

'Wow. Look at the stars.'

The four women stand together in the moonlight. It's not the time to mention that someone might be spying on them, and now, peering into the darkness of the wood, Orly can't even see the mound. It was probably just the lie of the land.

'I'm so glad we did this,' Mel says, taking Lenny's hand. 'Thank you.'

'It was Thea's idea.' Lenny takes Thea's hand, Orly holds the other one, and then Mel joins hers, until they are standing in a circle, like the bluestones.

Their smiles are self-mocking, but Thea's eyes are shining in the moonlight and Orly can feel her own sinuses pricking. She wonders if they are thinking what she is. The little-girl mantra, armour against the world.

Best friends for ever.

As one they all squeeze, then laugh and break away.

The night air is cold on her exposed flesh and Orly turns to go back to the tent.

'Wait!' Mel whispers.

She turns back.

'It's gone midnight. Happy birthday, Len.'

They all hug Lenny and it's a wonderful moment, and only the tiniest part of Orly enjoys a sense of smug satisfaction that Pandora has gone to sleep and missed it.

But then . . .

'Oh my gosh! It's your birthday!'

How is it possible to emphasise every single word in a sentence? Orly wonders as Pandora falls out of the tent flaps, staggers to her feet and throws herself upon them.

With no thought to those slumbering in the surrounding tents, she leads them all in a chorus of 'Happy Birthday to You', then announces that it's present-opening time.

174

'Oh no,' Lenny says. 'Let's wait till the morning.'

'No way. We are celebrating this birthday *right now* and I don't want to hear *another word* about it!'

The others surrender, following Pandora's taut behind back inside, but Orly stands for a moment in the moonlight.

She's been trying to draw the others' attention to how annoying Pandora is with sighs, rolled eyes, loaded glances. And yet she can hear them now in the tent, enjoying themselves, accepting and generous with their friendship. Laughing along with Pandora's silly foibles as they would laugh along with Orly's – if she ever did anything silly any more, instead of trudging around with a hangdog expression, bringing everyone down. Maybe Pandora holds a mirror up to Orly herself and she doesn't like what she sees. Considering what happened at school, what those events meant for Pandora's life, Orly should be going out of her way to be kind.

Determined to be better, she plasters a smile to her face and goes back in.

Lenny is sitting before a small pile of presents. Someone has gone into Orly's case and retrieved hers, which she tries not to be annoyed about.

'Sorry if it's crap,' Pandora says, picking up a rectangular gift and pressing it into Lenny's hands. 'I didn't have much to choose from here, unless you wanted weed or friendship bracelets, but I figured with the kids you probably needed some me-time.'

Lenny unwraps a glass bottle and reads the label.

'Relaxing pillow spray.' She sprays it into the air and there's a strong smell of lavender. 'Ooh, lovely. Thank you.'

Pandora picks up another present from the pile and looks at the label. 'This one's from Mel. Here you go.'

Lenny unwraps a tub of moisturiser for mature skin and grins at her friend. 'Bitch.'

It's beautiful, a ceramic container with a cork lid woven with a plait of corn, and must have cost Mel a fair amount from what must be a fairly tight budget, but before they can admire it,

Pandora is reading the label of the next gift. 'This one's Thea's.' She hands Lenny a flat box. At least all the presents are small, like Orly's.

'It actually *is* a friendship bracelet,' Thea says ruefully. 'Sorry.'

Lenny unwraps the silver paper, and then opens the turquoise box inside. Immediately she closes it again.

'Thea,' she says. 'No.'

'Yes,' Thea says firmly. 'You're my best friend and you deserve it.'

'No.' Lenny tries to give it back, but Thea puts her hands behind her back.

Orly can see Lenny trying to decide what to do. To drop the present in front of Thea would be unforgivably rude. In the end it's Pandora who saves the day. Snatching the box from Lenny – 'Let me see!' – she opens it and gasps. Upside down on the lid Orly reads the name of the shop. *Tiffany*.

'Oh my God! Gimme your wrist.'

Dipping her head, Lenny extends her arm and Pandora takes out a silver bangle with a heart-shaped padlock and key dangling from it. She fastens it to Lenny's arm, then twists it to let the charm glint.

'It's gorgeous,' she says.

'It is,' Mel breathes.

'Mmm,' Orly echoes.

'Lenny?' Thea says softly. 'Do you like it?'

Lenny says nothing, only leans forward and takes her friend in her arms.

Orly wonders if this is her opportunity to snatch up her own present and hide it. And for a moment it seems as if everyone really has forgotten the tiny matchbox, hidden under its brown luggage label filled with her looping handwriting, but then fucking Pandora spots it.

'Oh, wait, there's one more! This diddy one.'

Lenny picks open the gift, so small that it's almost completely encased in Sellotape, then throws back her head and laughs.

'How on earth did you find it?'

Orly shrugs. 'eBay.'

'Oh my days,' Mel splutters, taking out the little badge with its soulful face of a young bank manager gazing back at her. 'They actually made badges of Craig? You are such a freak.'

'God, yes,' Thea laughs. 'You liked Craig! Only human female in the universe who didn't fancy either Matt or Luke.'

'Well some other people must have done,' Lenny laughs, taking the badge and pinning it to her T-shirt. 'Or they wouldn't have made badges.'

'You only liked him because he was achievable,' Thea says. 'Like Ringo.'

Only Pandora is silent. Orly glances at her. She has picked up the discarded wrapping and is frowning at the luggage label inscribed with Orly's message.

Orly's blood runs cold.

Pandora looks up at her and their eyes meet. Around them the other women are talking. Thea is asking whether the moisturiser contains collagen, and Mel is saying something about natural flower serums.

Pandora's eyes hold hers.

She should smile. Smile and say *What?* Make Pandora doubt her eyes, and her memory. But it's too late. Orly's face must scream *Guilty!* because Pandora's expression has already morphed from suspicion to cold loathing.

Pandora gets up and ducks out of the tent.

GILLFEST DAY 3:

MIDSUMMER'S DAY

WhatsApp Group: Lenny's Birthday Fest

5 participants
Lenny (group admin), Orly, Thea, Mel, Pandora

Mel
Where are you Pan? You ok?
03.12

Mel
Thought u just went for a pee. U been ages.
03.26

Mel
Pick up Pan. We're worried.
03.43

16

Orly

The women huddle together in the inner tent, listening so intently for any hint of Pandora's return that they start at every sound. It's at least twenty minutes since Pandora exited the tent. Mel was the first to notice, and turned her phone back on to call her, but Pan's phone was off. This in itself is weird, and the atmosphere in the enclosed space has become thick with tension.

'Has she replied?' Lenny asks, and Mel looks at her phone for the twentieth time.

'No.'

'I'm sure she's fine,' Thea says. 'She's probably gone back to Jay.'

'Yeah,' Orly murmurs. 'And at least there have been no more threatening messages from Trey. That's something.'

'Orly thought there was someone outside,' Mel says. 'Watching us.'

'Seriously?' Thea says, and all eyes turn to her.

'I thought . . .' Orly stutters. 'In the wood . . . when I went for a wee. It might have been nothing. Just a bump in the ground.'

It's not convincing, and already Mel is pulling on her trainers.

'Stop,' Orly says. 'Don't go. What if there *is* someone?' She hopes the others are too preoccupied to notice the fever scarlet of her cheeks.

'We're no safer in here,' Mel says. 'And we can't just abandon her.'

'Let's have a look around outside,' Lenny says. 'She was very pissed. Maybe she's just blacked out.'

They crawl out of the tent. The stars are gone and the moon's face is wan against a yellowing sky.

It's brighter than earlier and Orly tries to pick out the mound, to reassure herself and the others that it's nothing more than a rise in the ground.

But she can't.

Aside from the odd grass tussock or rock, the woodland floor is uniformly flat. There really was someone there, watching her pee, and now he's gone. Because he got what he came for? A vulnerable, drunk woman stumbling out of the tent to make her way back to her boyfriend, alone. Could Orly be responsible for a second calamity befalling Pan?

No. She saw Pandora's face quite clearly, read her expression before she left the tent. Pan left because she was shocked and angry. If she'd been attacked, surely they would have heard her cry out. Surely.

They walk in silence to the treeline, then turn and scan the campsite.

'Is that her?' Thea is pointing in the direction of the gate, where a dark figure lurks in the shadows of the hedge. All four women stand perfectly still as the figure, equally motionless, watches them.

Then Lenny says, 'It's that jacket, isn't it? Didn't we see it on the way in, hanging on the gatepost?'

The others exhale.

Mel turns back to the wood. 'Should we split up, or search together?'

'Together, of course,' Lenny says.

But before she can move off after Mel, Orly puts a hand on her arm. 'Wait.'

At the tone of her voice, all three women turn to look at her. Orly can't bear the thought of those expressions changing, the eyes filling with disappointment, judgement. Will they like her just that little bit less? But the alternative is letting her friends wander round in the dark, frightened and worried and possibly in danger.

'I need to tell you something.'

183

She'd known it was wrong the moment she left the art room, and the feeling of dread grew over lunch, where she couldn't concentrate on the conversation being batted back and forth across the table. At one point Lenny asked her if she was okay. Friday was their special day, after all, when it was just the four of them once more because Pandora was at invitation-only art club. Pandora, who had only joined Summer Hall the year before, had muscled in on the group with no apparent shame. Because she did GCSE art with Orly and media studies with Mel, she seemed to think she was one of them. Orly had justified what she'd done as a bit of a laugh, a harmless prank, but it wasn't. She was jealous of the pretty new arrival. A younger girl would have said something spiteful, but what Orly had done was more sophisticated.

Could it be, she wondered, glancing anxiously at the clock, genuinely dangerous?

Before they'd even put the trays of pudding out, she excused herself and headed for the art block. They always teased Pan about Mr Newman fancying her, claimed that was the only reason she'd been invited to the club. That wasn't true. Pan was a talented artist, who made beautiful textile prints with leaves and flowers and embroidery, but he was in his late twenties, handsome and bright-eyed, and they clearly enjoyed one another's company. Pan was often on her own with him these days because the other girl in the club had been diagnosed with glandular fever at the end of last year, and was still unable to come in for a full week.

Orly rounded the corner past the French block, and the art building rose up before her. It was on the very edge of the school grounds for fire reasons, because of the kiln and chemicals that were stored in the cupboards, and now, in the middle of the lunch break, the whole area was deserted.

She pushed open the door and stepped onto the paint-spattered lino.

A corridor ran the length of the building, with rows of windows on the left and three doors leading off to the right. Next to her were the pegs holding the smocks, and just beyond them, the door to the large room for the lower-school classes. The second room was for messy stuff – pottery and papier-mâché – and the third was an intimate space where the GCSE and A-level girls came if they had close work to do – fine drawings or embroidery.

All was silent.

Orly almost turned round and walked out again, but then she started to worry that it was *too* quiet. What if she had started something with the letter? What if she walked up to the door and peered through the window to find them at it on the table? What the hell was she supposed to do then?

Pan was fifteen, so it was illegal, but maybe not if it was consensual. How old was Mr Newman? Surely no older than thir—

A cry echoed down the corridor.

A split second later, the door at the far end banged open and Pan burst into the corridor. Orly just had time to bury herself in the smocks as she came running in the direction of the door.

'Pan!' Mr Newman bellowed. 'You said! In the note! You said you wanted to!'

But Pandora just kept running, hurtling out of the door, her shirt flapping open, and stumbling down the path to the main block.

Orly froze in terror as a split second later Mr Newman pelted past. Then the door banged shut, the footsteps died away and silence settled once more.

She leant back against the cushion of smocks and wondered if she was going to be sick.

Her legs were wobbly as she stepped back out into the corridor. She was for it now. Pan was new and so wouldn't know her handwriting as they only had art together, but someone else could certainly identify it when they saw the note. Orly would be expelled. Could she be arrested?

Then she spotted the screwed-up ball of paper on the floor by the door to Room 3. Her heart jumped into her mouth as she hurried down the corridor.

It could be anything. A used tissue, a scribbled homework assignment.

But it wasn't.

Thank God.

It was the letter.

Though she immediately recognised her own looping handwriting, she picked it up to make sure.

Dear David,

I can't stop thinking about you. All week I look forward to being alone with you. I long for you to kiss me, to touch me. Please don't tell anyone, but I couldn't keep it inside any more.

Pan

Fresh horror at her stupidity gripped her. She tore the sheet into pieces, chewed it up and swallowed it, the hard wad making her gag before it finally went down.

Hurrying back to the form room, she found the English lit exercise book she'd used for the note. In case anyone found the imprint of what she had written, she tore out all the pages after it, then ripped them into little pieces and tucked them into the bottom of the bin.

Then she picked up her bag and went to history.

Afterwards, she watched as the fallout from her prank sent ripples through the whole school, but the note that both Pan and Mr Newman claimed had existed, and that exonerated both of them to some degree, was never found. Even when Mr Newman was fired and Pandora was hounded out of school, Orly never said a word to anyone.

Over the years that followed, she tried not to think about it all. Pan had been such a fleeting presence in their lives that they soon stopped talking about her. In the end, it was almost as if she had never existed, except as a phantom in the shadowy recesses of Orly's mind.

A phantom that has now stepped out into the light.

When she has finished speaking, there's a long silence, during which the air seems ionised with static. Orly can feel little charges exploding under her skin.

'Look,' Thea says finally. 'We all did stupid things at school.'

'It wasn't your fault,' Lenny says. 'The school dealt with it really badly. They should have kept it completely quiet.'

Orly nods, biting her lip.

Mr Newman had been so popular. The vitriol that rained down on Pandora was mostly due to jealousy. The other girls wished it had been them he'd made a pass at – or thought they did: being groped by an adult man in real life would have been another matter. They couldn't forgive her for being the chosen one. They believed his claim that there had been a note, but were sure Pandora had written it. As far as the authorities were concerned, a note was no defence when it came to the sexual assault of a teenage pupil, but in the court of her peers, the note proved her culpability.

He was fired, of course, and the police were involved. These days he would have been put on the sex offenders register, but back then it was just a warning. And Pan was spoken to about *leading him on*. A fifteen-year-old being blamed for her own sexual assault. Some things never change.

Nasty notes were slipped into her bag. Rotten food and, once, dog poo.

There were rumours that Mr Newman's wife had left him. That he'd tried to commit suicide. And in the end, Pan couldn't take it. Orly remembers with agonising detail that last school lunch with her, after their GCSEs. Pan's hair was unwashed and there were huge bags under her eyes. She'd turned up for the exams but knew she'd made a hash of them. It was no surprise when the results came in. They were not good enough for her

187

to stay on for A levels. Lenny argued that she should retake, that the school owed it to her to get her through them and take her back, but Pan was right in her assessment that she was an embarrassment to them. There was a meeting. It was felt that it was in her best interests to continue her education elsewhere. Except that she didn't. She went to hairdressing college, then dropped out.

Orly risks a look at Mel. The others keep their eyes firmly fixed on the ground, but she can feel them willing Mel to speak, to say something reassuring.

Mel obliges, but her tone is flat. 'You never meant for it to happen.'

Orly feels the comment like a slap. She wants to cry, to experience the release, to wallow in the attention again – herself as victim, not perpetrator – but she doesn't deserve it.

She clears her throat. 'I think she saw my handwriting on the tag and made the connection, and just left because she didn't want to cause a scene.'

'That was good of her, on Lenny's birthday,' Mel murmurs.

Lenny gives a half-hearted *mmm*.

'Maybe . . .' Thea says. 'Maybe we should keep trying her phone, just in case.'

The others listlessly agree, but when they go back inside the tent, nobody says much when Mel puts her phone away after the second unanswered call.

'Night, all,' she says, without looking at them.

'Night,' Thea echoes.

'Night, everyone,' Lenny says. 'And thanks for the lovely presents.'

'Happy birthday,' Orly says, then turns her face to the tent wall.

@GillingwaterFestival
We'd like to remind people to take care of themselves and their friends at #GillFest25. We want everyone to have a safe, fun time. Any concerns, please report them to the guys in the yellow jackets.

@Berniethehound
Replying to @GillingwaterFestival
Is this about the rape? I heard someone was attacked in one of the campsites on the outskirts and had to be taken to hosp.

@StevenBridge4433
Replying to @Berniethehound and @GillingwaterFestival
By 'take care of yourself' they mean don't get so pissed. Half the girls I see are out of it by 6 p.m. Not fair to accuse a guy of rape if you can't remember if you gave consent or not.

@Jacscrack
Replying to @Berniethehound @StevenBridge4433 and @GillingwaterFestival
So many women make false claims of sexual assault. All this for attention and extortion. #feminismiscancer #fuckfeminism #mgtow #redpill

17

Lenny

Used to a five o'clock start with the twins, Lenny wakes early. She can sense that Orly is awake too but won't acknowledge it. Orly probably needs some space. It was a big deal her coming here, probably the first time she's allowed herself to have fun since Harry died, and it's all been a bit of a disaster. First the tent-trashing, and then Pandora. It's as if evil gods are conspiring against her.

Lenny tries not to resent Mel for inviting Pan along. What was wrong with a hello, a hug and a pint or two? How did she end up as part of the group? It's not that Lenny disliked Pan at school: she was just irrelevant. Trivial. She may well have had hidden depths – the art talent hinted as much – but her relentless buoyancy got up Lenny's nose. She turns over.

Thea is awake and watching her.

Their eyes meet and Thea makes a face. Lenny mirrors it.

Disaster.

Mel sighs and sits up. 'Morning, all.'

There's a lot to be said for Mel's inability to hold a grudge. She might make snap judgements on people, but they rarely linger.

She's only a day into her forties but a night on the hard ground has made Lenny's bones feel a decade older, and the process of getting up is painful and protracted. Pulling on shorts and the T-shirt Greta made for her with the clumsily painted rainbow, she goes outside and has a puff on her inhaler. As she stands in

190

front of the tent breathing in the relatively fresh air, a definite tang of human excrement drifts from somewhere nearby. There's a tightness around her heart as she scans the wood for a blotch of colour – Pan's golden hair, pink flesh in a crumpled heap. But the undergrowth is uniformly green and brown, with only the occasional glint of broken glass.

Pan is almost definitely okay. But the niggling uncertainty is a shadow at the back of Lenny's mind. What if . . . ?

Mel and Thea emerge to clean their teeth with the bottled water, but Orly remains inside.

'Right,' Thea says, spitting her toothpaste into the grass. 'Let's get the birthday drinks in!'

Lenny grimaces. 'At this time?'

'Oh my *God*, you are not wussing out on your *birthday*?'

Thea's rictus grin makes Lenny's heart sink. Forced celebrations are the absolute last thing she needs today. A quiet day with Orly is all she wants. Reading in the sunshine or watching one of the lesser bands. To be honest, if she and Orly had made it out of here, she might even have crashed at Carol and Peter's for the night. But her friends have come all this way for her, so she'd better play her part.

'How about a yoga session? All those contortions might squeeze some of the poison from our bloodstreams.'

Thea stares in overdone astonishment. 'That's *my* line! Besides, I'm not sure we should subject Mel to it. Mel, wouldn't you rather just hit the pub?'

'I don't mind,' Mel says, shrugging.

'Great.' Seeing Thea's crestfallen face, Lenny adds, 'And then I'll get so pissed you'll have to put me to bed, pinkie promise.'

Thea's grin draws deep grooves either side of her mouth.

'I'll just go and get Orly.' Lenny crawls back inside.

Orly hasn't moved. Her knees are pulled up in a loose foetal position.

'Come on, we're going to yoga.'

'Bit hung-over,' she says thickly. 'I might just have a lie-in.'

Lenny climbs over her and lies down so that their faces are almost touching.

'It's my birthday,' she says quietly, 'and I want to spend it with my best friend. So have a snooze, take a paracetamol, then come and meet us later, okay?'

Orly nods, peering from half-closed eyes, the lids fat and red with crying.

'Attagirl,' Lenny says, patting her shoulder.

They don't talk about it until they have passed through the gate with its jacket sentinel, into the next field.

Mel is the first to speak. 'Well, that was a surprise, eh? Why didn't she say anything before?'

'Because she was ashamed,' Thea says. 'Besides, would you have? With all the shit that came afterwards?'

Mel shrugs. 'Poor Pan.'

Lenny stops walking. 'Yes,' she says, as the others turn to her. 'Poor Pan. Orly did a shit thing, but she's our friend, and sometimes you have to choose.'

Mel starts to protest, but Lenny speaks over her.

'I know what you're going to say, you shouldn't have to choose between friends, but this time, on this occasion, we have to. Who do we care about most? I like Pan, I really do. But I choose Orly. If we have to avoid Pan to make Orly feel better, then I will do that.'

'If she's still alive,' Thea mutters.

'Very funny,' Mel says. 'I doubt she'll contact any of us again, to be honest.'

'She'll just have to put up with Jay,' Thea says.

'With his six-pack.'

'And full head of hair.'

'And twenty-five-year-old libido.'

'Poor cow.'

Lenny has to stop halfway through the yoga class. The downward dog goes on for so long that all the blood rushes to her head and threatens to push her eyeballs from their sockets. Rolling onto her

192

back, she lies staring at the sail canopy above them, willing her lungs not to succumb to the fist she can feel tightening around them. She breathes carefully, in through her nose and out through her mouth in time with the female instructor's count, and the fist eventually relaxes its grip.

She's about to join in with a less intense position when she senses eyes on her and lifts her head.

Rich is leaning against a smoothie bar a hundred or so metres away.

Sitting up, she raises her hand. He doesn't wave back but pushes himself off the side of the van and walks away. She gets up, rolling her mat and stacking it with the others at the edge of the tarpaulin, before going to meet him.

'I've been looking for you,' he calls across to her as she approaches. 'I thought we were meeting at the cinema last night.'

'Oh God, sorry, I totally forgot. Were you there long?'

'An hour.'

She bristles at his tone. 'You could have called.'

'I didn't want to *speak* to you,' he says with a laugh, placing both hands on her waist. 'I wanted to *see* you.'

Lenny laughs too. 'Well, here I am.'

'Let's go somewhere private.'

'What for? We can talk here.'

He raises his eyebrows. 'Who needs talking?

She gives a sharp laugh. 'A morning fuck? I'm with my friends, Rich. I might see you later.' She slides out of his embrace, but he takes her by the upper arm, his fingers tight on her flesh.

'I'm not around later.'

A flash of anger sharpens her tone. 'Let go, please.' Apart from her children, it's a long time since someone has invaded her personal space like that. He seems to be under the illusion that she's still a biddable schoolgirl.

He holds her gaze for a moment, then releases her arm, shaking his head. 'Unbelievable.'

'What?'

'You haven't changed, Leonora, you know that? You pick me up when you feel like it and drop me when something better comes along.'

She stares, then hold up her palms. 'Wait a minute. You come here and basically demand sex. I say it's not convenient, and you act like *I'm* using *you*?'

Rich's upper lip curls. 'Oh what, so acting like we were boyfriend and girlfriend for a fucking year, then going off to uni without a fucking by-your-leave, and then never calling me again doesn't count as *using*?'

It takes her a moment to gather her thoughts.

'Whoa,' she says, shaking her head. 'Firstly, I didn't *act* like we were boyfriend and girlfriend. We *were* boyfriend and girl-friend. Secondly, I didn't have to ask your *leave* to go to uni. I wasn't your property.'

He gives a snort of derision.

'And I didn't ignore you. I was at uni two hundred miles away. There was no way we could have carried on.'

'Everyone else managed it. Tim and Elaina, Kiki and Paul.'

These are people she has no recollection of.

'I called you. I wrote to you. And not a fucking word.'

She can dimly remember some messages on the pad in the hall of residence, and a letter that made her laugh. It had a photo of the two of them that she kept for a while, then lost track of.

'Look, I'm sorry if you're upset, but it was more than twenty years ago. We were starting our lives. I—'

'Had better things to do,' he finishes. 'Like I said. Same old Lenny. Selfish and cold.'

His breaths are so heavy she can feel them on her chest.

To think that all these years she has got it so wrong. She really thought they parted on good terms. That Rich held a candle for her, as she did for him. You think you know people, and then *pow*.

'Hi.'

A woman walks up. Lenny recognises her. She was handing out the bags with Rich the first time they saw him.

'I'm Saeeda,' she says, stretching out a hand and smiling. The other arm she wraps around Rich's waist.

Oh, thinks Lenny.

'Hi.' She shakes. 'Lenny. Rich and I used to go to school together.'

'Yes,' Saeeda says. 'He's told me about you.'

Silence.

'Well, good to meet you. I should be getting back to my friends.'

Rich moves off without a word and the woman calls after him, 'I'll be along in a minute.'

Lenny glances behind her, but Mel and Thea are lying on their backs on the yoga mats, eyes closed, oblivious.

'I know what you're thinking,' Saeeda says quietly.

'Really?' Lenny smiles. It's a stupid, immature response, but she can't seem to help it.

'You think you can just come here and snap your fingers and Rich will come running.'

'The idea never crossed my mind, I assure you. I'm just here for my birthd—'

Saeeda moves her face close enough that Lenny can smell her unbrushed-teeth breath. 'Rich is with me now, and I'm here to stay. We're getting married, okay? So if you think you can just waltz back into his life, think again, bitch. Got it?'

Lenny's mouth is open but no words appear ready to emerge.

'I said, got it?'

'Yes,' she says. 'I've got it. Understood completely. You're the fiancée, I'm the bitch.' She smiles again, shaking her head with the disbelief of the only sane person in the room, but the fist is back, pressing, pressing.

Saeeda's face remains pinched with anger, and possibly fear. Beneath the flushed cheeks her skin is blanched. 'Fuckin' A,' she spits, then turns and goes after Rich, who must have almost run to have got so far away.

Lenny stares at her retreating back, then sits heavily on the nearest hay bale and takes out her inhaler.

195

A couple of minutes later, the others join her.

'You feeling okay, babe?' Mel says.

Lenny looks up in bewilderment. 'Is it beer time yet?'

'It's always beer time!' Grabbing her by the same arm that Rich bruised, Thea hauls her up and they head out to the main track.

Mel is predictably outraged at Rich's behaviour, Thea just as predictably forgiving.

'That woman, *Saeeeeeda*,' Mel stretches out the name mockingly, 'is clearly crapping her pants. You've probably been this bogeyman to her from the moment they got together.'

They're shivering on a bench by an organic beer van, waiting for the sun's rays to break through the cloud cover. Lenny hasn't looked at the weather app recently. She just assumed the relentless sunshine would carry on, like it did the last time they were here.

'But why on earth tell her about me, for fuck's sake? *Hi, nice to meet you, I like you and everything but I'm still really bitter about my first girlfriend.*'

'Maybe he just wanted to be straight with her,' Thea says. 'Tell it like it is. If you know what you're getting, you can't kick off down the line.'

Lenny swigs from the bottle of pissy lager. Is Thea talking about herself and Bruno? Lenny remembers when they met. Thea was at her most stunning, unattainable for women and unobtainable for men. Bruno was an ageing banker staring down the barrel of his lost looks and alpha-male status. Did Thea tell him what the transaction would involve right from the start? She never said so in so many words, but Lenny knew that, after Tony, she was holding out for the best possible replacement. Someone who would look after her and the kids long-term. And Bruno, who probably couldn't believe his luck, delivered: taking them into his home, paying for private schooling and lifting Thea into the echelons of the upper middle class. As far as Lenny's concerned, she's welcome to it. From what she knows of finance

196

wives, their lives are characterised by insecurity, suspicion and ultimately – when the inevitable happens – bitterness at being replaced by younger clones of themselves.

'What, and know that you're always being compared with this fantasy first love?' Mel says. 'No way. I'd run a mile. She must be mental.'

That might be Mel's problem, Lenny thinks. This black-and-white attitude to the world. If it isn't perfect, then it's worthless. She finished with Gary because he admitted to getting off with a work colleague at a Christmas party. A quickie in the toilets and that was it: a home shattered, a child's life turned upside down. It's hard not to judge her friend for that, but what does Lenny know about commitment? No relationship of hers has lasted longer than Rich.

'She loves him,' Thea says. 'And when you love someone, there's no limit to the pain you'll go through for them.'

Mel bangs her fist on the table. 'It's not about *love*. It's about self-respect. If you don't have boundaries,' she carves a line through the air, 'people will shit on you.'

'Depends,' Thea says, looking away, and Lenny suspects that the conversation is at risk of straying onto dangerous ground. 'It depends how much you love them.'

Mel jabs her bottle. 'You're talking about co-dependency, not love.'

Lenny tenses, waiting for Thea to bite, but she doesn't respond, and Mel clearly feels guilty for what she has said because she goes on: 'I mean, you and Bruno are in a balanced relationship. You both get something out of it. With me and Gary, I did everything. He thought that the fact he had a nine-to-five job entitled him to get out of everything else – housework, parenting, the finances, shopping, cooking. When he did what he did, that was the last straw.'

'You'd stopped loving him,' Thea says simply.

Mel nods. 'Yeah. I suppose I had. That was what killed it in the end. The way he was.'

197

Lenny realises she has nothing to add to this conversation. She decided a long time ago that she wasn't capable of romantic love. It was one of the things that kept her up at night when she was pregnant with the twins: was she incapable of *all* kinds of love? But she loved her parents, and she'd loved her childhood pet dog, so she crossed her fingers and hoped for the best. When the twins came along, for about three days she was in such shock – no, that's overstating it: she was adjusting to the fact of their being here, and being hers – that she felt nothing other than anxiety. The fear started to creep back: she had made a dreadful mistake. And then she took them home and tucked them into their little baskets and knelt on the carpet gazing at them, wondering at the fact that she, plain old Leonora and some unknown male, had produced the most beautiful, perfect children the world had ever seen. Unfamiliar as it may have been, she recognised the feeling. It was love. And she knew then that it would last for the rest of her life.

What she felt for Rich had been no more than a pleasant fondness spiced with adolescent lust. She honestly did not realise she'd hurt him. She always imagined he had tucked their relationship into a little box in a corner of his mind, to be taken out and gazed at wistfully every now and again, as she had done. But not this. Not this rage and bitterness. And Saeeda's hatred and fear that fed on it.

No, it was not her fault. Rich was mentally unhinged, and he had driven his girlfriend down the same path.

'I think I'll just stay out of their way,' she says, finishing the dregs of her beer.

'Good luck with that,' Mel snorts.

'What?'

'Well, he's clearly stalking you, right? And his girlfriend is stalking him. When it comes to the crunch, they'll team up against you. If you ask me, you should go to bed with a weapon of some kind.'

Lenny laughs. The idea of being the object of someone's obsession is ridiculous. If Rich spent more time with her, he would very soon realise how dull she is. And – perhaps he was right – cold. Except where the children are concerned.

She feels a sudden overwhelming urge to hear their little voices. Excusing herself, she gets up from the bench and walks away, tapping in Jeanne's number. Standing by the hedge, she scuffs her toe in the tangle of dry grass as she waits out the rings. She won't get much out of either of them, she knows, just a highly coaxed *hello*, and possibly a *When are you coming home?*

But Jeanne doesn't answer, and absurdly this brings tears to Lenny's eyes. She checks the time on the screen as she slides the phone into her pocket: 11.30 on a Sunday morning. They'll probably be in the park. Jeanne and Greta will be taking it in turns in goal while Jackson kicks the football at them. Lenny allows herself a moment's gratitude that she's not there – being told off for not saving the ball properly, or taking jarring strikes to the side of the head – before heading back to the table. She is almost there when the phone rings.

'Hello, Mummy.'

Her heart melts.

'Greta! Hello, baby. How are you?'

'I miss you.'

'I miss you too, but I'll be back tomorrow.'

Silence.

'Is that good?'

'Yes. Bye bye.'

'Bye, sweetie, see you tomorrow.'

'Oh, wait, Jackson wants to speak to you.'

'Does he?' This is a surprise. Perhaps Jeanne has told him to. Lenny waits while the mic rustles and thuds as the phone is passed between the children.

'Hello, Mummy.'

'Hello, lovely. Are you in the park?'

'I'm sorry, Mummy.'

199

'For what, darling?'

'For saying mean things about wanting a daddy and making you sad.'

'Oh sweetheart, that was ages ago, I'd forgotten all about it.' She turns back to the hedge, cupping her hand over the phone, unwilling to share this beautiful intimacy with anyone. 'And anyway, you could never, ever make me sad. I was sorry *you* were sad.'

'I miss you and I knew I would have to wait three days to see you. It made me think about all the things people want that they can't have. Like Auntie Orly not having Uncle Harry any more even though she really wants him. You have to be happy with what you've got. And I am. I'm happy with you and Greta and my friends and football.'

For a moment she can't speak. Such wisdom from an eight-year-old.

'There is something, though.'

'What's that?'

'Can we have a puppy?'

She laughs. 'I'll think about it, okay?'

'Okay. I like pugs. Like in the book where they race in the snow.'

'We'll talk about it when I get home.'

'Okay. I love you, Mummy.'

'I love you too.'

'I love you, Mummy.' The voice is Greta's now. 'See you tomorrow.'

'Love you too, baby.'

As she hangs up and goes back to the table, her heart feels as though it might burst from her chest and sail up into the clouds. Lucky her. Lucky Jackson and Greta, and Mel and Billy, and Thea and Lewis and Jade. There is love, and then there is the love you have for your children. They are as different as the moon and the sun. For Rich to be obsessed with their tawdry little barn-fucks all these years later, to have kept a pair of her knickers, for fuck's sake, she can only assume he doesn't have children. Poor him. And poor Orly.

'Where's Thea?' she asks.

'Gone for another round.'

She was going to suggest a break. This will be their third bottle and she is woolly-headed already, plus the cold beers are making her feel colder. There is still no sign of the sun coming out. She's ready to go home. The idea of going to bed sober and waking up warm with no aches in a bed full of sweet-smelling children is sheer bliss. It's been good to be with the girls again, but the days when they yearned to spend every second with one another, share every thought as if they were one entity, are long gone. There's a reason they only meet a few times a year. Mel is simplistic and impulsive: it gets exhausting being around her. Thea is desperate to hide her frailties – whether psychological or physical – and consequently there's always a barrier between them. Orly is the only one Lenny can bear to spend large amounts of time with. She experiences a fresh twinge of guilt. It was so easy to let the friendship slide after Harry got ill: what with her job and lifestyle and then the children, she told herself they had grown apart. But it was a lie. She was just being a coward. She'll do better from now on.

'Here you go.' Thea swings onto the bench, setting bottles in front of Mel and then Lenny.

Lenny glances at the label and her heart sinks: 6.8 per cent alcohol. She will definitely have to go back to the tent for a sleep this afternoon. But at least that will kill a bit of the day. She can't even be bothered to see a band now. She must be getting old.

'Should we call Orly?' Mel says.

'Shall we leave it a bit?' Thea says. 'Let her come when she feels like it?'

The other two nod.

'In that case . . .' Mel rubs her hands, grins. 'Beyoncé's on.'

Thea groans. 'That'll be absolutely thronged. Let's just stay here.'

201

They turn to Lenny, the birthday girl, who would far rather be opening clumsily felt-tipped cards with wild-haired stick men under a bristled yellow sun. But at least Beyoncé will give her a break from relentless drinking.

So they head to the Litha Stage, and it's predictably awful. They are a good quarter of a mile from the front and the singer is a glittering speck under flashing lights and a screen featuring images Lenny can't make out without her glasses.

Mel is dancing. Thea's body jerks to the beat as if she is being rhythmically electrocuted. Lenny looks around her and sees that everyone else, every single soul in this enormous field, is enjoying themselves. There's nothing for it. She will just have to get trashed.

Linking arms with her two friends, she allows herself to be drawn forward, into the heat and noise.

+44 7895 334552
How did you like my present?
11.03

Orly
Sorry think youve got the wrong number.
11.05

+44 7895 334552
The one I left outside your tent. I wanked on them first.
11.05

Orly
If this is you Rich youve got the wrong number.
11.05

+44 7895 334552
Whos Rich? Your name is Orly. Ive been watching you. When it gets dark Ill come and introduce myself.
11.13

18

Orly

Huddled in a nest of sleeping bags, Orly hopes that from outside no one can tell she's there.

At first the field was a hubbub of comforting noises – people brushing their teeth and talking, zips buzzing up and down, phones ringing, tinny music through travel speakers – but now the sounds have died away to birdsong and the odd rustle.

She's alone.

And someone is watching her.

The profile image by the stranger's number seems to be of a dark-clad figure with a black beanie on. Could it be Trey?

The next rustle is right at the back of the tent.

She rips open the zip, bursts outside and stumbles away across the field, not stopping until she reaches the gate. There, with one hand on the comforting arm of the abandoned coat, she pauses and looks back. There is no movement, no telltale splash of colour or suspicious shape. The place is deserted.

Someone could be hiding behind one of the tents.

She turns and runs. Only once she's got as far away from the campsite as possible and is safe amidst the bustle and crowds does she realise that she has left her phone in the tent. Along with her wallet.

She can't buy breakfast or a drink, watch a film, do a yoga class or even hail a cab home. And she daren't go back to the tent until late afternoon when people will start to return for a tactical snooze. All she can do is trudge about for the next . . . she doesn't even know what time it is without her phone . . . however long it is until that time, or until she finds her friends. Given the insane number of people, that doesn't seem possible, but she makes for the Village Green, the final place they drank last night.

All the way there she feels she is being watched, by a gaze that lifts the hairs on the back of her neck.

She dips her head, in case Trey or Pandora or Baldric are close by.

To have made so many enemies in just three days is quite something. Although of course only Trey is new. The other enmities have been brewing over twenty years, beginning before she even realised that things had a habit of coming back to bite you. Karma is an unfair bitch, punishing you when you've already changed from the person who committed the crime. Or perhaps she still is that person. Her jealousy of Pan verged on hatred. If she'd had the chance to do her harm this weekend without getting caught, perhaps she would have taken it.

She shivers. Clouds are massing above her. It looks like rain. And she has come out in the vest she slept in. Tears of self-pity spring to her eyes.

She's about to cross the track that branches to one of the toilet and refuse areas when, out of nowhere, a grim-faced Rich is striding towards her, with an equally grim woman at his side.

She turns her steps down the track, hunching over, trying to make herself inconspicuous. It's not hard. They pass within a metre or so of her but neither registers her presence. She might as well be a ghost. She makes for the toilets.

The tampon comes out almost completely white.

Her period has dropped down to three days this month. Forty is early to be perimenopausal, but her mother went through it early too. Orly remembers her at the wedding, slightly tipsy, telling her not to leave it too long before they had babies.

She sits there for a few minutes on the plastic seat, wondering if her life could get any shitter.

It can, of course. As she steps out of the little cubicle and sets off for the main track, it starts to rain. The beautiful girls tilt their heads back, swing their hanks of hair and dance like a photographer's watching.

Orly turns onto the main track.

What are the other three saying about her now? It would almost be satisfying if they were shocked and horrified: *We thought we knew her*. But no, they'll be pitying her: *Poor thing, she was just scared Pan would take us away from her*.

She straightens her back and glares defiantly up into the rain.

Yes, she was a bitch. Worse than any of them. But can't she just fucking own it? Does she really have to be tragic Orly for the rest of her life? Can't she be something else? Bitch Orly – don't cross her or she'll mess your life up.

The thought makes her laugh out loud, and as if in sympathy, the sky booms a laugh of its own. The beautiful girls stop dancing and run for cover.

Orly hurries through the rain, which has fallen like a bridal veil, giving everything a soft-focus glamour. Earthfields is a mist of colour and flame, the beer tent a fuzzy outline against the hedge. She runs towards it.

Inside is a heaving, steaming mass of noise and smells – of unwashed armpits and spilled beer. As the crowd shuffles and undulates, she makes her way deeper, grateful to be among warm humans again. But what if she was followed in?

She scans the faces, waiting for one to trigger a memory. Someone she hasn't seen for years, whose memory she suppressed because what she did was so very bad, but who never forgot . . .

How did you like my present?

Someone raises a hand. Her heart clenches, then relaxes.

Extracting himself from a group of men, Ben weaves through the crowd.

'Hey.'

'Hey.'

'Didn't have you girls down as real-ale fans.'

'I've lost the others. Although actually I do like pale ale.'

'Let me get you one.'

'No, no.' She grimaces at the thronged bar. 'It'll take for ever.'

'Come and keep me company, then.'

The crowd at the bar is four deep, but at least it's warm, and so noisy that they have to stand very close to hear one another.

'I can't get you one back,' she shouts. 'I left my wallet in the tent.'

'Shit. I hope it doesn't get stolen. Apparently there are gangs that go round looting stuff. Like that guy in your tent yesterday. I wish I'd decked him.'

'No, no, no. I'm glad you didn't. He was a drug dealer.'

The story sounds funny in narration – the binning of the drugs, the dance around the helter skelter – and the warm rush when she makes Ben laugh is like honey through her veins.

They ease forward.

'So where are your mates?'

'They started early. I fancied a lie-in.' She has no intention of recounting the whole Pandora debacle. He's a teacher himself, a good-looking one, and probably lives in fear of something similar happening to him. He will hate her for it.

Instead they talk about the festival, how surprisingly boring it can be unless you're a party animal like Mel, or Ben's friend Corey. Apparently, Corey was called up on stage by one of the lesser, but still quite famous bands, and actually sang a chorus with the lead singer, sharing his mic.

They both make a face. How annoyingly wonderful to be so lacking in inhibition.

He has to buy her next drink too, and afterwards he says, 'Look, I'm worried about your stuff at the tent. Shall we go back and get it? It is your round, after all.'

'If you don't mind . . .'

They pass out into the rain, and he covers her shoulders with his jacket, which entails walking with his arm around her.

But the spell is temporarily broken. She feels exposed, insecure, unattractive in the dull, flat light, and the thought of her phone, and the new messages it might contain, dampens her mood. She omitted to tell him about them too. Why shouldn't she play fun and sexy for once, instead of the victim?

The festival-goers slow to a trickle as they pass down the main track. The rain is a heartbeat on Ben's jacket, and without thinking, she sinks into his shoulder. The warmth of his body exudes a faint scent of sweat, a beautiful male smell untainted by chemicals or sickness. It makes her feel young again. Young and sleepy. If she rested her head against his chest, perhaps she would sleep peacefully for the first time in years.

Her thoughts elsewhere, it's a surprise when they come to the gate and the coat pointing the way with its outstretched sleeve. She stops walking. In the field beyond, the tents suck and billow under the onslaught of rain, as if there are people moving around inside them.

'You okay?'

'Just a bit . . . freaked out by that guy, what he did to our tent. I don't like coming back here alone.'

'You're not alone.'

He turns towards her, slipping the jacket over his head so that it covers both of them, and kisses her.

Her head spins and for a moment she thinks she might faint. When it's finished, she exhales from the deepest centre of her body. Something, some last thread, pulled so taut it has been cutting into her flesh, has been snipped away, and she feels light enough to float up into the rain.

'Come on,' Ben says. 'Let's get under cover.'

They run across the ridged mud, stumbling like conjoined twins.

As they approach the green tent, she sees that the door is flapping in the wind, and her chest tightens. Someone has been inside. But then she remembers that she fled in too much of a hurry to zip it up.

The grassy area inside the door is drenched, but the rain hasn't reached the inner tent. She crawls inside, relieved that the open doors have refreshed the atmosphere, and hastily tucks a stray bra into a case.

Her wallet is still in the pocket sewn into the tent wall, and there, face down on Thea's sleeping bag, is her phone.

She flips it over.

There are many more messages. She turns the phone off without looking at them as Ben crawls in to join her.

'Everything here?'

'Yep. All fine.'

Great. So do we . . . go back and get another beer, or . . .'

She swallows, and when she speaks, her voice trembles. 'I guess we could stay and warm up a bit . . .'

'At the risk of sounding pervy, you should probably get out of those wet clothes.' His grin gleams in the gloom. The light in here is low enough to be kind, and she pushes her wet hair out of her face.

'Your T-shirt looks pretty damp too.'

'Should I take it off?'

'If you want.'

The awkwardness is exquisite.

'Together, then. One . . . two . . . three.'

Sucking in her stomach, she pulls the wet rag of her vest over her head and feels a rush of relief that she brought the fuchsia-pink bra instead of the comfy white one.

Ben looks almost as self-conscious as she feels, sitting with his knees up, his white pant elastic showing over the top of his shorts, his sparse chest hairs smoothed straight and flat by the rain.

Shuffling forward, he takes her face in his hand and kisses her again, this time flicking his tongue against her lips.

The flashback – to Harry – is hard and sudden. She jerks away.

Ben pulls back. 'Are you okay?'

She's breathing very fast and has to pause to take some calming breaths before answering.

'Orly? Speak to me. Did I do something?'

She squeezes her eyes shut, wanting to cry. It was all so lovely, and now it's ruined.

No, no, it's not. Calm down. You're not poor Orly. You are a young widow who has every right to move on. Harry's gone and Ben is here, warm and funny and alive.

But there's no way of getting out of some kind of an explanation.

She forces a laugh. 'This may be . . . this may be jumping the gun, but before we . . . I feel like I should tell you something.'

He's looking at her intently.

'I haven't got a disease or anything like that.'

He chuckles. 'Well, that's something.'

'It's just . . . Oh, I don't know, forget it.' This is a one-night stand. They're never going to see one another again. She reaches forward and touches his chest.

But he lays a hand over hers. 'You've got me interested now.'

She takes a deep breath. Here goes. 'I was married. I'm not any more. My husband died of cancer last year.'

Ben's dark eyes glimmer in the half-light. 'What was his name?'

She likes that he is courteous enough to ask. 'Harry. He was thirty-eight.'

'I'm sorry. What kind of cancer?'

'Bowel.' Could there be anything less sexy to talk about? She feels around for her vest. The mood is definitely killed. She should go back. Find the girls.

'My dad died of that when I was twenty-one.'

'Oh.' She blinks and forces her mind out of the runnel it slots into so naturally – that of accepting sympathy. 'I'm so sorry.'

'Fucking shit, isn't it? I was still living at home – my brother and sister had left – so I got all the fun. Sometimes I get a whiff of it. Of the smell, you know?'

She nods.

'And it takes me straight back there. Did Harry die at home?'

'In a hospice, thank God. What about your dad?'

'Mum insisted on having him at home. It was a fucking nightmare.' He lies back on Thea's sleeping bag and gazes up into the apex of the tent. 'She just couldn't get the pain medication right when the nurse wasn't there. I'd be woken up by him screaming.'

Orly lies down beside him.

'In the end it was a relief when he died. I went straight to the pub with my mate. He thought I was drinking to forget what had happened, but for me it was actually a celebration. It was like the clouds parted and I could look up and see that there was blue sky again. That there might actually be something to look forward to now.' His head turns, his eyes wide with consternation. 'Oh God, I'm sorry. Of course it was nothing like that for you. Harry was your future.'

'It's okay,' she manages. She's on the verge of tears, but not of sadness. Of relief, that someone else, someone decent, good and normal, might empathise with her shame. She remembers that sense of elation too: that the corpse you had been carrying on your back for months was lifted. You hadn't laid it down through weakness or cowardice; you had done your duty, and then you were relieved of it. She remembers the taste of the meal someone cooked for her that first night of widowhood. For the first time in months, food had flavour. The sense of freedom didn't last long, and the guilt of it probably exacerbated the depression that followed, but it was there. She was just never brave enough to tell anyone about it. 'I felt the same.'

For a long time there's silence but for the wind flapping the tent, like the sails of a boat they're travelling on across rough seas. And then uneven footsteps come stumbling across the grass, and stop right outside. A moment later the nylon whispers and bulges inwards, as is someone if feeling for a way in.

Orly freezes, her eyes wide in the gloom. The guy who sent the messages has come for her and it sounds as if he's too drunk to walk. Drunk men are dangerous.

Taking her hand, Ben whispers, 'Maybe he's got the wrong tent too.' Then he calls out in a loud, deep voice, 'Hello! Can we help you?'

For a moment there's complete silence but for the patter of the rain on the roof, and then the dragging footsteps move away.

Orly exhales and looks at him. 'I'm glad you're here.'

'So am I.' He smiles. Then he leans forward and moves his hand to her face. 'Can we start again?'

Orly isn't sure what he means, or at least not until he pushes himself up onto his elbow and leans across her body. Soon she is warm again.

@stjohnambulance
Please be aware that fentanyl is being sold as heroin at #GillFest25. Just 3 milligrams of this deadly opioid can kill an adult male. If a friend seems disorientated or unresponsive, call 999 immediately.

19

Thea

There's a lot that Thea admires about Beyoncé. Her ability to be insanely gorgeous in a normal-sized frame, her stalwart fidelity when the father of her children cheated on her, the fact that she's almost the same age as Thea and still looks fantastic.

The only thing she doesn't like is that song, 'Independent *fucking* Women'. Anais loves to put it on the Alexa at home and then join in pointedly with the chorus: *The clothes I'm wearing, Dad bought it.*

But it's easy to be an independent woman when you have a talent – dancing, singing, brains – like Beyoncé, or Lenny.

Thea had a talent, if you define talent as a God-given attribute. It was beauty. The specific kind that attracts men: what has come to be seen as a Kardashian polish before they were even a thing – everything plump and glossy and golden. Her breasts grew early and perfectly full, her bottom had a peachy curve before it was even fashionable. Her hair was thick and wavy and – back then – naturally honeyed. When she was thirteen, she overheard her mother talking to her aunt, whose own daughter was off to college to study veterinary science.

'Thea will be fine,' her mum said. 'She'll just marry a footballer.'

And Thea believed this to be her destiny: so long as she kept up her side of the deal and stayed beautiful, her smooth path in life would be guaranteed.

The problem being that at first it was.

From the first whispers of puberty, boys were falling over themselves for her. While her friends distributed their virginities like sweets, she hung onto hers with ferocious pride. No boy would be allowed a second date if he did not open the car door for her, pay for everything, compliment her and call her the following day.

And they all jumped through these hoops with enthusiasm. Even the boys who called girls slags and rated their physical attributes suddenly became perfect gentlemen where Thea was concerned, shaking her mother's hand, getting her home on the dot.

Then Tony sealed it for her. A couple of years older than her, he had a proper car – leather seats, alloy wheels, only one previous owner – and a flat of his own. His parents had a holiday home in Spain.

Yes, she could have waited for her footballer, but she fell in love.

And for a while it was perfect. Tony's business thrived. They bought the house in Essex. There were weekly hair and manicure and spa appointments, expensive gym memberships, holidays, parties, champagne. Then, after she got pregnant, a £10,000 engagement ring.

It never occurred to her to ask where it all came from. It was her dues. As her grandad always told her: only the best for his beautiful princess.

So what are you supposed to do when it's all taken away and you're left with nothing to your name except those attributes that brought you everything in the first place?

The only thing you can do. Put them back on the market.

Fuck you, Beyoncé. Just because someone else pays for it doesn't mean you didn't buy it.

After the set, they're all sweaty and glowing: even Lenny.

'Anyone else thirsty?' Thea calls over the final chords. 'We should hit the bar now before the rush!'

But it's not the rush that fills the nearest beer tent. They've just got inside and found a table, and Thea is up at the bar, when the heavens open. People immediately crowd in as the rain hammers the canvas like artillery.

She glances along the line of people waiting to order, to see who's looking at her.

No one.

The barman doesn't even make eye contact as he takes her order for three Beck's. She can see her face in the brushed aluminium barrels behind him: a blurred outline of pink and beige. The same as she's always looked, but of course it's the details that matter: that micrometre depth of shadow beneath her eyes and the almost imperceptible coarsening of her skin. Swipe left.

'Fourteen twenty-five, love.'

She pays and makes her way back through the crowd, setting the bottles down on the table, one in front of each woman.

'Sorry, can we squeeze in?' a young man says. He's drenched, as is the girl with him, but somehow they've managed to find two chairs. The women shuffle along, Lenny lifting the three bottles of beer and placing them down again a little way up the table.

'Cheers, Thee.' Mel picks up the one that is now nearest to her and drinks.

'I'll call Orly and get her to meet us here,' Lenny says.

Mel grimaces as she swallows. 'Do you think she's okay?'

'She'll be fine,' Lenny says.

'If not, there's always sertraline.'

'What's that?' Lenny says, gulping down a mouthful.

'Antidepressant. I took it after me and Gary broke up. Worked like a fucking dream.'

Lenny makes the call, leaving a message telling Orly to meet them.

Just as she hangs up, there's a creaking noise and everyone looks up. The canvas roof is swelling towards them. Through it Thea can see the currents and eddies of the water, like some grotesque pregnancy.

A man is running at them with a spear.

'Out of the way!'

Drawing back the spear, which Thea now sees is actually the wrong end of a broom, he jabs it into the distended belly of the tent. 'Look out!' A moment later, a cascade of water gushes from the roof, practically knocking over a woman in a maxi dress and flowery rain hat smoking in the threshold.

People point and guffaw as she gasps and staggers.

'Sorry, love!'

The woman turns and looks at all the jeering faces. Make-up streaks her cheeks, and without the hat, which has been knocked into the mud, her hair is rats' tails. Her cheeks twitch as she tries to laugh along; to be fun and easy-going. *It's a festival, chill out.* But she can't. She fucking can't. Pressing her lips together, she turns and flees into the rain.

'Bugger me, this beer is strong,' Mel says, rubbing her eyes and setting the empty bottle back on the table.

Lenny peers at the label, then shows it to Thea. 'What's the alcohol percentage?'

'Erm . . . four point eight,' Thea says.

'That's not too bad.'

Lenny's short-sightedness would be simple enough to sort out, but instead she's choosing to succumb to middle age, like her owlish mother.

Thea remembers Lenny's mother, old but not as old as she made out, mystified by the modern world. Lenny is not mystified just uninterested. She always was in her own private world, with its pathways, its mountains and valleys that only she could see: her gaze fixed on the final destination. She reached it so quickly and sure-footedly.

Back in the day, but before Lenny's kids came along, they would sometimes meet in secret, without the other two. They would eat at expensive sushi restaurants and go to shows, Thea's bills all put on the credit card Tony had given her. But Jackson and Greta changed everything. Despite the fact that Lenny could have afforded it with no problem, she wouldn't get a full-time nanny or even a babysitter in those early years. And so when they did meet for coffee or lunch, the inevitable happened. The only thing Lenny had to talk about was the kids.

Thea felt it as a kind of insult. The sacrifices she herself had made to stay young and fun, rejected as worthless by her best friend.

Bruno always said it was important for a woman to have a social life of her own, rather than just hanging onto a partner or trailing round after children. Looks weren't everything. You needed a spark to keep things alive. And Thea kept her spark. When they went to parties, she never whined about getting home to put the children to bed, never complained that she was too tired to go out. She made sure to remain the type of woman men wanted, and as a consequence her children were safe, well cared for, well fed and clothed, and with the specialist education Lewis needed: not muddling through on benefits with a single mum, one bill or breakdown away from homelessness.

When they're older, Lewis and Jade will thank her for the sacrifices she's made for them. The sacrifice of their company. Because when she's twerking with Bruno's work partner as the other partners cheer and whoop, no one would ever guess that she'd rather be curled against the warm backs of her sleeping children.

She gazes moodily into the neck of her bottle. The bubbles have lost their liveliness. Soon the beer will be flat and tasteless.

'Right,' Mel says, slapping her palms onto the table. 'It's the last day and I need to get something for my Billy.'

'Now?' Lenny says. 'In this? Why don't you wait till it clears up a bit?'

'Oh, I don't mind the rain. It might clear my head. Meet you back here in about an hour.' She staggers a little as she gets up, and rolls her eyes ruefully – 'Can't take it like I used to' – then weaves away.

Thea watches her stumbling through the crowd, occasionally leaning on someone for support and exchanging some laughing comment.

'Cheers,' Lenny says, clinking bottles. 'Just me and you. Like the old days.'

Thea lifts her bottle and drinks, then puts it down.

'You're quiet. You okay?' Lenny says.

'Fine.'

'Any luck with . . .' She nods at Thea's stomach, and Thea lays a protective hand over it, as if there were something fragile and precious inside.

'Not yet.'

'You thought of trying IVF?'

Thea shakes her head. She has, but not any more.

Lenny says something else, but Thea doesn't catch what it was. The clock hanging behind the bar clicks past the hour.

'. . . if you had this with Lewis, but Jackson has suddenly made this jump in maturity, like he's had some kind of hormone surge. Testosterone, I guess. I think they said in that Steve Biddulph book that boys get one at seven—'

Thea interrupts her, with a sharp drawn-in breath. 'Shit.'

'What?' Lenny turns in the direction she is staring.

'Don't look!' Thea hisses. 'It's Anais. Over by the blow-up Trump.'

'Anais is here?' Lenny peers surreptitiously through the curtain of rain, but she's never met the teenager so wouldn't know who she's looking for. 'Did you know she was coming?'

'No! Fuck, she's coming this way!' Thea ducks. 'I need to get out of here!'

'Go,' Lenny says. 'I'll hold the table. If you come back and she's still here, just message me and we'll head somewhere else.'

'Will you be all right on your own?'

'Orly'll be here soon.'

'Okay. See you later, then.' Thea leans forward and kisses her friend's cheek. Lenny's eyebrows have stuck together with the rain and are drooping like an old man's, and without make-up you can see age drawing its fine matrix across her brows and cheeks.

Happy birthday, old friend, Thea thinks, as she slips out of the side entrance into the rain.

WhatsApp Group: Lenny's Birthday Fest

5 participants
Lenny (group admin), Orly, Thea, Mel, Pandora

Lenny
How come you're not picking up Orls? You okay?
14.01

Lenny
Call me when you get this Orly.
14.17

Lenny
Ladies? Anyone? I feel like a right Norma no mates here.
15.04

Thea
On my way back.
15.13

Lenny
Look out for Mel. She was quite pissed. She might be lost.
15.17

20

Lenny

Now that she's alone, Lenny can't help replaying the confrontation with Rich.

It's so strange how you can go through life sure that your version of history is the authentic one. Rich was her lapdog, slightly contemptible, his faithfulness preserved in aspic over two decades. And yet in his version she is something other than the aloof love object patiently accepting worship.

She is cold, arrogant, a user.

She was never cruel to him, she simply never realised she'd hurt him, but perhaps she's been as guilty as Mel of oversimplifying things.

You don't have to be nasty to hurt. The opposite of love is not hate, it's indifference, and Rich must have felt her indifference like a knife blade. A woman like Saeeda, with all her jealousy and passion, is a far worthier mate. At least she has feelings.

Passion is something Lenny would like to possess. But what can you do when your neat, calm personality has been carved into your muscle memory over forty years? With the exception of her children, affection and fondness is all she can manage. She knows full well she is missing something. To love with grand, Shakespearean passion, to feel it just for a moment, in all its bloody colour and heat and chaos, would be quite something.

For that one moment she is tempted to call him. Just to set something off. To see what someone – Rich, or Saeeda or even herself – is capable of doing to keep hold of what they love.

Instead she takes out her phone and texts the others to come back. To enclose her in their affection, to pin her down to the earth again and dispel the sensation that her presence here will leave no trace.

Beside her the couple are leaning so close their foreheads touch. Their eyes hold each other's with mesmerised intensity, their lips breathe each other's exhalations.

She knocks back her beer and asks them to save her place while she goes for another.

'Blimey, I thought you'd died!'

Thea is walking towards the table, hair plastered to her head, cheeks mottled, her long sleeves stuck to her bony arms.

When she sits down, Lenny feels the chill radiating off her.

'You okay?'

'Just cold.'

More than cold, Lenny thinks. Thea looks properly unwell. Beneath the red splotches her face is sickly white.

'Has she gone, then?' Lenny looks around. The tent is still packed. People have settled in for the long haul.

'I couldn't see her when I came in.'

She leans across the table. 'If she's really that bad, shouldn't you say something to Bruno?'

Thea shrugs, dully. 'Say what? *Your daughter's a bitch? It's her or me?*'

'Maybe he needs to hear it. Sounds like she could do with some boundaries.'

'Bit late for that.' Thea draws patterns on the table with the rain dripping from her hair.

'Still, you only have to put up with her for another few months, right? And then she's off to uni.'

Thea nods.

This flat mood is uncharacteristic. Perhaps Thea's been doing some soul-searching too. It can't be easy, being the bit of stuff with the big four-oh approaching. Has Bruno got it in him for one more trade-in?

'Want a drink? Maybe a shot to warm you up?'

Thea shakes her head. *After all that big talk earlier*, Lenny thinks about saying, then decides against it.

'Wonder where Mel is. She's probably pulled. Maybe that guy at Earthfields.'

'Yeah.'

'Do you think we should go looking for her?'

Thea looks up. 'This place is over a thousand acres.'

'Did she turn her phone off again?'

'I guess so, in case T . . . Tr . . .' Thea breaks off as her body is gripped by a shudder strong enough to rock the table.

Frowning, Lenny takes her friend's hand. It's ice cold. There's not enough flesh on Thea's bones to keep her warm. If they don't get her into dry clothes, she might very well develop hypothermia.

'Put this on, right now.'

Thea doesn't protest, just takes the hoodie Lenny passes across the table and pulls it on over her thin top.

'Have you been wandering about like this for an hour?'

Thea nods. 'I was looking for something for the kids.'

'I suppose I should get something for my two. Did you find anything?'

'No.'

'Okay.' Lenny stands. 'Let's get you back to the tent. We should check on Orly anyway. She's not picking up her phone or checking messages.'

The rain has lightened but the relentlessness of the drizzle is almost worse. People are no longer running and shrieking for shelter, but huddling outside bars and stalls, their expressions etched with a grim determination to carry on enjoying themselves. All the colour has leached from the flags and banners, and they hang drab and limp.

The two women trudge under the metal sign and out onto the main track, blotched with puddles and almost deserted. Those who are out are swaddled in disposable yellow macs, their heads down, hopping from high ground to high ground.

They have outstayed their welcome and the land wants rid of them, Lenny thinks as her flip-flops sink into the mud, to tend its wounds and cleanse itself of the contaminants they have left behind.

She thinks of her children. They'll be having their tea in the warm. As a consolation for her absence, Lenny asked Jeanne to give them their favourite: macaroni cheese with bacon followed by tinned peaches and squirty cream. It was always Lenny's favourite food too. The 1950s fare her parents had been brought up with and didn't have the imagination or inclination to stray from when it was their turn to provide.

They didn't understand when she told them she wanted to come here that first time. They watched from the doorstep as Mel came to collect her, their faces etched with anxiety that over the course of that three-day period she would get pregnant or drunk or addicted to hard drugs. Or that her Christian faith – long dead by that time, as it happened – would be corrupted by the Bacchanalian revels.

She feels a stab of sorrow that her children came too late to meet them. Perhaps an extra generation would have sloughed off their awkwardness and worry and made them wonderful grandparents. Old-fashioned indulgent: cakes and sweets and inappropriate gifts like Swiss Army knives and pellet guns. The musty comfort of a polyester hug.

She pauses for Thea to catch up. The sandals that must be expensive – everything of Thea's is – are caked in mud and the water has already began to peel up the insole. But Thea doesn't seem to care. Her gaze is directed straight ahead, and it seems to take great effort to place one foot down in front of the other. Sometimes she winces.

As they approach Earthfields, Lenny can smell the savoury

musk of the bonfire. She pauses beneath the metal sign and scans for Mel. As soon as the smoke drifts over, her chest tightens and she pats her pocket for the inhaler the medic gave her. Still there.

There's something hellish about Earthfields in the rain: slick dancing bodies are silhouetted against red flames, the only colour left in the landscape.

Thea comes to stand beside her.

'Can you see her?' Lenny says.

'No.'

But Baldric's inscrutable gaze is fixed on them from beneath the awning of her stall. She has painted her face with a swirling Celtic design and the effect is intimidating. Why would you do such a thing? There seems to be some huge expanse of human experience that exists behind a door Lenny will never have the key to.

They carry on down the track, which is growing busier with people heading back to the campsite to seek shelter. The coat has slipped off the gatepost and been trampled into the mud. The tractor runnels have flooded and they must step into dark water to cross into the field.

Lenny has to clench her toes to keep her flip-flops on as they trudge across the grass. The day has become so gloomy that some of the tents are aglow with torchlight, but not theirs. She walks faster, leaving Thea hobbling along behind. Reaching the tent, she drops to her knees in the wet grass and pulls up the zip. Inside, all is silence. She crawls to the inner tent and unzips the door.

Two figures are curled like bulky caterpillars under the sleeping bags.

She exhales.

'They're here!' she calls back to Thea, then crawls inside with a sense of relief that is out of proportion to the short-lived separation.

The interior of the tent is blessedly warm and fugged with body smells. Beneath the drumming of the rain is the sound of deep, peaceful breathing, amplified in the enclosed space. Lenny takes a jumper out of her case and pulls it on.

Mel stirs and rolls over, nudging off the sleeping bag that covers her.

It's not Mel.

Thea comes in and stops. She stares at the good-looking man lying naked on her roll mat, then her eyes meet Lenny's.

'Well, well,' she breathes. 'Someone's a dark horse.'

Leaning across the stranger's body, Lenny strokes Orly's hair. 'Rise and shine, sleeping beauties.'

Orly murmurs and shifts.

The man grunts and turns over and his eyes flutter open. 'Shit!' He tugs the sleeping bag over his nakedness.

'Oh . . .' Orly is blinking, heavy-lidded. 'Hi, you guys.'

Thea sits down as far as possible from Ben, who is now attempting to dress himself beneath the slippery sleeping bag.

Orly sits up and rubs her eyes. 'What time is it?'

'Gone four. You've nearly missed my whole birthday.'

'Sorry. Oh my God, I didn't realise it was so late. Did you?'

Ben is pinned to the spot by the attention and shakes his head rapidly.

'Won't your friends be missing you?' Thea asks him, and Lenny catches Orly's wince.

'Sorry, yeah. I should . . .' He pulls his T-shirt on over a muscular torso and starts patting around for, presumably, his phone and wallet.

'Has Mel been back here?' Lenny says. 'She went off to look for a present for Billy but didn't come back to the bar where we were supposed to meet.'

'I wouldn't worry about it,' Orly says a little sharply, perhaps understandably, considering this abrupt end to her liaison. 'You know Mel. She's probably bumped into someone she knows.'

She detaches the hooks of her bra from the lining of the sleeping bag.

'Right,' Ben says breathlessly, his T-shirt label flapping beneath his chin. 'See you later, then.'

They all watch him depart, waiting until he has closed the zip behind him and his squelching footsteps have been lost in the pattering of the rain, then Lenny turns and raises her eyebrows.

'We leave you for a couple of hours . . .'

Orly just smiles and fastens her bra.

Back in the day, they would now have been given a blow-by-blow account of the intricacies and embarrassments of the encounter. They would know the size of Ben's dick, how quickly he came, any embarrassing noises or bodily imperfections. Lenny can remember cackling with them about Rich's desire for her to talk dirty to him. All she had to do was say *cock* to make him whimper like a baby. They would all try and slip it into conversation when he was with them. *Look at that guy, what a cock. Don't be so cocky, Lenny.*

But loyalties change. They never heard about the size of Harry's dick, or Bruno's, and Lenny can't remember why it ever seemed so necessary or hilarious to share such details.

Thea has climbed into her sleeping bag, without any apparent squeamishness at what recently occurred there. Hopefully a rest will perk her up. When the cold gets into your bones like that, it takes a while to feel better. Lenny does likewise, crawling gingerly into the sleeping bag that abutted the one they were fucking under, hoping they were considerate enough to use a condom. Orly is humming to herself as she gets dressed. Even if she never sees Ben again, this is a huge step. And who knows, maybe it will be the start of something.

The warmth and alcohol work better than any lullaby, and she only dimly hears Orly telling her that she's off for a wee before sleep whisks her into darkness.

She wakes to a cold glow filling the tent like moonlight.

Orly is looking at her phone, but as soon as she notices Lenny stir, she hits the off button and the tent is plunged back into gloom.

Lenny blinks a couple of times, letting her eyes get used to it. The ever-present radiance of the festival means it's never completely dark. She can see well enough to know that there are still just the three of them in the tent.

She checks her own phone, now very low on battery. There are no messages from Mel.

Thea is lying in the same position as when Lenny went to sleep, but a certain tension in her shoulders and her shallow breathing makes Lenny thinks she's awake too.

Sitting up, she turns on the torch dangling from the loop in the roof and the tent is washed in an LED glare.

'What time is it?'

'Ten past eight,' Orly says.

Lenny rubs her face and feels, as she has these past months, the compressed skin take longer to smooth out again. 'I guess Mel must be having a really wild time.'

In the distance, the unresting beast is still roaring, its enthusiasm undimmed. Lenny can't remember who's supposed to be on tonight. Coldplay perhaps. A band you can neither hate nor love. Vanilla, like herself, perhaps.

Thea sits up and swigs from the bottle of water in the tent pocket. She looks about as thrilled as Lenny feels at the prospect of restarting the festivities. She's about to suggest going for some food when she notices Orly's expression. Has something happened with Ben? Shuffling her sleeping bag closer, she lays a hand on Orly's hunched back. 'Hey, what's up?'

'I'm a bit worried about Mel.'

Lenny chuckles. 'Don't be silly. She'll be off somewhere having a great time. She's probably forgotten we even exist.'

'I've been . . .' Orly begins, quietly. 'I've been getting some messages.'

'From Mel?'

She shakes her head.

'What kind of messages?' Thea says.

Orly hands her phone to Lenny, and Thea shuffles over as Lenny touches the screen to make it light up.

They read silently, until the low battery warning flashes up.

'Why didn't you tell us?' Lenny says.

Orly shrugs. 'I didn't want to put a downer on things.'

'Any idea who they're from?'

'I don't recognise the number.'

'We should call it.'

'No!' Orly snatches the phone back. 'Please. Don't. I don't want to . . . hear him.'

'Could it be Trey?' Lenny says. 'Did he have your number?'

Orly shakes her head.

'Oh my God,' Thea says quietly. 'You don't think he might have done something to Mel?'

'It's me he's been threatening,' Orly says.

'Yes, but it sounds like he's been watching us. If it is Trey, then he could have grabbed her when she was on the way back to the tent.'

'How would he have got my number?'

'Let's think about this,' Lenny says. 'Mel goes off in broad daylight to get a present for Billy and hasn't come back yet. You start getting these messages when, Orly?'

'Around eleven.'

'Right, so we'd just got to the bar about that time. If he was watching you, like he said, then he couldn't also have been watching Mel. And if he wasn't watching you, if he just sent the messages to freak you out, then it's probably not Trey, because *he* was targeting Mel.'

'It could still be some psycho who was waiting for one of us to be alone,' Thea says.

'We should call the police,' Orly says.

Thea snorts. 'Are you serious? You think they haven't got better things to do in this place than investigate creepy messages? Leaving a pair of knickers isn't really up there with assault and rape.'

'Yes, but that might be exactly what's happened to Mel.'

'In which case, what are we doing sitting here?' Thea says. 'We should go and find her.'

They emerge from the tent into the damp evening air. The sky is asbestos grey, the air misted with rain. Lenny suppresses a prickle of anxiety. Her breathing is never great in this weather.

'I doubt she'd go to any gigs without us,' Orly says. 'So maybe check the bars. The Village Green and Earthfields.'

'Someone should stay here,' Thea says. 'In case she comes back.'

'One of you will have to do that,' Orly says. 'My phone's almost out of juice.'

'Mine hasn't got much either,' Lenny says.

'So no one make any calls unless it's absolutely necessary,' Thea says. 'I'll stay here.'

Orly and Lenny start trudging back to the gate. The water has penetrated the crust of mud and turned it to slurry, and Lenny's flip-flops suck and pull at every step.

'This is madness,' she mutters. 'She could be anywhere.'

'What else do we do, though?'

'Mel's a grown-up. Even if she stays out all night, she'll be back in the morning. All her stuff's at the tent.' She sighs. It's not Orly's fault. 'Look, Billy's leaving for uni soon, right? She's bound to be feeling a bit weird. She was pretty drunk when she left us. She probably just wanted to party, drown her sorrows, and celebrate too. She's lucky she's still young enough. By the time my kids leave, I'll be getting my bus pass.'

She clamps her lips together, kicking herself at her tactlessness. Orly may never know the bittersweetness of losing a child to adulthood.

They walk on in silence, past the trampled coat, and onto the track. To change the subject, Lenny says, 'So you and Ben, then?'

Orly smiles. 'He's lovely.'

'Did you get his number?'

'He took mine, but I doubt I'll hear from him again.'

Lenny chuckles. 'That's the spirit.'

'Well, look at me. I'm pushing forty.'

'I would.'

Orly laughs.

'Well, whatever, there's plenty more where that came from.'

Orly stops, so Lenny does too. Orly takes her hands. 'Thank you.'

'What for?'

'For this. Bringing us all here. I wasn't really looking forward to it, and it's had its moments, but I'm glad I came.'

'Yes, it's been a laugh.'

'More than that. I'd forgotten I had friends. Good ones that I didn't need to hide things from. I should have known you'd always have my back.'

'Always,' Lenny says, and pulls her into a hug. Perhaps she hasn't been such a bad friend after all.

They reach Earthfields and make a cursory check – after all, she and Thea looked here earlier on – then move on to the Village Green.

The little hill they basked on yesterday is now churned mud and rubbish. Some of the bunting has come down in the rain and been trampled underfoot. The clientele has aged, greyed and sagged. A few bedraggled revellers stand around the folk stage nodding their heads in time to mournful fiddle music.

After a pass through the beer tent, they trudge round every stall and food outlet. The air is filled with the sour smell of proving dough: one stall boasts it will have fresh bread by 4 a.m. Lenny thinks of taking the kids to GAIL's on a Saturday morning and buying a seeded rye and cinnamon buns to munch on the way home through the park.

They're passing back out onto the main track when Lenny's phone rings. She snatches it from her pocket. It's Mel.

'Hello, stranger!'

It's a video call, and for a moment Lenny can make no sense of the image on the screen. There's no answer from Mel, only a rasping sound that she eventually works out must be heavy breathing, very close to the mic.

'Mel?' Orly says, leaning over Lenny's shoulder. 'Where are you?'

Now Lenny can make out that what they are seeing is Mel's face, very close to the camera. The part not covered by a cascade of hair is squashed against something. It's the ground. Yes, the lines on her cheeks are blades of grass. She's lying on the ground.

'Mel?' Orly says again. 'Say something. Are you okay?'

But Mel's eyes are closed and that rasping breathing is the only sound. Behind her head there's a blotch of grey, against which dark bars or lines are drawn. Tree trunks?

'What's that coming out of her mouth?' Orly says. 'That white stuff?'

Lenny squints at the screen. 'She must have been sick. Mel, can you—'

The call ends.

She immediately tries to call back, but the line is now dead.

The two of them stare at their reflections in the dark screen, waiting for it to burst into life.

'Do we call the police?' Orly breathes.

'We should keep the line free in case she calls back.'

They go over to a food van and stand in its radiated warmth, staring at the phone. Every now and then Lenny touches the screen to make it light up, but there are no more calls and no messages.

Then, finally, after several minutes, it does ring.

Lenny immediately swipes to accept the call, but they both have time to see that the image onscreen is Thea's profile picture.

'Any sign of her?' Thea says. Lenny puts the phone on speaker.

'She video-called us. She's collapsed somewhere. It looked like she was off her face on drink or drugs.'

'Mel doesn't do drugs,' Thea says.

'Maybe her drink was spiked,' Orly says.

'If it was,' Lenny says, 'we need to find her, quickly. Get her to the medic tent.'

'Wouldn't the police find her quicker?' Orly persists. 'With dogs or heat-seeking equipment?'

'This is the last night of GillFest,' Thea says. 'They'll be rushed off their feet. One more pissed woman isn't going to get them jumping to it. Could you see where she was?'

'It was really dark,' Lenny says. 'And quiet.'

'Did you see the shapes behind her?' Orly says. 'I thought they were trees.'

'So she could be in a wood,' Thea says. 'There's the one here – she might have tried to get home and got disorientated. Wait a minute. I'll get the site map up on my phone.'

In the silence they can hear her breathing and the rustling as she shifts position in the tent.

'Right, so there's a strip of woodland by the teepees, where you shagged Rich . . . and also a sort of copse behind the fairground.'

'Okay,' Lenny says. 'We'll look there.'

'You should split up,' Thea says. 'It'll be quicker, and if she has taken drugs we need to find her as fast as possible.'

Orly starts to say something, but Thea speaks over her. 'I'm here, so I'll search the wood by the campsite.'

'Okay,' Lenny says. 'In that case I'll do the one by the teepees, and Orly, can you do the bit by the fairground?'

'Umm . . .' Orly's eyes are wide and fearful in the gloom. 'What about Trey? If he's still at the fair, he might recognise me.'

'He could be anywhere,' Lenny says. 'Just keep your eyes peeled.'

'Right,' Thea interrupts. 'No luck and we meet back at the tent, otherwise call each other.'

'But my phone battery . . .' Orly says.

'Just borrow someone else's.' Thea hangs up.

'Okay,' Lenny says briskly. 'I'm going this way. You need to go that way, past the toilets and then right. Just stay in the well-lit areas until you get there. It doesn't sound like that wood's too big.'

Orly bites her lip, nods and sets off. Lenny starts walking in the opposite direction.

'Len.'

She turns back. Orly is a dark shape silhouetted against the lights and colours beyond, but her voice is so quiet Lenny has to strain to hear her.

'Mel honestly looked too fucked to make that call. This is going to sound mad, but you don't think somebody else made it to try and . . . and lure us into the woods?'

Lenny's arms droop at her sides. What she thinks is that Mel is pissed or stoned or both, and is drifting in and out of consciousness. She's lying face down, so if she vomits again she won't choke on it. Either someone will find her or she'll creep guiltily back to the tent feeling like death whenever she sobers up. What Lenny does *not* think is that it's a good idea to go wandering about in the ever-shifting crowds, in encroaching dark, looking for a needle in a haystack. They're not children any more. They're no longer responsible for one another's safety. She'll give it half an hour, and then she's going back to the tent.

'Let's just try to keep calm,' she says. 'I'm sure she's absolutely fine. Just have a quick look around, then come back.'

'You don't think,' Orly murmurs, 'that Trey might have done this to her?'

'Please stop worrying. Everything will be fine.'

Orly nods again, then turns and walks away.

Lenny passes out of the field and into the craziness of the festival's last night.

@GillingwaterFestival
Glad you're all having such a great last night, but the police have asked us to remind you to please be sensible when it comes to cooking and the management of the bonfires that are such a brilliant and atmospheric part of the festival.

@GillingwaterFestival
We know this sounds obvious, but please don't throw fireworks onto your fire. Don't use petrol. Don't let it spread or get too high. If you can see it over the hedges, it's too big! Cheers, all!

21

Orly

Orly walks quickly along the edge of the track, where the shadows are deeper. It might be her state of mind, but the atmosphere seems to have changed tonight. The festival-goers look different: their grins are leering, their eyes skitter, their voices are loud and braying. She feels like a sane person trapped in an asylum.

She passes the entrance to the standing stones. Through the willow fronds orange light is flickering. A midsummer bone-fire. She thinks of what the puppet man said about evil spirits. Perhaps they haven't performed the correct rites, or chanted the right incantations, and the spirits have been let loose on them.

She hurries past to where the track branches off to the right. Diving across the relentless surge of people, she passes under the colourful banner and into the buzz of the fair. Everyone is drunk. Men bellow like steers when they win a keyring from the hook-a-duck. Women screw their faces up as they lean over and release darts that end up on the rubber floor. The Ferris wheel creaks round, a black skeleton against the cloud mass.

And everywhere she seems to see Trey: lurking amongst groups of men, in the shadows behind the rides, or reflected in the windows of the operators' booths. It must be him sending those hateful messages. When she was with the others they receded from her mind, but now the fear is back. It's not just the spitefulness of the words but the intent behind them that makes her blood run cold. Either the texter wants to frighten her or he genuinely means her harm.

She stops by the swing chairs and clutches the barrier rail. Trey must be a psychopath. If they had just given him the case when he asked for it, they would have been fine. Why did Mel have to be so bolshie about it? She always did get them into trouble with her gobbiness.

A surge of anger at her friend makes her turn on her heel and head back towards the entrance.

But as she passes a stall, there is a loud bang followed by a metallic clatter. She staggers, almost floored by shock, and her head snaps round.

This time it really is Trey, aiming a rifle at a whey-faced boy in a red-curtained box. The gun fires. A stack of cans behind the boy collapses. Trey punches the air and the girls beside him whoop. The boy hands him a giant Winnie-the-Pooh with the flat milk-eyed stare of the habitually stoned.

Orly hurries away but doesn't get far.

Blocking her path is a looming wall of badly drawn grins bleeding spray paint. The fun house.

She looks back. Trey is turning away from the stall, the stuffed toy riding proudly on his shoulder. She hurries on, but she's not looking where she's going and clatters into the queue barriers outside the fun house.

Trey looks up.

Their eyes meet.

Slapping a five-pound note onto the counter of the ticket booth, Orly sprints past and enters the lurid gloom of the ride.

The first part of the fun entails squeezing her adult body through foam rollers intended for children and landing awkwardly on her neck. She doesn't pause to see if he has followed her in, but runs on to the hall of mirrors. She could stay here, slipping in and out of the mirrors, her reflection confounding him at every turn. But this is not a film and it's perfectly obvious which is the real flesh-and-blood her, and which a tinny, warped reflection. She bursts out onto a moving walkway and manages to keep her feet until the moment she steps off the other side, when the sudden solidity of the ground makes her plunge forward into curtains of scarlet fabric.

Feeling her way through the swathes of material, she makes contact with the wall. Sliding down it, she sits with her knees pulled up to her chest. In the muffled darkness a feeling of calm comes over her. She is safe.

The fabric that brushes her cheek smells of winter months spent folded in containers in damp warehouses. What might once have been velvet pile has worn away to the webbing beneath.

Closing her eyes, she drops her head back. The metal wall clangs dully, but no one would hear it over the music.

She goes still. A man's voice, from the direction she just came from.

The voice gets closer. Complaining that he is too big to get through the rollers, that he will jar his back. A woman tells him laughingly that he shouldn't try and walk out on his arms but must do a roly-poly like James Bond when he jumps off a high building.

There is an *oof* and the man cries, 'Mish Moneypenny, you're a genius!'

A moment later the curtains waft as the pair run through, laughing, before settling back against Orly's face like art smocks on pegs.

Trey has not followed her in. In which case, he must be outside waiting for her to emerge. She could just stay here until he gives up or thinks she has crept out another way.

But what about Mel?

Twenty-four years ago, Orly was in this same position, too ashamed and scared to do the right thing. Is she really going to do that again? Let down her friend in her hour of need, out of sheer cowardice? During the long months of Harry's illness, she witnessed true bravery. Isn't it about time she did something worthy of his memory?

She gets up.

The webbing tears as she draws the curtain back and steps out into the final room. There up ahead is the exit. A dark arch milling with shadows.

She betrayed Pan, but she will not abandon Mel. If Trey is there, she will confront him, find out what he's done to her, and rescue her. Striding across a floor that revolves beneath her, she steps out into a fairground night that smells of burnt sugar.

Trey is nowhere to be seen.

She turns in a circle.

He's gone, along with his female companions.

But beyond the bouncy slide, down which people are hurling themselves whilst managing to hold their bottles of beer upright, she can make out the outstretched arms of tall trees.

Crossing the threshold of the wood is like stepping through a door that closes behind her. For a moment the darkness is total, and all sounds – the dizzy Wurlitzer, the howling of the ghost train, the ringing of the test-your-strength machine – are deadened to silence.

She stands still, waiting for her eyes to adjust.

Slowly, trunk by pale trunk, the trees shape around her. The copse is denser than the one at the campsite, and looks far older. The trunks are broad and gnarled, the branches huge, heavy and moss-covered, criss-crossing one another, locking arms to repel intruders.

Before she can change her mind, she sets her feet in motion, ducking under a branch to pass deeper into the wood.

The outer ring smells of piss, but the smell fades as she moves deeper in. No one wants to go far to relieve themselves, and it soon becomes apparent why. The forest floor is covered in ivy or some other creeper that loops around her feet as she walks, and sometimes rears up to trip her. There are thorns too, snagging the thin skin of her ankles. The coloured lights of the fair are swallowed almost immediately, leaving her in near-total darkness.

Taking her phone from her pocket, she is about to turn on the torch app when she remembers there's barely any battery left. She'll have to manage with the light from the screen.

She hits the button and blue light spills across the woodland floor.

Each leaf and thorn is picked out in graphic detail. She just manages to avoid treading on a huge slug the shape and colour of a corpse's thumb.

Don't think about corpses.

Raising the phone, she directs the light higher, between the trees. The effect is unpleasant. An invitation, almost, for someone to step out from between those sharply drawn trunks.

It is only now that she remembers that in the video call, behind Mel's head, there was sky. There is no sky here, just the dense canopy pressing down on her. This is the wrong wood.

She turns and begins to walk, as quickly as she can, back towards the lights. How did they get so far away? Her breathing and the snap of twigs beneath her feet are loud in the close silence, but in the noise of the fair, a scream out here would be as faint as an owl cry.

And then she does scream, dropping the phone into the undergrowth, where it lies, bleeding light. A message has come through, the alert cutting jaggedly through the silence.

It's not necessarily him; it might be one of the others.

She picks it up.

I'm watching you.

Her whimper is that of prey.

The phone trills again.

I'm coming for you.

WhatsApp Group: Lenny's Birthday Fest

5 participants
Lenny (group admin), Orly, Thea, Mel, Pandora

Thea
Mel we got your message. Stay where you are we're coming for you.
19.24

Thea
Mel darling, I dont know if you can see these messages but we will find you I promise.
20.17

Thea
Can you try and call us Mel please?
20.23

Thea
Hang in there darling Mel. Stay awake for us xxxx
20.35

22

Lenny

Lenny tramps down the track, back towards Earthfields, her flip-flops sinking into fag-strewn sludge and God knows what else.

But the momentary irritation at Mel passes when she remembers that Thea is right: Mel would never willingly take drugs, not after the death of Billy's friend. Nor has Lenny ever seen her in the sort of catatonic state that she seemed to be in on the call. Booze always gives Mel a sort of demonic vitality that enables her still to be dancing on the tables when the sun comes up. Or at least it did when they were teenagers. Which leaves two options: either someone has spiked her drink, or she's been attacked.

In either case the most obvious suspect is Trey.

After that one glimpse at the fairground, Lenny doesn't know if she would recognise Trey again. This is probably for the best, because she'd be sorely tempted to confront him, and that sort of arsehole might very well be carrying a knife.

Fucking men. You only have to look at the games and films they enjoy to realise they're only interested in screwing and fighting.

A fresh stab of guilt.

She has her own little man. A boy who draws dogs with flowers in their ears, and apologises for upsetting his mummy. No, for every Trey and Rich there is a Jackson, a yellow daisy opening its face to the sun.

People stream past endlessly, screeching and cackling and

singing. There's a smell of unwashed bodies, dirty hair and woodsmoke. The atmosphere is febrile. She'd dismissed what the puppet guy said about pagan rituals and human sacrifice, but passing among these revellers, a collective murderous madness seems infinitely possible.

This is not her world. The world of sensation, risk and wild abandon belongs to the likes of Mel. Lenny doesn't know the rules.

A woman turns her ankle in a pothole and sprawls into her path. Lenny reaches down to help her up.

The woman snarls, 'Fuck off,' then clambers to her feet and limps off.

It's not often that Lenny feels intimidated. At the start of her career, when people were still challenging her in meetings, trying to step on her to get a leg up in the eyes of their superiors, she would simply wait patiently for them to finish speaking, a faint smile on her lips. Because even if they were factually correct, she would always be able to turn the argument around, make herself look good and her challenger stupid. It wasn't a method she continued with for long. Once she had underlings, she was sensible enough not to undermine them, but to build them up, to reward them, to possess their loyalty. No, clever, powerful people have never bothered her. It's the weak that scare her. People who have been pushed into a corner they see no way out of, apart from through you.

She was mugged once, by an emaciated woman who might have been twenty or a hundred and twenty. So desperate was she for the next hit of whatever ravaged her body that she held a knife to Lenny's throat.

What a waste was all Lenny could think as she waited for the woman to complete the search of her bag. To die here in a gutter at the hands of the type of person she had forgotten existed. Snuffed out by the most basic human animal to feed its basic wants.

And now she feels it again, that vulnerability: the softness of the body that surrounds her diamond-hard mind. One of these

243

drunk, stoned revellers might be made murderous by something as innocuous as being helped up.

As she steps out to cross the track that leads to the toilets, she's almost run over by a tractor.

Its trailer is full of overflowing drums and the driver makes no concession to the drunks shambling up the track by beeping his horn or slowing; just trundles across to the hedge on the other side, gets out and opens a gate.

Beyond the gate is a fallow field.

Lenny brings up an image of the site map in her mind. The field is out of bounds, but if she crossed it, it would bring her directly to the wood behind the teepees in Earthfields, cutting off the corner.

The driver is climbing back into his cab.

Before he can close it, Lenny runs up to the door. 'Excuse me!'

He turns. It's the bearded guy who took the drug bin away, without his cap tonight.

'Are you going to Earthfields? It's just I think my friend might be in difficulties in the wood there. Could I have a lift across the field?'

He jerks his head. 'Get in.' His strong West Country accent brings with it the sweet aura of her childhood, and she thinks again of her quiet, aged parents awaiting her return from the wild escapade of her first GillFest.

Jogging through the vehicle's headlights, she climbs up and perches on the edge of the seat.

The door closes differently from car doors. Some mechanism clicks into place and there doesn't appear to be a handle, just a series of mysterious knobs and levers. Presumably one or more of them has to be manipulated to allow egress.

The man settles beside her and performs a series of purposeful movements that make the engine roar. They jump forward and begin trundling across the mud, puddles bouncing glare from the headlights. After they've passed through the gateway, he brings the vehicle to a halt once more, yanks up the handbrake – that at least she can recognise – and gets out. She hears a clang and, glancing in the rear-view mirror, sees that instead of the usual five-bar construction, the gate is a solid slab of grey metal, half as tall again as the driver. Closing it immediately extinguishes the lights of the festival, and the field beyond the headlights becomes a lake of darkness.

He gets back in and shuts the door with enough force that the whole cab shakes. This sets off a little tinkling from the clutch of keyrings hanging from the rear-view mirror. A sleepy-eyed turtle is smiling at her. Beside it a grubby yellow emoji winks.

They move off, bouncing across the rutted field. There is nothing else in the world except for their little sealed box and the illuminated cones of mud ahead of them.

'Want me to come wiv you to look for yer friend?'

She glances at him. 'Really?'

'S'no problem.'

'Thanks.'

Silence descends once more.

They hit a particularly deep rut and she gasps and instinctively clutches the dashboard. The jolt makes the keyrings revolve and the friendly face of the turtle disappears.

She glances at the driver. He's still facing forward, but a smile plays at the corner of his mouth, and the consequent stretching of his lip exposes a line of bare skin in his moustache, running down from his nose. A scar. There's a little notch in his upper lip that keeps it from meeting the lower one. He has a hare lip.

The keyrings continue to swing and a new one comes into view. It's just like one she used to have on her school bag. A pink Care Bear called Love-a-Lot that Rich bought her – she'd assumed ironically. She leans forward and squints in the poor light.

The teddy's right eye has been painted over with dripping blobs of red nail varnish.

She sits back sharply.

It's her keyring. She is one hundred per cent certain. She defaced it for a joke and Rich was upset. So upset, she thought at the time, that he'd taken the keyring off her bag.

The driver's eyes are fixed straight ahead, but she senses a fresh alertness in him.

'Are you Farmer Woollacott's son?' In the close atmosphere of the cab, her voice is swallowed immediately.

The smile becomes a grin. 'Wondered when you'd figure it out. I remember you. There were always a nice view from upstairs in the red barn.'

Her breath speeds up and her hand moves automatically to the door handle, but there isn't one.

'Did you like the present I left you? Thought you might want 'em back.'

She opens her mouth and closes it again. He took her keyring, and he took her knickers, which he left outside the tent the day before yesterday. He has been spying on them, just as he spied on her and Rich twenty years ago.

She pictures the child creeping across the dusty floor of the barn towards where they moved rhythmically, oblivious, absorbed in one another's face and skin. Stretching out an arm and clawing the scrap of fabric towards him. Cosseting it, sniffing it, possibly even masturbating with it for twenty years, until he found a new and unsettling use for it. A fist closes around her chest.

The tractor slows to a halt. The keyrings chatter. Darkness laps at the windows.

'Why have you stopped?'

She tries to get out, but her panicked fingers bump like moths against the glass and plastic. Her breath is coming in sharp gasps that make her vision jump.

Without replying, he gets out of the cab and disappears into the darkness.

Is he coming round to her side to drag her out into the middle of the field and rape her? Kill her? Is that what he did to Mel?

She breaks out in a sweat as she rattles every lever and knob, and it immediately chills on the exposed parts of her skin, thanks to the cold air pouring over her back.

The other door is open!

Throwing herself across the jutting arm of the handbrake and out of the open door, she lands with a jarring thud on the wet grass. She scrambles to her feet and stumbles away from the search beams of the tractor, into the darkness.

'Where you goin'?' calls an affable voice.

There is a metallic clink behind her. A shotgun? Fuck.

Now that her eyes have got used to the darkness, she can make out the faint line between hedge and sky. He is bigger and heavier than her. If she can make it to the hedge and crawl through, he won't know which direction to follow her. Unless he has a torch.

Stupid. Of course he has a torch.

It switches on behind her, picking out her shape in stark detail.

She runs faster, legs and arms wheeling, lungs screaming.

She sees the ridge of mud a split second before her foot lands on it, but has no time to change direction. Her ankle twists and she is thrown to the ground. Without pausing to catch the breath that has been knocked out of her, she starts crawling across the rutted ground. When she does try to breathe, barely a sip makes it past her throat. She is on the brink of an asthma attack.

Behind her there is music and chanting, as if she has been offered up to some hellish coven.

She stops moving.

Beneath the music is laughter, the murmur of voices. A voice shouts that the meditation class will begin in five minutes.

Rising to her knees, she turns round.

It's not torchlight that's throwing her trembling shadow onto the mud. The metallic clink was the sound of another gate opening, to reveal the pretty lights and bonfire glow of Earthfields.

Farmer Woollacott's son is standing by the open door of the tractor cab.

'You wanna go through, then?'

Her chest relaxes. She gets to her feet and starts walking towards the lights.

As she passes the cab, she feels his eyes on her. If he were going to do something, surely he would have done it in the seclusion of the field, but as she passes through the gateway, back into the warmth and light of the festival, she cannot shake the thought that she told him where she was going. Into the woods. Alone.

The tractor growls across the mud behind her.

Rich

Saeeda has finished with me. Thanks a bunch Len. Youve royally fucked up my life for a 2nd time.
19.14

Rich

Are you seriously going toignore me?
19.23

Rich

In that case Ill drink that fucking rum Igot you myself.
19.29

Rich

People like you make me sicj you think you are Such a london bigshot you can shit all over nobdies like me? You need tyo be taught a lesson
20.45

Rich

Im sorry didnt me an that
20.47

Rich

We have top talk about this faceto face
20.47

Rich

I fucking love yoy len. We should be together I need to make you see
20.49

23
Mel

Dark. Hurt. Help. Billy. Colours. Said you would come back.
Sick. Water, stars. Cold. Would help me. Billy. Don't leave me.
Cold, scared . . . said you would come back. Wet, sick, dying.
Can't move. I can't feel my hands . . . am I dying?
  Billy.

@SimonJJ1975
Anyone know what happened to that woman they just pulled out of the woods? She looked pretty fucked up @GillingwaterFestival #GillFest25

@GingerNSpicey
Replying to @SimonJJ1975 and @GillingwaterFestival
Is she dead?

@MaddoxMaddoxMaddox
Replying to @GillingwaterFestival @SimonJJ1975 and @GingerNSpicey
Am literally watching the paramedics treat her. Theres a lot of blood. Looks like a head injury.

@Kulio42069
Replying to @GillingwaterFestival @SimonJJ1975 @GingerNSpicey and @MaddoxMaddoxMaddox
Shouldnt have got so wasted. Prob fell over trying to piss in the woods.

@MaddoxMaddoxMaddox
Replying to @GillingwaterFestival @SimonJJ1975 @GingerNSpicey and @Kulio42069
They just pulled a sheet over her head.

24

Thea

She waits, rocking backwards and forwards on her jutting sit bones, the ground unforgiving beneath the roll mat. Her breathing is so loud in the stuffy little prison. She tries to steady it, but forcing it only makes her chest shudder.

She can't remember much about what happened in the wood, she was so scared. In and out, that was it, and then a dash back to the tent. Her face and bare shoulders are damp and she takes a jumper from her case and mops them, then pulls the jumper on. The touch of the luxurious fabric is an immediate comfort. A soft mother's hand on her back. There, there. It will be all right.

Her fucking mother.

Never a glance at her school report. Taking her for her first sunbed session at thirteen. Always putting her on a diet because they were 'both' too fat. All your fault, you stupid bitch.

She checks her phone to see if there have been any messages or calls from the others.

Nothing.

Bruno hasn't called either. Not in three days. It proves she was right.

Don't cry, don't cry, don't cry.

Think of the children. They're the important ones. Everything she does, everything she *is* is for them.

They don't understand, the others. They think she hankers after money and attention. The proof is right in front of them

– her body, her face. They don't understand that this is work: her job is to be beautiful and thin and vivacious, and that isn't easy, and it isn't painless.

All she wants is to save her children from suffering.

She messages first Lewis, then Jade.

What you doing?

Watching TV in my room

What you watching?

Predator

Turn that off, baby, it's really scary!

Soc said I could. He said it was good

Where's Bruno?

Out

The curt monosyllable has the power of a jab to her solar plexus. Out where? With who?

Hey, Jadey Button, how are you doing?

Socrates helped me cut my hair

Ooh. Show me a pic!

Jade sends a selfie. It's clear from her red eyes that she has been crying. And clear why from the tufted remains of her fine blonde curls.

She looks so awful, so utterly, comically ridiculous, that Socrates is bound to have put it all over his social media.

Thea left her children in Bruno's care, and they are being worse than neglected; they are being tortured. For a game. Soc and Anais have sensed that the wind has changed direction. Thea and her children don't matter any more and can be tormented like mice in the claws of a cat before having their heads bitten off.

She was right to do what she did.

She was right.

She was right.

@GillingwaterFestival
Are you all ready for Coldplay to close #GillFest25?! What a way to end our quarter-century. We hope you've all had the time of your lives. Sleep tight and travel safely tomorrow! We love you all.

25

Orly

The phone screen blinks off and the message disappears, but the words are seared into her brain.

I'm watching you. I'm coming for you.

Dropping to her knees, Orly curls into a foetal position, arms protecting her head, waiting for the blow.

The tiny rustles her shivering produces in the damp undergrowth are magnified by her terror. A shiver becomes a spider becomes a fox becomes a man.

And yet the blow doesn't come. She cannot make herself any smaller, cannot screw her body into a tighter contortion, and soon her neck starts to hurt.

She raises her head a fraction to listen. The sounds are there, but now she hears them for what they are: the wary starts and stops of tiny animals. There's no hint of a larger creature nearby, unless he's keeping very quiet.

Another minute passes.

She unfurls and gets to her feet, breathing as shallowly as she can. Her phone is still glowing from the last, horrible message. Holding it out in front of her, she turns in a circle.

Tree trunks.

More tree trunks.

Knots and boles look momentarily like heads and faces, and the sudden swoop of an owl between them almost stops her heart.

Is anyone there? she wants to call, but her vocal cords won't work.

She stumbles forward, towards the lights. Then the phone buzzes, insectile. Another message.

Your gonna die bitch.

The fear hollows her out. She feels so light she might float off into the trees, snag in the branches like a helium balloon.

With numb fingers she presses the call button.

A larger version of the thumbnail picture comes up onscreen. Now she can see that it's not a person at all, but an extended middle finger with a face drawn on the nail between a felt-tipped beanie and a coloured midsection.

The image blurs as the little arrow scrolls upwards.

She listens so hard the silence becomes an audible hiss, but there is no sound of a phone ringing. Then again, if he were stalking her, he would turn it off.

The call connects. She raises the phone slowly to her ear.

'Hello?' A man's voice, normal pitch, without a real-world echo. He is not here in the wood, then.

Her breath bursts out in an inarticulate sob.

'Hello? Who's . . . Oh, wait a minute . . . Fuck!'

The voice moves away from the phone. 'It's her! She's fucking crying!' The man on the other end starts to laugh, a cruel hyena squawk. Behind the laugh she hears music, chatter, laughter – all the ambient noise of the festival.

'Give it here,' says a voice she recognises. Then the voice comes close. 'Hello, Orly.'

Orly blinks at the rising arc of the Ferris wheel visible through the trees, its precarious little rusting boxes moving through the dark.

'Mel?' she breathes.

'Try again.'

Her body is no longer light. She slumps against a tree trunk, her mouth slack.

'I know what you did and I know why you did it, you pathetic cow. You were just so jealous when I joined, weren't you? Terrified that your precious friends might like me better.' Pandora is drunk enough to be slurring, and Orly can hear little bullets of spit hitting the mic. 'Because you knew how boring you were, even back then. And you're still boring now. Count yourself lucky you're a widow. It's the only thing that's vaguely interesting about you . . . What's the matter, Orly? Cat got your tongue?'

Orly swallows. Her throat feels like it's been coated in bonfire ash.

'You tried to ruin my future, but I've got news for you. I'm fine. Fucking fine. See how much my boyfriend loves me? I had to stop him from coming round to beat the shit out of you. You, on the other hand, what have you got except for—'

Orly ends the call, pushes herself off the support of the tree trunk and walks unsteadily out of the wood.

The lights blur and pixelate as she passes through the fair.

She just needs to be cuddled and comforted, but there's no one here to tell her that everything's going to be okay, no one who loves her unconditionally. Only two of those people exist now, and they are curled on the sofa, watching *Foyle's War* in the warm comfort of her childhood home.

The others have been good about it – what she did to Pan – but they had no choice. They wouldn't want to ruin Lenny's birthday, so they're pretending sympathy, but she suspects she might never hear from them again – well, not Mel at least, with her diamond-cut morality. Thea will be looking for an excuse to dump the frumpy friend who has always been a downer, even back when they were young. Always crying over a crush, or paranoid about a friendship, the one who vomited or fell over drunk and had to be looked after all night.

She can think of no reason any of them were ever her friend, except for the one Pandora so clearly articulated. Pity.

She's nothing but a burden to everybody. Perhaps she should terminate these stale relationships before they do. Delete them all from her phone to save them the trouble. Then they'll be able to sneer and judge her without guilt. It will be a relief for all.

Yes. After tomorrow, she won't contact them again. But first she'll let them know who sent the messages. At least it might short-circuit any sympathy they've been feeling for poor hard-done-by Pandora. *See, Orly was right all along, she* was *a bitch*.

But when she takes out her phone, the screen refuses to light up.

She jiggles it, scribbles across the screen. Nothing. She tries to restart it, and for a moment it wakes and performs its swirling light show, then the battery warning comes up and it dies.

That's it. No more phone.

It's almost liberating.

She considers making for the nearest bar and getting completely trashed. Alone. Free from judgement, from the pressure of trying to be good company.

Head down, she hastens her steps and soon draws near to Earthfields, but though her vision is blurred with tears, there's something different in the quality of the light, something harsh and unnatural that makes her wipe her eyes and look up.

An ambulance is parked beneath the metal sign, its blue lights strobing the darkness. She stops and stares at the stretcher laid on the floor between two crouched medics. Her blood turns to cold jelly.

A sheet has been drawn up to cover the face of the person lying there. She takes a step towards it and her knees almost give way.

Then her mind starts working again.

It's not Mel. There are no dark curls spilling out from the sheet, no suggestion of their bulk beneath it. The legs outlined by the fabric are longer and more solid than Mel's.

Relief drains all her remaining energy. As the medics lift the stretcher and load it into the back of the ambulance, Orly sits heavily on the corner of a picnic bench. The four other occupants of the bench are talking in hushed, excited tones.

'Apparently they were doing a meditation session when some-body heard a scream. Looks like she fell over and hit her head.'

'My God,' a woman says. 'Like that guy in London who got killed with one punch.'

'Didn't he bang his head on the pavement? I guess there are rocks and stuff in the wood. If she'd used the proper facilities, she'd have been okay.'

'Kills all the vegetation, apparently. Uric acid.'

They fall silent as the ambulance begins to crawl through the crowds, which part before it. The lights are still flashing but there's no siren. Too late for that.

'Why would she scream, though?' someone says quietly. 'If she fell.'

Orly totters to the nearby bar, returns with a small plastic bottle of red wine and swigs it straight down. After a few minutes it starts to work, spreading like syrup through her thoughts. She tips her head back and inhales.

The starlit sky spread out above her is beautiful. She knows from those few blissful moments with Ben that she is still capable of happiness. It has just slipped out of her grasp, drifted to the bottom of the sea: she must dive for it. At least she still has the chance. Unlike that poor woman on the stretcher.

Tipping the last wine dregs into her mouth, she gets up and sets off back to the campsite. The rain has freshened the air, and it feels somehow lighter and less dense than before, as if the sky has more room to breathe.

As she approaches the field, a wave of optimism washes over her. Everyone is fine. They will all be waiting for her in the tent, impatient to get back out and hit the festival bars for the last time. Perhaps they should watch the last-night band. Coldplay's soaring melodies will lift her out of herself, speak to her heart and her spirit. Promise her that one day everything will be yellow again.

Someone has picked up the coat, shaken off the worst of the mud and draped it back over the gate. A glove pokes from one of the sleeves, its fingers folded around a fat spliff. The other glove holds a beer bottle. She smiles as she passes, her feet sinking into ground softened by the rain.

Ben's tent is silent, its cheerful scarlet darkened to the colour of old blood, but it doesn't dampen her mood. She will catch

259

up with him later, when they're both drunk and high on the last-night vibe. Perhaps they will make love again. Somewhere completely inappropriate and spontaneous, like Lenny and Rich did.

Their own tent is lit up by phone light, and she can see shadows moving inside.

The flap is open and she ducks through.

Thea is there. Alone.

She has been crying.

Orly's good mood collapses. Thea doesn't cry. Ever. Not when Tony was put in prison, or when they kicked her out of the flat. On the phone she would say things like 'It's all good . . . things'll work out.'

Now things are clearly not good.

'What's happened?' Orly manages.

Thea shakes her head rapidly, as if trying to dislodge a fly buzzing around her skull. 'Did you find Mel?'

'No. Maybe Lenny did.'

'I can't get through to Lenny.'

'Maybe her phone's died. Mine has. Maybe she found Mel and took her to the medic tent. In which case, I guess we just wait for a call.' Orly's tone is as reassuring as she can make it. It's not often these days that she has to be the strong one.

She sits down beside Thea. 'The messages I got were from Pandora's boyfriend, so we don't need to worry about them. We're not being stalked. And I guess the medics are pretty busy tonight. I saw someone being taken off in an ambulance. Not Mel,' she adds quickly. 'Maybe someone's already found Mel and taken her to hospital. That's why Lenny's taking so long. We just need to wait for her to call.'

Thea nods and curls up on her sleeping bag. Orly lies down behind her and wraps an arm around her waist, resting her forehead on Thea's hair, still damp from the rain.

*

Time passes. Without her phone, Orly cannot tell how much, and she can't bring herself to ask Thea to look at hers. She couldn't bear to see no new messages. That would make it real, the feeling that's tugging on her sleeve, more assertively with every minute that passes. That two of her friends are now missing.

She can't stop the thought from blooming like ink in water: they're being picked off one by one.

Don't be silly. Who the hell would want to cause them harm?

Trey?

Okay, he threatened them and trashed the tent, but that would only make sense for Mel. He's never even seen Lenny.

Rich?

The outburst Lenny described suggests he's harbouring some serious resentment, and the knickers were probably left by him. But why would he bother hurting Mel?

Jay?

But as Pandora promised, her boyfriend would have come for Orly first.

She rolls over and stares up at the apex of the roof, then wrinkles her nose. There's a smell in here. Coppery, plucking at the back of her throat.

Oh God, it's the period knickers she stowed in her case. Ripened by the heat, they've made the whole tent stink like a butcher's shop. Her face burns with shame. Is that why Ben made such a fast exit earlier on? Sitting up, she leans towards her case. But the lid is shut and the smell doesn't seem to be any worse over here.

Beneath the increasingly febrile sounds of the festival night, Orly can hear Thea's rapid shallow breathing. This is stupid. How long are they going to wait here, going mad with worry? They need to do something, anything.

'We should call the police now.'

Thea says nothing.

'I haven't got any battery left. Can you do it?'

Thea sits up. In the dim glow of the tent, her face is green. She holds up her phone and taps the screen. 'No signal.'

261

'Shit, shit, shit.'

'I've been getting it on and off, so maybe I just need to move. I could walk around for a bit, see where I get some.'

'Okay.'

As Thea crawls towards the doorway, fear grips Orly at the prospect of her frail, scared friend going out there alone.

'Thea, wait. That person who was being taken away by ambulance . . . they died of a head injury.'

Thea stops and looks back, her eyes round. 'What?'

'What if . . . what if someone hit them? What if there's some psycho hanging around the woods just waiting to attack people. What if Mel and Lenny—'

'Stop, Orly. Stop. Lenny's phone's out of battery, that's all.' The chattering of Thea's teeth belies her tone.

'Yes,' Orly says. 'Yes, you're right. They're probably together somewhere. Lenny'll be helping Mel sober up. Imagine how shit she'll be feeling tomorrow!' Her laugh sounds like a sob.

'Wait here.'

She nods.

'Wait, okay? Don't go anywhere.'

The two women reach out to squeeze hands. Thea must have been gnawing at her cuticles, because blood has drawn dark lines around her fingernails. Her face has sunk back into the bones of her skull, ageing her ten years in less than an hour.

Orly tries to smile with a reassurance she doesn't feel, but Thea's expression is odd. Her eyes seem to glitter with fever as she ducks out of the tent, and Orly is left alone.

Alone, but surrounded by the mess of her friends. Overflowing cases and discarded underwear, stained facial wipes and smelly T-shirts. It should be comforting, but the rainstorm has chilled and dampened everything, stripping it of the warm scent of her friends, replacing it with the must of abandonment: charity shop rubbish.

As she shuffles into her sleeping bag to keep warm, Orly tries to remember the feeling of Ben's body pressed to hers. It's gone.

The feel and smell and taste of him so impossible to recall that it might never have happened. Perhaps it didn't. Perhaps all their drinks were spiked and it was just some fevered dream.

Minutes pass.

How long does it take to call the police? Did Thea have to go a long way to get signal?

Christ, Orly needs a cigarette. She hasn't had one in eighteen years, but the craving is so strong. Back at school they would always have one whenever anything stressful happened, the melodramatic announcement 'I need a cigarette' making them feel so grown-up. She thinks of the lighter she saw in the pocket of Thea's case. Perhaps Thea's going through a stressful time too and has started smoking again.

Sitting up quickly, she opens the case.

There, tucked down the side. Not a lighter, a power pack. Why the hell didn't Thea mention it before? Too expensive to lend, probably.

Orly plugs in her phone and waits impatiently for it to juice up enough to turn on. It doesn't take long. The power pack, like everything else of Thea's, must be a good one.

She's about to message Thea when the phone rings. She drops it in fright and it lies face down on the sleeping bag, twitching in a pool of red.

Lenny.

She snatches it up. 'Hello?'

'Orly?'

Not Lenny. Her heart jumps. 'Ben!'

'Oh my God, Orly . . .' He sounds like he's about to cry. Fear grips her.

'What? What's the matter?'

'I'm so sorry, so sorry.'

'W-why?'

'About your friend.'

Orly's breaths become rapid little gasps. Mel is dead. Lenny didn't find her in time.

'Orly? Oh my God, you did know, didn't you?'

'We knew . . .' she manages, 'that she was in trouble. We were t-trying to f-find her.'

'I'm so, so sorry. They took her away by ambulance, but I think it was too late. I saw them bringing her out of the wood. I was having a drink at Earthfields. I'm still there. I've been trying to call you.'

'Did you speak to Lenny? Is she okay? Did she go to the hospital with Mel?'

For a moment Ben doesn't reply. In the background she can hear the raucous hubbub of the beer tent.

'Orly,' he says finally. 'Did you understand what I just told you? I saw Lenny being pulled out of the wood. I'm so sorry. She's dead.'

'Lenny?' Orly says, frowning. 'No, you saw Mel.' Ben was only introduced to them once. He's got them mixed up.

'Oh God,' Ben moans. 'Oh my God. I could have sworn Mel had long curly hair.'

'Yes.'

'And Lenny is taller, with short hair. She was wearing a T-shirt with a rainbow on it.'

There is a roar in the background, as if something exciting has happened in the bar. A dropped glass perhaps. A woman dancing on a table.

'Orly . . .' He says something else, something about her not being alone, asking where she is, telling her he will wait at Earthfields, but she can't really hear him over the wail rising up from her throat.

Eventually it breaks and she sits, howling, until finally the tent opens and Thea returns. They cling to one another, rocking and sobbing.

'I want to go home,' Orly whimpers eventually, drained of energy and tears.

'Yes,' Thea says. 'Yes. I'll c-call a . . .'

A what? thinks Orly. A taxi? It must have dawned on Thea

at the same time that they are no longer free to leave this hell. The police will want to speak to them. Arrangements must be made to take Lenny's body back to London. There will have to be a funeral.

'What about the children?' Orly wails into her hands. 'Oh God, who's going to tell Jackson and Greta? I'm their guardian, so I guess it'll have to be me.'

Thea doesn't reply. Orly takes her hands from her face and looks up. Thea is looking back at her. The tears have stopped and she is frowning slightly. Her cheeks are viral scarlet, but the rest of her face is deathly pale.

'I'm their guardian,' she says. 'Lenny asked me when they were born.'

Orly's mouth opens. Oh fuck. So, Lenny already had a guardian in place before she asked Orly. And clearly she didn't get around to telling Thea she'd changed her mind.

Orly begins hesitantly, 'I think Lenny . . . She asked me at the funeral . . . I guess because she thought that what with all the attention Lewis needs, I'd have more time and . . .'

Thea is staring at her intently.

'I guess she knew I'd always wanted kids with Harry and so . . . It's not going to be easy.' *That's it, big up the negatives to try and outweigh the massive slap in the face that Thea has just been given.* 'They'll be traumatised. And there'll be loads of logistical stuff to deal with. Schools and stuff. I wonder if I'll have to move in with them for a bit. God, the last place I want to live is London.'

Thea takes her hand, squeezing until the bones crunch. 'Poor you.'

'Did you get through to the police?' Orly says quickly, to change the subject. 'When you went out?'

'No. The signal was really bad and I was worried about leaving you here alone for too long.'

'Try again. I'll be okay. I found your power pack, so just call me as soon as you get through to them.'

When Thea has left the tent again, Orly sits in the silence and thinks about the girl she made friends with that first term at Summer Hall. Back then, she was sure they would be best friends for ever, and then they drifted apart and Orly got jealous of Thea. All that time wasted being resentful when it was just distance and lack of time that separated them. And then, right at the end, she and Lenny had found each other again.

A tear rolls down her cheek.

If only she had lived, they could have—

Her phone leaps to life in her lap as a text comes through.

After the shock has passed, she exhales. Thea must have got through to the police.

But it's not Thea.

It's Mel.

Orly opens the text.

Help me.

Thank God. She's alive, and lucid enough to be able to use her phone.

Where are you?

A long minute passes.

The wood by the tents. Cant walk.

Im coming

Orly scrambles outside. The wood looms above her. Has it got closer?

There's no sign of Thea, and beneath the ever-present layer of festival noise, all is silent.

The tents surround her like a mouth full of sharp teeth. There are too many blind spots. Thea might have had to walk miles to get a signal, or she might be just a few metres away: it's impossible to see from here.

Fuck fuck fuck.

Should she call Thea and they can look together? No. If Mel has been lying out in the rain, drugged and sick, she will be in a terrible state. Those minutes it would take Thea to get back might make the difference between life and death.

She hurries across to where the trees begin, and peers into the shadows until lights explode in her vision. The darkness beyond the first regiment of trunks is impenetrable. What if Mel is confused and she's not actually in the wood she thinks she's in? What if she's back at Earthfields, or the copse by the fair?

Orly will just have to start here and hope Mel was right.

She takes a deep breath, then steps across the treeline and into the darkness. Only then, as she's stumbling through the rustling undergrowth, does the strangeness of Mel's message strike her.

Mel couldn't know anything had happened to Lenny, so why didn't she send the message on the group text? Why only to Orly?

@GillingwaterFestival
Would anyone who was in the vicinity of #Earthfields when the incident in the woods occurred please make themselves known to the festival police. Thank you.

@ZummerzetZoe
Replying to @GillingwaterFestival
Is this about that woman that died?

@LillyLovesReading
Replying to @GillingwaterFestival and @ZummerzetZoe
Prob drugs.

@MotocrossManiax
Replying to @GillingwaterFestival @LillyLovesReading and @ZummerzetZoe
My brother knows one of the medics. He says she had 2 head injuries. As if she fell over, got up, then fell over again.

@MotocrossManiax
Replying to @GillingwaterFestival @LillyLovesReading and @ZummerzetZoe
Unless it wasnt a fall at all.

@ZummerzetZoe
Replying to @MotocrossManiax @GillingwaterFestival and @LillyLovesReading
What do you mean?

@MotocrossManiax
Replying to @GillingwaterFestival @LillyLovesReading and @ZummerzetZoe
They found an item of bloody clothing in a bin, as if someone tried to hide it.

26

Orly

Orly's fear is like an animal crouched inside her ribcage. If it wasn't Mel who sent the message, then she might be walking right into a trap, the dry leaves and twigs announcing her approach at every step.

The sounds of the festival are so muted in here it might be another world, but one of the bonfires has grown so huge that she can see the red flame tips licking the top of the hedge. At this distance the glow it casts is feeble, but at least it's there, relieving the absolute darkness.

She steps gingerly, hands paddling the air to give her some warning of lurching trunks or stabbing branches. After a while she can distinguish some light and shade: the pale glow of a food wrapper against the dark undergrowth, a patch of raw wood where bark has been scratched off.

And then suddenly she's walking on air. Her leading foot lands in a ditch with a jolt that sends a shudder through her whole body. Clambering out the other side, she's gone no more than a few steps before stubbing her toe on a rock. She stops and bends double until the pain recedes.

The quest is hopeless. As in the wood by the fair, she will simply stumble around blind, no use to anyone. She might even have an accident. The third friend comes to harm going after the second, who went after the first. Like some fable about fools. Is this what happened to Lenny? If Orly had been walking faster, she might have fallen badly, banging her head instead of merely stubbing her toe.

She goes still. She's sure she's heard a new sound – not rustling or her own breaths; a tiny whine.

She listens for a few minutes, but it doesn't come again.

An animal, perhaps, or a distant orgasm from one of the tents behind her. Or maybe just tinnitus. She gets that sometimes when she's feeling stressed.

She walks forward.

There.

The sound comes again, closer now.

Not a whine, but a gurgle.

She turns in a circle, arms stretched in front of her. Now that her ears are tuned to its wavelength, she can hear that the gurgle was just a spike in a series of choked breaths coming from somewhere to her right.

'Mel?'

The breaths stutter, then speed up, accompanied by frantic rustling.

She moves towards the sound.

Her sense of time and space has shrunk to a bubble enclosing her, magnifying her grunting gasps and clumsy footsteps. But that other breathing goes on, the thread of its distress yanking her forward until finally she's within what feels like touching distance. Lowering herself to her knees, she stretches a blind hand out into the darkness.

It makes contact with something soft as flower petals.

The moans are cut off in an intake of breath.

Under her palm, Orly feels the unmistakable brush of hair. She lowers it and the bouncing curls give, until it is resting on a cool, clammy forehead. A cheek, a neck, a shoulder, a hand.

She fumbles with her phone and touches the screen. The glow falls on a face. Mel's face.

'Mel, it's me, Orly!'

Mel moans.

271

Her chin is covered with foaming vomit, which has trickled into her hair and across the dark leaves beneath her. Moving the phone up and down, Orly scans her body for injury. Nothing. Neither are Mel's clothes disordered: it doesn't look as if she's been assaulted. The only evidence of harm is the vomit. Was it too much alcohol, or some kind of drug? Surely the only point in spiking someone's drink is to render them helpless to fight off your advances, but Mel has just been left here, or she's staggered here on her own, attempting to get back to the safety of the tent.

Perhaps there was no attacker at all.

'Hey,' she says, gently stroking Mel's face. 'It's okay. I'm here. You're safe now.'

Mel's eyes are unfocused, but when she hears Orly's voice, she raises a hand to bat the air. Orly takes it.

'Did someone do this to you?'

It's like trying decipher the cries of a baby, but the increased urgency of the moans make her lean closer.

'Yes? Who was it? Was it Trey?'

Probably Mel doesn't even remember, but her eyeballs, with their pinprick pupils, swivel to Orly's and her lips twitch as if she's trying to speak. She's so out of it it's a wonder she managed to send the text – and where is her phone anyway?

Orly leans forward, trying to understand what Mel is trying to tell her.

She's listening so intently that at first she thinks the sound is merely the rushing of her blood in her ears. But when it comes again, it is closer and clearer.

The quiet rustling of footsteps.

Someone has come into the wood after her.

The siren of the fire engine is what saves her. That brief rising wail momentarily drowns out all sounds, including the telltale protests of the undergrowth as she attempts to drag Mel by her arms towards the feeble glow of the campsite. Under its cover, she's hoping they can reach the tent before their pursuer catches up with them, but Mel is a dead weight, and on the rough ground Orly can't get any momentum going. She manages no more than a few centimetres at a time as those footsteps get closer and closer. But then what difference will it make if they do reach the campsite? The place is deserted. Everybody's off having a wild time on Midsummer's Night.

Then she loses her footing and stumbles back into the ditch, pulling Mel with her.

She's done, she thinks, pressing her body into the leaf mulch. She will lie here until those footsteps catch up with them, cover her face and await her fate.

Same old pathetic Orly.

Fuck you.

Is it pathetic to nurse your husband in his final hours?

To hold him as he bucks with pain?

To comfort him as he whimpers that he's frightened, that he isn't ready?

No.

The voice in her head isn't Pandora's, or Harry's parents', or her own treacherous inner demon, picking away at her self-esteem and her courage. It's her mum. Her lovely mum, who always believed in her despite all the evidence to the contrary.

You can do it.

Don't give up.

I'm so proud of you.

Is it her mother who has led her here, to this little dip in which Mel can be concealed from the thing that hunts them? Is it Harry, protecting her from beyond the grave? Or is it just good fortune that needs to be grasped with both hands and wrung dry?

'Quiet,' she breathes in Mel's ear. 'Stay quiet. I'll be back with help.'

She squeezes Mel's hand, and somehow Mel manages to squeeze back.

As the siren dies away, Orly sprints towards the treeline with steps as light as the terrain will allow. Only when she's put a good distance between herself and Mel's hiding place does she become heavy-footed again, making no attempt to mask her crashing passage through the undergrowth.

As she runs, she offers up a prayer to the pagan gods whose images decorate every hand-made soap wrapper and artisan beer bottle label in this place. Gods not of essential oils and yoga, but of rock and storm and fire. Perhaps they still have some power here.

The hedge rises before her.

She must make a ninety-degree turn and run along the edge of the campsite to the gateway. If she can make it onto the main track, there might be someone sober enough to help.

Possibly.

Although who would be lingering on the tracks and passage-ways now, as the festival reaches its climax?

She can hear whoops and peals of laughter, but they're not coming from the track beyond the gate. They're drifting over the hedge directly in front of her, and if she peers closely, she can see tiny snatches of flame. The bonfire at Earthfields. The most popular part of the festival after the Litha Stage. Where people go to pretend there is something more spiritual to them than their boring jobs and mundane lives would suggest. People who can help her.

She throws herself at the hedge.

The first few branches give, raking her arms with thorns as they are forced to part before her, but the next bramble does not surrender so easily and she feels the flesh of her arm slice open.

Barbed wire.

She tries to turn back, to take the route along the edge of the campsite.

She's stuck.

A whimper escapes her as she twists around, trying to free herself from the brambles that have caught her in an evil embrace, as if determined to hold her until her pursuer's arrival.

She can hear his approach now in the cracking of twigs, ever closer.

Mel's hiding place must have been overlooked. She at least will be safe. Orly will be the sacrifice that ensures her friend's survival.

But of course she won't. Mel is in no fit state to go for help, and once Orly is dealt with, her attacker will go back to finish the job.

No, she must keep fighting.

Thrashing at the vicious barbs, she searches for a way through. And then her hand breaks out into air on the other side of the hedge. The wire is strung along the hedge in rows. She can crawl between them! Except that the distance between each wire is no more than a handspan.

Parting the brambles before her face, she takes hold of a wire above and below and pushes her head through. The tension is so tight that when she loses her grip, the upper wire springs back, jabbing barbs into her neck. Biting her tongue to stop herself crying out, she eases it away and begins trying to manoeuvre her shoulders through.

The barbs cut through her clothes to rake her flesh, and her progress is so slow that every moment she expects a hand to close around the ankle still supporting her weight on the camp side of the hedge.

But at least some of the gods are with her.

A firework show has begun.

An expensive one, not like the ones on the Newton Collard recreation ground, where each tiny rocket must be oohed and ahhed over for at least a minute before the next one is released. Once these start, they do not stop. The sky explodes into crimson and gold rain, and an artillery barrage begins. The light flares help her locate useful branches to lever herself through her narrow escape route, and she finds herself visualising the fun house again. Curl forward. Don't try to walk out on your hands or the entire weight of your thighs will press down on the lower barbs. Just let yourself do a roly-poly. Like James Bond.

There's rustling behind her and branches brush her ankles. Someone is crawling through the hedge after her.

She screams and throws herself forward, and for a split second she's falling, the barbed wire tearing her thighs as they flip over her head. Landing heavily, she rolls onto her back, her legs thumping onto damp grass.

She's in a field. Above her the sky is a fantastical apocalypse and smoke rolls across the uneven ground. It's coming from Earthfields. A huge bonfire licks the sky above a solid metal gate set in the hedge on the other side of the field – no more than the length of a football pitch away. She's nearly there, nearly safe.

But she's so tired. If she could just lie here for a moment in peace . . .

Another firework lights up the hedgerow, leaving an after-image like a photographic negative.

A bone-white hand has burrowed its way through the wire.

27

Thea

The tent is empty when Thea returns.

There was no sign of Orly on the way back here, so there's only one place she can have gone. Into the wood, just as Thea intended with the messages from Mel's phone. Opening her case, she slides a belt from one of her pairs of shorts: thin but good-quality leather. It won't snap under tension. A laugh bubbles up from her chest as she fastens it round her waist. To think it has come to this. She suppresses it and ducks back outside.

Crossing the strip of grass to where it roughens to scrub at the edge of the wood, she enters the shadows of the trees. Her eyes instantly adjust to the darkness she has become so used to today. She listens, and after a minute or so hears the snap of a twig. She sets off in the direction of the sound.

If her first plan had worked, none of this would have been necessary. Lenny gave her the idea herself back in April, just days after she found out about Bruno's vasectomy, when she told Thea about the near-fatal asthma attack she had suffered at home the night before. *If the inhaler had fallen just out of my reach, that would have been it. Orphaned children.*

And in that tragic scenario, the poor orphans would be handed over to their legal guardian, along with the expensive London property and Lenny's substantial capital and investments, which would be put in trust to be used for their care. Well, Thea couldn't very well care for them without moving into that big

277

London house. And a reasonable expense would be providing for her own children.

The little blue device was sticking out of Lenny's handbag in the footwell on the drive down here. All Thea had to do was pop to the toilet when they stopped at the petrol station and empty it. Lenny even did her the courtesy of remaining asleep the entire time and failing to notice the way Thea's hands trembled on the wheel for the next hour. An asthma attack was always going to be the thing that got Lenny in the end, a tragic accident that would allow Thea to grieve; the Tiffany bracelet proof that she had loved her friend dearly and would never seek to do her harm.

But Orly somehow managed to rescue her. After that, Orly's mood had changed, and only worsened after the tent was trashed. Thea knew she would be whining at Lenny to take her home. But what if Lenny didn't come back afterwards? No, they both had to stay. That was why she'd dunked the Range Rover fob into the stream when they were washing the sleeping bags: nobody was going anywhere.

The second chance came at the fairground, this one purely opportunistic. Knowing that Orly was too chicken, Thea persuaded Lenny to go on the Ferris wheel. When they got to the top, she would simply push Lenny out, to crash-land in the snarl of metal and machinery below. But it was probably a good thing that Orly changed her mind. Lenny was bigger and stronger than Thea. If the element of surprise failed and she fought Thea off, that would have been it. Game over. A prison sentence for attempted murder and the children put into care.

In the end, she had to use the fentanyl she'd stolen from Socrates in case the asthma attack didn't work. A spiked drink was not unlikely in the chaos of a festival. A fatal one would cause more of a stir, but the perpetrator would never be found. The fates had even given her Trey to pin it on.

Gel extracted from two of the fentanyl patches she'd found in Socrates' drawer was more than enough to kill someone when ingested. Thea spent hours practising squeezing gel-filled pipettes into bottles, until she could do it under her sleeve, swiftly and unobtrusively, up at a crowded bar.

It was the rain that fucked everything up.

The beer tent was too crowded; they had to move up to allow another couple to sit down.

She didn't realise what had happened until, after only two bottles, Mel was drunk. Mel could always take her drink, far better than the rest of them, but almost immediately she was bleary-eyed and slurring. Somehow, when they moved up the table, the bottles must have been switched and Mel had drunk the one laced with fentanyl. The horror of what Thea had done paralysed her. She watched helplessly as Mel staggered to her feet and left the tent. Poor Mel, who had never done anyone any harm, who had slaved and sacrificed everything for her child just as Thea had. Eventually she managed to get up herself, pretending she had spotted Anais and wanted to avoid her, but her dismay was not feigned as she blundered out into the rain and went in search of Mel.

Everything had gone wrong. Her plan seemed so simple back in London, but it was spiralling out of control. She should stop now. Rescue Mel, then give up. Accept what was coming to her. To Lewis and Jade. Perhaps Bruno would be kind to them, set them up in a little flat, give them an income, maybe even continue to pay the Hoare House fees.

Who was she kidding? His wife had spent a decade trying to squeeze money out of him, and the only reason he'd wanted custody of Anais and Socrates was so that he didn't have to pay her maintenance. No. He would unleash the power and unscrupulousness of his lawyer friends and Thea would be lucky to keep her shoe collection. At least she could sell those, and her clothes.

Finally she spotted Mel, slumped against a waterlogged hay bale. Was she dead? Thea hurried over. No. She was still breathing. Perhaps there was time to save her if Thea got her to the medic tent.

Somehow she managed to haul Mel upright and, taking her full solid weight on her shoulders, staggered away from the stalls and onto the main track.

Eventually the sign with the red cross swam out of the grey mist. She stopped, breathing heavily from the exertion.

Mel's eyes had rolled back into her head and white foam flecked her nostrils and the corners of her mouth. Could she already be past saving?

If so, if Thea got her to the medics and Mel died anyway, it would all be for nothing. The police would be involved. They might find evidence of what Thea had done. Worse, there was no way she'd be able to carry out what she intended with Lenny.

Rain crept down her back, like cold fingers down her spine.

She shifted Mel's weight to ease her aching shoulder. She was so tired. She was getting old. Her days of being able to charm her way to a good life were gone. No, the good life was over for all of them, leaving only the alternative.

Thea and her children would be out on the street again, their departure watched with triumph by her stepchildren. Not stepchildren – she and Bruno were never married. And they had never been going to have a child together. He had lied to her all those years, or at least never told her the truth – that condom, pill or not, she was never going to get pregnant. He'd had the vasectomy to protect him from women like her.

There was no safety net for her, no rich mummy and daddy, no property or savings, no skills or experience, and a worthless education. All she had was her fading beauty and the precious burden of her children. And, back in mainstream education, all the progress that Hoare House had achieved with Lewis would be undone. She would have to watch, helpless, as he grew into a vulnerable, troubled adult, dependent on her for the rest of his life.

Unless.

Bracing herself, she hoisted the slumping Mel back onto her shoulder and walked on, past the sign, into the grey.

Nobody saw them stagger down the track, Thea blessing those long hours spent in spin classes, where she'd learned to embrace physical suffering. Eventually the campsite shimmered into view.

She propped Mel's floppy body up on the gate to catch her breath for the final push over the churned ground. Mel's skin was ice cold and turning blue. She was obviously dying, but if Thea got her to the tent, the alarm wouldn't be raised for a while. She would have time to do what she came here to do. It could all still be okay.

She almost broke down as she pictured Billy, one of the last times she had seen him, as a round-faced twelve-year-old with a thing about Egyptian mummies.

At least he was a grown man now, away to university.

But Lenny's children weren't.

Don't think of her children. Think of yours.

Manoeuvring herself back into position, she hauled Mel into her arms.

There was a muffled clump behind her as the coat someone had hung on the gate bars slipped to the ground to lie face-down in the mud, stretching an arm towards her.

You.

Shivering, she turned and set off for the final part of the ordeal.

Navigating the treacherous dips and tussocks would have been hard enough in her stupid sandals, even without Mel's dead weight on her back, but eventually the little green pyramid swam into view, almost camouflaged against the wood beyond.

Her legs were about to give way, her arms were numb, her lungs ached, and all she was thinking about was the moment she could drop Mel, but as she approached the tent, she heard voices.

There was someone inside.

Fuck.

She thought Lenny had spoken to Orly, telling her where to meet them, but Orly was still here. And she wasn't alone.

Thea's legs gave out and she sat heavily, unable to stop herself flinging an arm out to steady herself. It brushed the nylon and the whole tent quivered. The voices fell silent.

'Hello,' a man's voice called. 'Can we help you?'

Her brain made rapid calculations.

If she'd been seen, she should just pretend she'd found Mel like this. But this man – she was pretty sure it was Ben from next door – would no doubt take charge, as men did, and insist on getting her to a medic. As Thea recalled, he was a big enough guy: it wouldn't take long.

Mel would get a reversal drug and they would all accompany her to hospital, and then it would all be over and Thea would have lost her chance.

A rustling inside the tent made her heart stutter. Were they about to open the door?

In hindsight, it was a crazy decision, but she was panicking. Scrambling to her feet, she hoisted Mel up by the armpits and began dragging her towards the wood, her eyes never leaving the tent, her breathless thoughts constructing a sequence of events that could, at a push, be credible.

Mel had upset Trey, and as punishment he had spiked her drink. She felt ill, tried to make it back to the tent, got disorientated, got lost, died.

Died. Dead. Murdered. By one of her best friends.

Thea pushed down the wave of nausea that rose into her throat.

Finally she made it to the cover of the trees. With her last ounce of strength she inched deeper and deeper into the darkness until the veil of rain concealed all but the merest spectre of the coloured tents in the field beyond. And then they were gone, and there was only Thea and the friend she had murdered.

She laid Mel's body down as far in as she dared, given the time limits, and ran back to the bar. By the time she got there, she was ready to vomit or faint.

Tony had always told her that the person most likely to betray you was yourself, through stupidity or nerves or an attack of conscience, and when she sat down, she was sure her crime must be written all over her face. She shrank from Lenny's gaze, shivering as waves of nausea washed over her. But thank God Lenny thought she was just cold: she was so worried, she gave Thea her hoodie.

But even after the waves of horror and shock had passed, Thea could not rest. If she didn't deal with Lenny, if she chickened out now, everything had been for nothing: Mel would be *dead* for nothing. Back in the tent later, pretending to sleep as they awaited Mel's return, her brain worked like it had never worked before, concocting scenarios and dismissing them, searching for the holes and risks in each idea she came up with. Nothing held water.

It was the texts that saved her. Those spiteful messages that had got Orly so worked up allowed Thea to sow fear into the hearts of her remaining friends, convincing them that Mel must be found before Trey got to her. While the other two left to go looking for her, Thea retrieved Mel's phone. She switched it on and traced the ludicrously simple unlock pattern. Sure enough, there were more threats from Trey. Perfect.

By this stage, panic had made Thea careless. Anyone could have seen her burst from the tent and race into the woods.

To her great shock, Mel was still alive, just. Her eyes were rolled back and the undergrowth was spattered in vomit.

When the video call connected, Thea was careful to ensure no part of her was visible. Only the trees behind Mel's head. It all worked perfectly. She didn't even have to prompt them to suggest searching the woods. All she had to do was get to the one behind Earthfields before Lenny finished looking there.

The first blow, with a rock she could barely lift, was a glancing one. Lenny screamed and stumbled forward, but remained on her feet. Her head started to turn. Terror at the thought of having to look into her eyes flooded Thea's blood with adrenaline. As Lenny's head moved into profile, she brought the rock down on her temple with such force that Lenny was dead before she hit the ground.

Thea knew, because she crouched beside her oldest friend and took her pulse.

Finally she'd done something right.

Afterwards, she washed her hands and face as best she could in the puddles that remained after the rainstorm and pushed the hoodie that must surely be blood-spattered deep into one of the overfilled bins.

She was only just back inside the tent when Orly returned.

They waited for Lenny, and eventually Orly said they should call the police. Orly had no battery, so Thea would make the call. Except that she wouldn't. The more time that elapsed before they found the bodies, the better, especially if more rain was coming. When she got back, she found that Orly had managed to charge her phone. She told Thea that Lenny was dead.

And then Orly told her something else.

Something that made Thea's heart shrink and her flesh crawl.

Lenny had changed her will to make Orly legal guardian of the twins. It was almost funny, really. After everything Thea had gone through: stealing drugs, spiking drinks, dragging a body through a wood, beating her best friend to death. Like a hapless stooge in a crime caper. All of it was for nothing. Orly would inherit everything.

No. Thea couldn't let that happen. She had come too far now. There was no hesitation this time: she had to go on. Finish the job. Remove the final obstacle in her path. For her children.

After leaving the tent once more, on the pretext of trying the police again, she used Mel's phone to send a message begging Orly for help. *The wood by the tents*. Christ, could it be more obvious Orly was being duped?

But she never was that quick on the uptake.

Thea stifles laughter as she follows the sounds of her prey blundering through the trees.

28

Orly

It takes every ounce of Orly's energy to make it across the field and burrow through the hedge to Earthfields. Every moment she's expecting a knife to slash down her back. At one point she considers turning to face her pursuer, to try and tackle her with a rock or her own brute strength. Because the hand was small and hairless, like a woman's.

Could Pandora have taken her revenge this far? But why hurt Mel?

Bursting through the hedge, she falls heavily onto her stomach, winding herself, and lies there a moment trying to muster the breath to scream for help.

Then she sees that no one would hear her anyway.

Earthfields is in uproar.

The oversized bonfire has caught the row of hay bales surrounding it, and flames are roaring into the sky. The stall-holders shout frantically to one another as they try to move their vehicles and produce to safety. Some festival-goers try to help, while others kick out at the flaming bales, sending more sparks and ignited stalks up into the night.

In the shadows of the hedge, Orly is invisible to them.

She staggers to her feet. She must cross the fire to get to safety.

Something pale moves in the corner of her eye. She twists round.

Someone is slithering like a white worm out onto the grass.

As the figure gets to its feet, straightening up, and the curtain of messy hair falls from its face, time stops.

Orly stares, her mind blank.

Then she exhales with relief.

Thea must have got the same message from Mel and come into the wood to help. Orly has been panicking for nothing. She almost laughs. So silly.

Thea's eyes lock onto hers and she starts moving at a lurching lope.

But why didn't Thea call out to her? *It's only me, don't panic.*

The distance between them is closing. Orly takes a step back, and the warmth of the fire laps at her thighs.

On Thea's face is a look of such burning determination. And now she reaches for the belt looped oddly around the outside of her top and unhooks the buckle, letting it fall like a whip by her side.

Orly turns and runs towards the flames, now swaying like corn stalks as they are struck with sacks and flags. The flames directly in front of her bow down under the assault, and for a moment she catches sight of the people on the other side.

Ben is there. She feels such a swell of emotion her legs almost give way. He's helping a young woman pull a flower-laden bicycle from the blaze.

Then the flames leap up again and Orly skids to a halt, shielding her face from the heat, feeling her skin shrink, smelling her hair as it singes.

A glance behind reveals she has dithered too long.

Thea, an arm's length away, is reaching out for her. Orly has a split second before the other woman grabs her hair and pulls her back into the darkness.

At that moment, the flames die. She catches a glimpse of a huge man bringing an entire awning down into the heart of the fire, momentarily cowing it.

Now. She must go now.

But she's always been a coward. Too scared to own up to what she did to Pan, to stand up to Harry's parents, to admit the truth to her friends. And even now, the thought of trying to leap over the seething white-hot heart of the fire is terrifying. But what choice does she have?

A sob breaks from her chest as she hurls herself forward.

She can actually hear the flames hissing in rage as she flies over them. Under the waft of oxygen, they resurge, and the backs of her legs burn as they roar upwards in renewed fury.

She lands heavily on the other side, scrabbling back as the fire surges into the sky. For a moment she can make out Thea's figure, spindly as a corn doll, blundering after her, before it is engulfed in flame.

A voice bellows. 'There's someone in the fire!'

'Oh my God!'

'Get them out!'

As figures crash past her, bravely kicking and trampling, Orly can only stare. There is no sign of movement from the heart of the fire.

'Orly! Oh my God, Orly! Are you okay?' Ben is on his knees beside her. 'Come away. Come away. Don't look.'

But she has to. She has to look.

Now something is being dragged from the flames. Orly makes out tufts of hair and scraps of fabric, patches of black and red flesh. The rescuers drop the burnt thing, then hurl themselves to the ground to extinguish the flames now licking their own clothes.

The hand that flops down beside Orly's foot is completely still; the face is, mercifully, pressed into the grass. A smell of barbecued meat fills the air.

'Ambulance, please,' Ben says. He has moved away from her, his phone to his ear. 'Gillingwater Festival. The Earthfields area. Someone's been burnt. Badly.'

A hand closes around her ankle.

Orly's shocked cry is lost in the noise.

A face has risen from the grass. The bald, charred thing is barely recognisable as human, let alone as her friend, and yet the strength left in those blackened fingers is incredible.

287

Orly moans.

'Look after . . .' The breath squeals in and out of the creature's burned lungs. 'Lewis and Jade.'

Orly tries to shake the hand off, but it's impossible.

The milky eyes blink and a tear draws a pale line down the black cheek. Beneath the soot is smooth skin, plump and youthful from years of diligent care.

And she is Orly's friend once more. Beautiful Thea, who taught them all how to apply eyeliner, who held Orly's hair when she was vomiting into the Oak's toilets, who whispered the answers to the Latin test when Orly had forgotten every single one.

'Swear . . .'

Orly reaches forward and lays her hand over the burnt claw.

'I swear,' she whispers. 'I swear. I swear. I swear.'

She repeats the phrase over and over, her sight so blurred that she cannot see if the terrible intensity in Thea's eyes has softened to something more peaceful. All she knows is that the iron grip slackens and the squealing becomes no more than the whine of a mosquito, and then nothing at all.

@I_Got_Bills_02
Thanks for all your good wishes about Mum. She's making a good recovery and should be out of hospital soon. Drug dealers killed my best friend and almost killed my mum so if that's where you are in your life then think hard. Peace and love.

@KieranRoyale
Tell her we love her Bills.

@I_Got_Bills_02
It'll be a comfort 2 know ur still stalking her m8.

@GaryStephenSergeant
Your mums a fighter. I should know. Still got the bruises LOL.

@I_Got_Bills_02
Cheers Dad x

@JennniferJelllybean
Sending so much love Billy. Cant wait to meet her. Xx

@KieranRoyale
WOOOOOOOOOOOOOOOOOOOHH Billys got a ladeeeeee!!!

@I_Got_Bills_02
Grow up oaf.

29

Orly

Arranging three funerals in as many years was not something Orly expected to have to do.

But orphan Lenny had no one else to do it for her, and Elaine, Thea's mother, had no inclination to help with her daughter's.

The older woman sat at the front of the church, stony-faced, occasionally patting down the thinning hair that was still worn long and bottle-black.

This was a double funeral. If Elaine minded, it was not enough to take on the responsibility herself. Her involvement extended to providing childhood photographs of Thea, in which Orly could trace the development of a plump-faced toddler to a seven-year-old in full make-up, pouting at the camera, to the immaculate teen Orly remembered from school, whose smiles were tightly controlled to ensure the best angle.

By contrast, Lenny's childhood pictures, searched out by the wonderful au pair, Jeanne, who had been a mother to the children for the past month, showed a studious girl whose dark eyes, though dutifully directed towards the camera, seemed firmly fixed on a point far in the future. It was as if someone had cut out her picture and glued it onto an image of the drab little sitting room with covers on the chair backs to protect the brown fabric from her father's oiled quiff.

Thea's children had remained with Bruno, being cared for by a full-time nanny, which he had told Orly was the very least he could do under the circumstances. The very most, too, it seemed, as he'd already informed Elaine that if she did not arrange for Lewis and Jade to be picked up soon, he would contact social services.

Elaine tells Orly this over the buffet table as she helps herself to avocado crostinis.

'I can't have them. Not at my age.'

Orly does not remark that she's not even sixty yet.

'If you're gonna have children, you gotta look after them. Not rely on other people to do it.'

As if by dying, Thea has somehow wriggled out of parenting.

Orly says nothing. She does not trust herself not to spew her grief and rage over this foul, petty hag, who so failed her daughter.

'Can't you take them?' Elaine whines, spitting a fleck of green slime over Orly's top.

'I'd love to,' Orly says. 'I really would. But I'm living with my parents at the moment.'

Elaine's thin eyebrows rise. Orly can hear the nasty little thought passing through her shrunken brain. *And you was supposed to be a career girl.*

The truth is, it causes Orly such pain to imagine Lewis and Jade in a children's home that she's been forcing herself not to think about it. She speaks to them every night, and comforts them as they cry, until the brisk nanny tells them it's time for bed. Sometimes she will ask the nanny to prop the phone by their beds so that she can read them a story on FaceTime.

Jade is so like Thea in appearance, but Thea has not inflicted upon her daughter what she herself suffered. Jade is a little girl. She wears dungarees and Crocs, her hair is a raggedy ponytail, and her favourite hobbies are pond-dipping and minibeasts.

Man hands on misery to man.

Orly remembers the poem from an English lesson. Everyone else remembers the line with *fuck* in it, but Orly remembers this part. Because she disagreed with it so completely. Her own parents have given her nothing but love and support. And Thea

291

never handed down that miserable world view – that a woman is nothing but a walking ornament to be displayed upon the arm of as rich a man as she can find – only her pure white-hot love. Thea, Orly suspects, never loved Bruno. She lived with him and suffered the humiliations of his vile teenagers because it was the absolute best thing she could do for her children, and Elaine had ensured that there was no other way for her to support them.

As if reading her mind, Elaine says, 'If she'd got herself a job, like everyone else, then she wouldn't have had to lie on her back for—'

'Excuse me,' Orly says. Elaine's eyes have filled with tears, as if she's been chopping onions, and Orly knows that this bitterness is the only way she can express her grief, but she can feel no sympathy.

Turning away, her amnesiac heart leaps. Thea! But then the woman with the caramel hair turns, and though her perfect features resemble those of Orly's old friend, the face blooms with genuine, glowing, impossibly perfect youth.

Bruno is looking at her with a sort of possessive hunger, like a greedy schoolboy.

How could he have moved on so fast?

Don't be stupid. He was having an affair.

Orly inclines her head politely as he sets off in her direction, primed to deliver his polished public-school patter about her being a wonderful friend and blah blah blah, and walks straight past him.

Mel is sitting in the corner, clinging to the rock of Billy's arm. She still looks frail, as if the overdose of the drug has had more lasting effects than the cheerful doctors promised.

Orly sits down beside her. 'Thea's mum should be humanely put down.'

Mel smiles, but it doesn't reach her eyes. The trauma of that terrible weekend will stay with both of them for ever.

'Go and get us another drink, Bills,' Mel says, and her huge son obediently gets up and ambles to the bar.

'I just can't stop thinking that this was all my fault,' Mel murmurs when he's out of earshot. 'If they hadn't been looking for me, then—'

Orly takes her by the shoulders. 'It is not your fault, okay? Your drink was spiked. You were a victim, same as Lenny. Thea too.'

'Have they charged Trey?'

'Only with cannabis possession.'

'For fuck's sake! He probably just ditched the fentanyl somewhere!'

'There's no proof.'

'I don't want this happening to another woman!' The last word shatters into a sob and Orly pulls her into her arms.

She doesn't like lying to Mel, but the truth will be far more painful, the injuries it would cause far harder to recover from.

It was Ben who raced back to the spot Orly had described to him while they waited for the ambulance. He carried Mel all the way back to Earthfields, where the paramedics immediately diagnosed an opiate overdose and gave her a drug called naxolone to reverse the effects.

He accompanied Orly to the hospital, shared her relief when Mel was pronounced out of danger, comforted her in her grief.

Since then, she has kept him at arm's length.

When they first met, she'd feared that he would run from the emotional baggage of a young widow, but now that she knows him better, she fears the opposite. That he's such a kind, caring person he'll willingly take on all her distress and grief and rage, be there for her whenever she needs him. It isn't fair to do that to him. She didn't even tell him about the funerals.

There's a lot she isn't telling people these days.

Billy gets back with the drinks, but before Orly has taken more than a sip, a small, neat man with a cap of red hair approaches.

'Mrs Goldstein? My name's Oliver Wormley; I'm Leonora's lawyer.'

All three of them shake his hand, but his next comment is directed at Orly alone.

'May we speak?'

Orly allows herself to be led out of the room into the corridor and through a door that opens onto a smaller, more intimate space with patio doors to the garden. Despite the mildness of the late-summer day, a fire burns in the grate.

'Take a seat, Mrs Goldstein, if you would.'

Orly sits down on an armchair that looks out across the lawn. Wormley sits opposite.

'As you know, Leonora's parents died many years ago and her children are without close relatives. It was for this reason that she was keen, as a relatively young woman, to ensure that a guardian was put in place should anything happen to her. The guardian she chose was Thea D'Agnelli.'

'I know.' Orly looks away.

'Should Lenny die prematurely, Thea would have been given control over her estate – the house, investments and cash – until the twins' maturity. Any reasonable costs would have been paid by the trustees and a pension provided to support her after the children reached eighteen.'

After delivering this information, Wormley pauses. Orly turns to look at him.

'Leonora may not have had the chance to inform her, but she had decided to make a change to her will. It might have been an awkward conversation, so perhaps she had been putting it off, or it's possible she decided not to mention it at all.'

Orly blinks, and Wormley's words become muffled and distant. How can she have been so slow? She'd let herself believe that Thea had suffered a psychotic episode from the stress of the weekend, but Thea had weathered worse storms and emerged the other side. No, her actions had far more pragmatic motives. She must have known that, being the children's guardian, on Lenny's death she would take control of Lenny's entire estate.

Wormley is still speaking. 'It was Leonora's wish, Mrs Goldstein, that you should become guardian of her children. She didn't have the chance to complete the necessary paperwork, but

I can take the email she sent me as an expression of her wishes. From a legal standpoint, so long as there are no objections by the executors, her decision that you should be guardian to the twins will stand. If possible, you would move into her London house, for the sake of stability for the twins, or the house could be sold if you wished to base yourself elsewhere.'

Orly gazes out of the French doors at the garden. In full bloom with swaying hollyhocks, clouds of hydrangeas and peonies like huge lollipops, it makes her think of four children, two boys and two girls, running around a different hotel garden.

'All my legal costs will be paid for by the trust. I can explain the terms in more detail another time, but essentially you would have control of the estate, to use in any way you see fit, to the ends of the children's care, until they reach maturity.'

Wormley puts his glass on a small table of deep green marble.

'I don't want to pressure you, Mrs Goldstein, but if you feel unequal to this task – and I understand it is a great one – then the twins will be sent to boarding school and a stranger will be appointed to accommodate them in the holidays.'

Orly flinches.

'You will need time to think about it, I'm s—'

'No.'

Wormley's face falls. 'Very well. I understand.'

'No, I don't need time to think. Yes, of course I'll be their guardian. And I'll do my best to love them as their mum did.'

He turns away and blinks rapidly, wrinkling his nose as if to hold back a sneeze. 'Well, that is . . .' he continues in a slightly gravelly voice, 'that is marvellous. Really. Lenny . . . Leonora would be so happy.'

'So are you my lawyer now too?'

He flashes a brief but not unfriendly smile. 'If you wish.'

'I know all Lenny's money will go to Jackson and Greta, but it's a big house, right?'

'Eight bedrooms.'

'In that case, I want to take Thea's children too.'

Wormley opens his mouth and closes it again.

'Lewis and Jade's father is in prison and I know Thea would never have wanted her mother to take care of them, so I'd like to apply for guardianship of them too. I'm going back to work, as a teacher, so I can pay for their care – the trust won't have to.'

'Four children, Mrs Goldstein. Four traumatised children. Are you sure you're up to—'

'What would you prefer?' Orly's tone sharpens. 'That they're taken into care? All children are equal, Mr Wormley, rich or poor; all of them deserve the best life possible. I nursed my husband in his last hours and my hopes of a family died with him. I'm forty years old. This isn't a burden, it's a blessing. So allow me to make some terms of my own: it's all of them or none of them.'

Wormley raises his eyes to meet her gaze. 'Very well. I'll draw up the paperwork.' He takes out his phone and begins tapping away at the screen.

Orly gets up and goes over to the French doors. A man is walking up the drive. Handsome but uncomfortable-looking in a black suit that constricts his broad chest. He pauses and looks up at the hotel, as if seeking the least obtrusive way in. Then he spots her in the window and raises a tentative hand.

Wormley comes to stand beside her.

'A friend?'

'Yes.'

'Well.' Wormley holds out his hand. 'I look forward to working with you in the future.'

Orly takes it. It's warm and dry, dependably solid, and as Ben crosses the lawn, Wormley dips his head and turns away.

At the door, he pauses and turns back.

'For what it's worth, Mrs Goldstein, I think Lenny made the right decision.'

Orly opens the French doors and Ben comes smiling up the steps.

Interview with Orly Goldstein, 17.7.2021, 15.27

DI Spenser Scale: In light of new information given to us by the son of Thea D'Agnelli's former partner, I'd like to go over a few things with you, if I may. [Ms Goldstein nods] Socrates Haslett-Mowbray told us that a quantity of fentanyl, prescribed for chronic back pain, was removed from his room three weeks prior to the festival. Tests have shown that it was of the same purity as that used to spike Melanie Court's drink. Can you think of a reason Ms D'Agnelli would have drugged Ms Court?

Orly Goldstein: No.

DI Spenser Scale: Do you think the death of Leonora Clarke is in any way linked to what happened to Ms Court?

Orly Goldstein: Lenny tripped in the wood and banged her head and Thea fell when she was trying to jump the fire to summon help. They were both terrible accidents. We were all drunk.

DI Spenser Scale: Right. Yes. I get that – you had been partying hard, so your memories might be a bit hazy – but the thing we just can't figure out is the bloodstained top. The one that belonged to Leonora that was found dumped in a bin. Can you explain to me how it ended up there?

Orly Goldstein: No.

[Long pause]

DI Spenser Scale: Who benefits from what happened, Orly?

Orly Goldstein: Sorry?

DI Spenser Scale: Who's living in an eight-bedroom London house with a trusteeship worth several million pounds?

Orly Goldstein: And four traumatised children, Detective. Don't forget that. Now, if you don't have any more questions, I should be getting back to them. Jackson has a counselling session at four thirty.

DI Spenser Scale: It was very good of you to take over the responsibility for those children.

Orly Goldstein: That's what friends do.

DI Spenser Scale: I think friends do a lot more than that sometimes.

June 2000

The exams are over.

Lenny shrugs when people ask how they went, Orly thinks she messed up history, and Thea covers her face and groans that they were a disaster.

On the last day of school, Mel picks them up in her beige Ford Fiesta, with cards and flowers and a bottle of cheap fizzy wine, and the following weekend they head off to GillFest.

Those days at the festival pass in a blur of alcohol and sleep deprivation.

There is plenty of drama: when Orly vomits over the side of the Ferris wheel, the liquid dispersing on its way down to fall as orange rain on the heads of the festival-goers beneath; when they have to take Lenny to the first-aid tent because she's forgotten to bring an inhaler and the sexy young medic asks for Thea's number; when Mel mouths off to the hog-roast seller because there isn't enough hog in her sandwich, and they have to run away as he bursts out of the van with a meat cleaver.

Articles of jewellery fall into the pit of the long-drop toilet. Casual sex is had in the tent, while those not partaking creep around outside giggling. Wees are taken in the wood, holding hands so as not to overbalance into the mulch.

The last day comes far too soon. Of course, they will remain friends, but they're not yet ready to turn over the page of their childhood. Each young woman wishes that time could stand still, just for a few more days or weeks, before the next chapter, with all its mystery and promise, begins.

But the sun rides inexorably across the sky and soon the only light is from bonfires and lanterns. By midnight on Midsummer's Day they are exhausted. Little girls who have stayed up too late too many nights in a row and are starting to get crotchety. They head to the standing stones for some peace and quiet, lolling on the grass in the centre of the circle, unable to take another sip from the plastic cups of cheap cider that is all they can afford from their meagre Saturday jobs.

Thea lies back with a groan.

'Look at that, I've never seen so many stars.'

The others lie down too, feet touching, unconsciously mimicking the cross shape of the festival site as they gaze up at the night sky. They have not lain there long when a burning white slash tears through the night sky.

'Shooting star,' Mel says.

But it is not like the shooting stars they have seen in films. This thing is dangerous, its will is destruction. It comes with an audible hiss and a smell of sulphur.

'Quick, make a wish!'

Orly wishes.

For someone, anyone, to pour her brimming love into, for ever. A wedding, a handsome prince, a happy-ever-after. Everything her teachers and the hatchet-faced headmistress have striven to drive from her soft little-girl heart.

Thea wishes.

Not to have to worry about money like her mother does, crying to the bank manager every month over an unexpected bill or a broken-down car. And to be free of her mother's disappointment with life. Thea has seen what life can be from the American movies she loves so much. She wants to live like the beautiful people.

Lenny wishes.

To become a woman of substance. A name on the school alumni board that people will recognise and murmur that *she* came here.

That captain of industry. The one whose opinion newscasters seek with every new prime minister or economic calamity.

Mel wishes.

For fun and excitement and the sort of sex she reads about in her mother's magazines. Fingers that know how to manipulate her to orgasm instead of plunging into her as if probing for a lost coin. She wishes for travel to exotic destinations, out-there experiences, knowledge, wisdom that cannot be taught. A life of discovery.

The angry star burns itself out, taking the dreams with it. To plant them in the fertile soil of the night, or to discard them like grains tossed on stony ground.

The four girl-women sit up and look from face to face, bright eyes gleaming in the darkness, the standing stones gazing on impassively. Their futures seem so far away, so fantastical. No more than a bedtime story. And yet they know they are on the cusp of something, a tipping point, and when they fall, this moment will be travelling away from them for the rest of their lives. But there is one thing they are all certain of. Nothing will ever come between them.

Acknowledgements

As always, thanks first and foremost to Eve White and Ludo Cinelli for their constant support and guidance.

This book was lucky enough to be hammered into shape by two fantastic editors, Katie Ellis-Brown and Rachel Neely. So many talented people worked on it, in fact, and they are listed overleaf, but particular thanks to Georgia Goodall for her unwavering patience and good humour.

In my going days I attended a fair few festivals. I used to like the little ones best – impromptu gatherings in fields, organised by elderly hippies. Enough cider was consumed that I usually slept through the music and had to be woken up when it was time to get back in the band van, though on occasion exciting incidents would occur. To my partners in crime through those heady days, I salute and thank you: Bex, Caroline, Lynne, Nick, Will.

I hated every minute of my one and only trip to Glastonbury.

Credits

Trapeze would like to thank everyone at Orion who worked on the publication of *The Festival* in the UK.

Agent
Eve White

Editor
Rachel Neely

Editorial Management
Georgia Goodall
Charlie Panayiotou
Jane Hughes

Copy-editor
Jane Selley

Proofreader
Ilona Jasiewicz

Audio
Paul Stark
Amber Bates

Contracts
Anne Goddard
Paul Bulos

Design
Lucie Stericker

Finance
Jennifer Muchan
Jasdip Nandra
Rabale Mustafa
Elizabeth Beaumont
Ibukun Ademefun
Afeera Ahmed

Production
Claire Keep
Fiona McIntosh

Marketing
Tanjiah Islam

Publicity
Ellen Turner

Sales
Laura Fletcher
Victoria Laws
Esther Waters
Lucy Brem
Frances Doyle
Ben Goddard
Georgina Cutler
Jack Hallam
Ellie Kyrke-Smith
Inês Figuiera
Barbara Ronan
Andrew Hally
Dominic Smith
Deborah Deyong
Lauren Buck
Maggy Park
Linda McGregor
Jemimah James
Rachel Jones
Jack Dennison
Nigel Andrews

Ian Williamson
Julia Benson
Declan Kyle
Robert Mackenzie
Megan Smith
Charlotte Clay
Rebecca Cobbold

Operations
Jo Jacobs
Helen Gibbs
Sharon Willis
Lucy Brem
Sneha Wharton
Steven Dennant
Lucy Olley
Rochelle Dowden-Lord
Isobel Sheene

Rights
Susan Howe
Richard King
Krystyna Kujawinska
Jessica Purdue
Louise Henderson

Help us make the next generation of readers

We – both author and publisher – hope you enjoyed this book. We believe that you can become a reader at any time in your life, but we'd love your help to give the next generation a head start.

Did you know that 9 per cent of children don't have a book of their own in their home, rising to 13 per cent in disadvantaged families*? We'd like to try to change that by asking you to consider the role you could play in helping to build readers of the future.

We'd love you to think of sharing, borrowing, reading, buying or talking about a book with a child in your life and spreading the love of reading. We want to make sure the next generation continue to have access to books, wherever they come from.

And if you would like to consider donating to charities that help fund literacy projects, find out more at **www.literacytrust.org.uk** and **www.booktrust.org.uk**.

THANK YOU

*As reported by the National Literacy Trust